ESSENTIAL MAGIC

THE THORNE WITCHES BOOK 8

T.M. CROMER

Cover art: Deranged Doctor Designs
Editor: Trusted Accomplice

BOOKS BY T.M. CROMER

Books in The Thorne Witches Series:

SUMMER MAGIC

AUTUMN MAGIC

WINTER MAGIC

SPRING MAGIC

REKINDLED MAGIC

LONG LOST MAGIC

FOREVER MAGIC

ESSENTIAL MAGIC

MOONLIT MAGIC (coming soon)

Books in The Stonebrooke Series:

BURNING RESOLUTION

THE TROUBLE WITH LUST

A LOVE TO CALL MINE (coming soon)

THE BAKERY

EASTER DELIGHTS

HOLIDAY HEART

Books in The Fiore Vineyard Series:

PICTURE THIS

RETURN HOME

ONE WISH

Look for The Holt Family Series starting March 2020!

FINDING YOU

THIS TIME YOU

INCLUDING YOU

AFTER YOU

THE GHOST OF YOU

DEDICATION

Sometimes we find our tribe in the least likely of places. This book is
dedicated to those women: Gen, Kate, and Sara!

Find out more about my talented friends:

Genevieve Jack - http://www.genevievejack.com
Kate Bateman - http://www.kcbateman.com
Sara Whitney - http://sarawhitney.com/

CHAPTER 1

Ryanne Caldwell woke, heart pounding and mouth dry. What the hell had she just dreamed about? Two sisters—goddesses at that—and a cursed object? Snippets really. Someone declaring her "the Chosen," and then a vision of a necklace. The rest of the nightmare faded to obscurity.

A trip to the bathroom provided a much-needed drink of water for her sore, parched throat. She'd woken herself screaming, which was rare enough to make her question what she'd eaten the night before that might've triggered a nightmare of such magnitude. Nothing out of the ordinary jumped out at her. No caffeine after four p.m. No sugary goodness past noon. Yep, not food related.

Next, she ran through the list of shows she'd watched on TV. No murder mysteries, time travel, or unconventional movies to warp her thought process.

Dismissing the bizarre dream as simply that, she checked the clock.

Four-twenty a.m.

She swore under her breath, threw on her ratty old robe, and padded to the living room. No getting back to sleep after a dream of that nature.

"A full workload today on only three hours sleep is going to suck," Ryanne complained aloud to no one.

The sound of her own disgusted tone echoed off the barren walls of her tiny two-bedroom apartment. Plain white—ugh! She cast the room a distasteful look. Really, after three years in the same place, she could add some damned artwork or colored paint. Anything to make the space more habitable. More home-like.

Even after thirteen years, a home without her sister, Rylee, didn't bear thinking about. Maybe she should consider getting a cat?

With a dismissive shrug, Ryanne headed for the coffee maker.

Milk and sugar in the mug, she waited for the single brewer to work its magic and make her the drink of the gods. A shudder shook her. Yeah, better not to think about gods or goddesses. That dream had been wack. Who in their right mind would consider her a *Chosen*? What did that even mean?

She toyed with the idea of calling in sick to work. A mental-health day. As a star employee of Thorne Industries for the last two years, she'd been the perfect little worker bee. She always showed up on time, stayed late, and hadn't used one single day of vacation.

"Maybe I'm due," she muttered.

Perhaps her brain was on overload and, as a result, was fried. It would explain the freaky visions her mind had conjured.

The more the idea of playing hooky bounced about, the more she warmed to it. She could lounge around, eating ice cream and catching up on rom coms. Let Nash pull a research assistant from the main floor. All his female workers were eager to be singled out. Her coworkers would backstab each other with letter openers in their desire to catch his eye.

And who could blame them? Nash was, well, *Nash.*

A sigh escaped, followed by a self-deprecating snort.

Working for the great Nash Thorne had made her immune to his charms. *Or nearly immune.* If, on occasion, she became short of breath in his vicinity, only she was the wiser. And if there were times when she would look up to find him standing over her, staring with those intense, all-knowing jade eyes, she was quick to suppress her lustful feelings.

Ryanne was certainly not as naive or as starry-eyed as she'd been when she first started working for him. A relationship was off limits. The arrogant little speech he'd honored her with on her first day made that quite clear.

"If you intend to be my top research aide, there will be no hanky-panky." He'd gone further to state that he didn't want her drooling over the ancient tomes in his possession.

Jerk.

Really, who used the term "hanky-panky" in today's day and age? He'd acted as if she'd be unable to control her baser urges in his presence. The conceit of the man had cured her of her brief fantasy almost immediately.

If she were forced to be brutally honest with herself—which she would go to the grave avoiding—she'd have to admit that on the days when he crowded in next to her to help translate a text, his unique scent turned her body into a live wire.

The musky, citrus smell of his skin had her wanting to bury her nose against his wide, muscular chest and inhale for all she was worth. And if, on her loneliest of nights, she fantasized about running her tongue along his corded neck or nuzzling his firm jaw with its perpetual two-day beard growth, who could fault her?

The blame could be firmly placed at the door of her dating dry spell. God, how long had it been since she got laid? She'd lost track around the two-and-a-half-year mark. Her vajayjay was ready to stage a strike.

Overly warm, Ryanne put the back of her hand to her sweaty brow. Maybe she really *was* coming down with something.

Screw it. She was calling off work today. Decision made. She grabbed her smartphone, whipped off a concise email to Nash, and copied Liz in Human Resources.

Both Nash and Liz tended to arrive early to work and would take the extra half-hour to check for new messages. They'd be shocked Ryanne had asked for a day to herself, but her absence shouldn't cause a hardship.

She'd settled into her plush leather couch with her second cup of coffee and palmed the remote when a banging on her door caused her to jump. The splash of scalding liquid on her hand brought a curse to her lips and tears to her eyes.

Ryanne raced to the sink and ran her hand under cold water.

"Sonofabitch!" she muttered.

The banging sounded again. Who the hell was at her door before five a.m.? She ignored the intrusion.

The cold water took a small portion of the pain away.

"Ryanne?" Bang, bang, bang. "Ryanne! Open the door!"

Shock and Nash's frantic voice made her hustle to comply with his demand. Wrapping a dishtowel firmly around her right hand, she hurried to open the door.

Damned if she didn't have to catch her breath when she took in his tousled head of blond hair on top of those well-formed shoulders that made her mouth water. Clearing her throat was a necessity.

"Nash? What are you doing here?"

"Your email said you were sick."

"Oh-kaaay. And you're here *why?"*

His slashing dark blond brows dipped, and a deep frown line appeared in the center of his forehead. The scowl indicated he didn't appreciate the fine art of snark. If she hadn't been used to his thundercloud expression, she might've been a bit intimidated.

"You're never sick," he stated as if he was speaking to a dim child.

"Still not getting why you're here, Nash. It's not life or death if I was able to take the time to email you."

"You're ungrateful, you know that?"

She closed her eyes and counted to ten.

Really, she shouldn't be surprised. The man hardly slept and only

4

lived twenty minutes away. She should've known he'd show up on her doorstep. Hell, if she'd taken the time to consider it, she would've been shocked if he hadn't.

That was the essence of Nash. He needed to control every aspect of his life. Nothing was allowed to derail the day. But the man seriously tried her patience. If he weren't her boss... well, if he weren't her boss, she'd probably be all over him like—*nope! Not going there!* That road was forbidden.

With a heavy sigh, she opened her eyes.

The intensity with which he was studying her caused her to swallow—*hard.*

When his frown deepened and he slowly raked her form with his gaze, her body went on high alert. Her breasts tightened with want, and her vagina became uncomfortably wet.

Crap!

She hated his ability to turn her on. No encouragement needed. For God's sake, he was only checking out her sleeping attire. Mr. Always-Impeccably-Dressed probably mentally faulted her mismatched tank, sleep shorts, and tattered robe.

Once again, she felt her brow to see if her forehead was overly warm.

"Do you feel faint?" Nash surged forward, scooped her into his arms, and kicked the door shut with his foot. "I've got you."

JesusMaryandJoseph! She was going to do it! She was going to lose control and lick him. As she leaned in, ready to take the plunge, he dumped her on the couch. Literally *dumped* her.

"*Dude!*" she yelped.

"Sorry. I lost my grip."

Nash nearly laughed at Ryanne's incredulous glare.

Whew, that was close! He'd nearly lost his ever-loving mind and succumbed to the overwhelming urge to kiss her.

He perused her scantily clad body at length for a second time.

While some people would consider her clothing cover enough, her ugly robe opened just enough to show off the outline of the hardened tips of her breasts and created havoc in his mind—*as well as other parts of his anatomy.* She possessed the type of body to make a grown man weep. She had a petite, hourglass figure that short-circuited his brain.

Okay, focusing on her curves was not the smartest course of action.

In an effort to protect his sanity, he grabbed a quilt from the back of the sofa and tucked it around her. When she was wrapped from neck to ankles, he stepped back and silently praised his quick thinking. A second glance showed that even her purple-painted toes were sexy as hell. He was in deep trouble.

Clearly irritated—her burning eyes said as much—Ryanne struggled to free herself from the heavy material.

He perched on the edge of the couch, hip to hip, hands on either side of her body, and held the quilt in place. "If you're sick, you should stay bundled up."

"I'm not that kind of sick, Nash."

Once again, he studied her—his favorite pastime when she wasn't looking.

Purple highlights blended perfectly with the nearly black hair. Her dark brows were shaped in a sharp arch, and her eyes were almost as dark as her hair and eyebrows. One had to look closely to make out her irises. They were a dark coffee-brown, practically black in appearance. Currently, they blazed with an unholy light.

Nash's lips twitched.

Ryanne's pique was a common enough occurrence—almost daily in fact.

Call him twisted, but he absolutely loved to see her fired up.

Those magnificent eyes would flash, and color would flood her cheeks. Her plump cherry lips would part in outrage and inspire fantasies no boss should entertain. Her passion brought to mind long, steamy nights spent in front of a fire, making love in every position known to man, then discovering a few extra for good measure.

His gaze fell to her mouth.

Whenever she smiled, her mouth split wide and showed a generous amount of white, lighting the room with its brilliance. But right now, when she was irritated and her lips were compressed as a result, he wanted to kiss the ever-loving hell out of her to bring back the joy to her face.

He recalled the first day he'd seen her in the conference room where she was being interviewed.

A goddess among mere mortals.

She'd looked up and beamed at him from her seat, clearly excited at the prospect of becoming his assistant.

Because he'd been in serious danger of falling at her feet and begging her for sexual favors right on the spot, he'd drummed up some stupid little speech about no romance and not drooling on his important papers or books. If he'd have dumped cold water over her head, he probably couldn't have shocked her more. His cousin Liz, who was conducting the interview, had shot him a horrified look as if he'd lost his damned mind.

Maybe he had. Maybe he hadn't been able to find it since meeting Ryanne two years previously. Really one year, eleven months, and twenty-two days if one wanted to be exact. When he wasn't thinking about business, he was consumed by thoughts of her.

And wasn't that the crux of the matter? He'd been smitten the moment he saw her in all her technicolor glory, and nothing she'd said or done in the interim had changed his mind. No, time had only worked to reinforce his feelings. He was a Thorne, and family legend held that Thornes only loved once.

Oh, screw it! He was going in for the kiss. He'd waited long enough.

Angling his head, he shifted closer and released the blanket to allow her partial freedom. "I'm going to kiss you, Ryanne. If you object, speak now or forever hold your peace."

Her indrawn breath and wide eyes curled his lips. He couldn't help his self-satisfied smile. The sheer wonder on her face was a sight to behold.

"I'll take that as a yes."

He lowered his head to hers, and when her lips opened to accommodate him, he explored the depths of her mouth. The very earth seemed to shake when their bodies connected. Somewhere in the close distance, dishes rattled. Oxygen left his brain, and his lungs went into overdrive when she gently sucked on the tongue invading her mouth. Christ, he could lose himself forever in the incredible taste of her.

Lightning lit up the sky beyond the balcony door. Thunder boomed within a second of the flash, and a woman's laughter echoed about the room.

Icy fingers caressed his spine, and he nearly came out of his skin.

His head whipped up and about.

No one was there.

"Did you…hear that?"

Confusion apparent, she asked, "What?"

"I thought I heard…a woman…laughing," he panted out, short of breath from their kiss.

Ryanne jackknifed to a sitting position. Her forehead connected with his chin.

"For fu—" Nash bit off his curse and rubbed his throbbing chin. "Are you okay?"

"Yeah, sorry," she muttered. "This morning is getting weirder and weirder."

Her words caught his complete attention. Weird was never a coincidence in the Thorne world. "How so?"

"I had a strange dream. It's nothing."

"It's not *nothing* if you had to call in sick during the early morning hours." Unable to help himself, he traced her kiss-swollen lips with the pad of his thumb. "That's unlike you."

Her bewilderment was adorable. Did she not believe he was

aware of his surroundings? Aware of her? Hell, most nights he couldn't get a full night's rest because he lay awake, replaying the day's events. He'd spend the entire time recalling every word they exchanged, every gesture she'd made. Of course, those thoughts brought to mind his ever-present desire for her. He nearly snorted in self-disgust.

All strangeness forgotten, he leaned forward. With his free hand, he cradled the back of her head in his palm. "Are you interested in picking up where we left off?"

Her soft whimper encouraged him to run the tips of his fingers down her long, graceful neck. He halted at the lacy edge of her top. "Say the word, Ryanne."

"No," she whispered seductively.

"Yes, I—wait, what? *No?*" Poleaxed, he pulled back. The husky quality to her tone had him wondering if he should go old-school alpha male and try to persuade her. He attempted to keep his petulant attitude in check when he asked, "Why not?"

"Because it could get messy at work. You know, I could drool all over your papers and books. We can't have that, Nash."

This time when he heard a woman's laughter, there was a wicked quality to the sound.

CHAPTER 2

Two days later, the taste of Ryanne was still taking up residence in Nash's memories. In addition, he'd spent the better part of his waking hours obsessing over the silky softness of her hair and how olive her skin had looked against the coral top she'd worn, as well as how smooth her legs had felt when he'd scooped her into his arms. Added to the mix was her smell. That night she'd smelled of clean, fresh pears. He'd developed a new affinity for pears.

When Nash wasn't consumed with thoughts of Ryanne, he recalled the odd laughter and the strange earthquake. An internet check had shown no seismic activity in the state.

If he didn't know better, he would've suspected a brain tumor. Regardless, he didn't broach the subject with Ryanne. If she hadn't felt or heard any of it, he would be forced to consult with his sperm donor, Alastair, to see if there was another reason for what might've taken place.

Of course, Nash could always kiss Ryanne again to see if he could recreate the earthquake and otherworldly laughter. He grinned. The idea had merit.

As if his thought had summoned her, Ryanne sailed through his office door. She'd said something the other morning that had been tickling his brain ever since. He'd also had a nightmare the same night and wished to compare notes with her. Surely it couldn't be a coincidence? Not when the Witches' Council had declared the time was at hand to retrieve the Red Scorpion necklace from Victor Salinger. And while he was at it, Nash hoped to rid the world of that evil shithead forever.

"I brought the—"

Nash cut her off. "Fine, fine. Set them on the table and come here. We need to talk."

"That sounds ominous. What have I done this time?" She approached the small table he was looming over.

He straightened and met her halfway. "Do you know what happens to a sassy-mouthed woman who can't curb her tongue?"

"I'm sure you're going to enlighten me," she retorted as he pulled the files from her hand and tossed them on the nearby surface.

"This." He pulled her close, paused long enough for any objection to his kiss, then claimed her mouth for his own pleasure. When Ryanne tangled her fingers in his hair to hold him in place, Nash was flooded with an amalgam of happy emotions. Once again, thunder boomed, but this time no resulting laughter tormented him.

Forgetting why he'd started the experiment, he became lost in the kiss. His tongue explored the recesses of her mouth and continued its erotic dance with hers. Moving one hand from the small of her back, he cupped her ass and pressed his budding arousal against her. A caveman-like urge overtook him, and he had the desire to throw her right down on the floor to have sex.

"Well, so much for no fraternizing with the hired help. This is an HR nightmare."

His cousin's comment had the effect of a wet blanket. He jerked away and scowled at her. "Don't you know how to knock, Liz?"

"I've never had to in the past. But then you've never made out with employees on company time before."

"None of that matters. Come in. I need you both to sit down. I think I'm onto something."

Of course, Liz—his cohort in the Red Scorpion Retrieval Plan—immediately comprehended the seriousness of his tone and to what he referred.

Ryanne, on the other hand, wore a bemused expression and continued to touch her lips as if she'd been burned.

His gaze dropped to her mouth. The bee-stung look made her already pouty lips larger and more tempting than ever. Had Liz not interrupted, he wasn't sure he would've stopped with only that single mind-drugging kiss.

"What's going on? What do you know?" Liz demanded.

"An inside source reported Salinger definitely has the necklace. And based on some recent events, I believe we need to act swiftly to get it back."

"Wait, what? *Victor* Salinger? The man my sister works for?"

"Yes."

"I don't understand." Ryanne perched on the edge of the nearest chair. "Thorne Industries is branching out into jewelry heists?"

Her confusion was delightful. Nash laughed. He couldn't have held it back even if he wanted to. "Only for one job. Then we're out."

"You're joking." When Nash shook his head, Ryanne straightened and shot Liz a sharp glance. "You're okay with this?"

He shared a speaking glance with his cousin. Without breaking eye contact, he answered for Liz. "She is."

"I'd like to hear it from her if you don't mind."

Liz nodded. "I am."

"Okay, who's been drinking the crazy Kool-Aid? Because I'm telling you here and now, there's no way in hell I'm letting either of you commit a crime."

"Isn't she adorable? It's like she thinks she has a choice."

A gasp of outrage greeted his statement.

Ryanne was quick to rally and jumped up from her seat. "I damned well *do* have a choice. I can call the authorities."

"Liz, will you excuse us for a minute?" he asked, tone silky and full of menace.

"Don't you dare leave me here alone with him." Ryanne held up a hand. "And don't *you* dare come any closer, Nash. I recognize that look. You think you're going to seduce me into a life of crime. No how, no way! I've been down that path, and I don't look good in orange."

Her pronouncement brought Nash up short. *She'd been down that path? With whom?* He shoved aside those nagging questions and asked, "When have I ever seduced you into doing my bidding, babe?"

"When have you ever kissed the living daylights out of me or called me 'babe' before? I'm not having it, Nash!"

Ryanne had a point. Nash had never touched her or indicated affection in any way, but once he had, there was no going back. At least, not for him.

He shrugged and asked, "What if I told you the fate of the world was at stake? That if we didn't do something soon, your sister's life would be in danger?"

She sank back into the closest chair. "You're insane, aren't you?" she whispered. "I'd suspected it on occasion, but this proves it."

"Oh, for pity's sake!" He stormed across the office, locked the door, and strode to his private liquor cabinet. With a scan of his thumb, the door slid down and revealed a row of perfectly aged spirits. A single shot of Glenfiddich for each of them should help calm everyone's nerves.

Some would wonder why he had high-tech security on his liquor cabinet, but a man had to have priorities. A few of those bottles ran to a hundred years old.

He handed her a tumbler with an inch and a half of the amber liquid. "I'm not insane, Ryanne. I think deep down you sense that."

When Ryanne remained quiet and continued to stare into the

whisky, Nash cast a pleading glance at Liz. His eyes went wide, and he nodded his head in Ryanne's direction as a clear "talk to her" signal.

Liz scrunched up her face in some semblance of a grimace. "Fine," she mouthed. She downed her drink in one move and slapped the conference table.

Although he'd been watching, Nash still jumped.

"Ryanne, Nash is not insane. Or not completely anyway."

"Thanks a lot," he muttered and took a sip of his drink.

"He's a warlock."

Nash spit the liquid in a Jackson Pollack styled pattern across the table. Had there been a canvas in front of him, it would've created the perfect spatter effect.

It was tough to determine if Ryanne's horror-filled expression was due to the news of what he was or because of his unsanitary spewing of alcohol halfway across the room. It was possible her appalled expression was the result of his repeated hoarse coughing from the whisky burning his pipes.

Liz's wicked delight wasn't lost on him. The twinkle in her bright amber eyes gave her away. She was going to pay. Next training session, he would work her over and burn her magical behind.

He almost swore, which would've shown everyone exactly what he was when the local population of raccoons came to call. With a sigh of disgust, he pushed off the edge of the table, hiked up his slacks, and squatted in front of Ryanne.

"She's telling the truth. It's not the way I would've wanted you to find out, but—"

"Am I being punked?"

He opened and closed his mouth. A demonstration was in order. "Ryanne, I need you to keep an open mind here, okay?" He rose to his feet. "Stay calm no matter what."

"You're scaring me."

"Just know that magic *does* exist and don't freak out on me. I'm counting on you to be as level-headed as you normally are."

Ryanne's alarmed gaze locked onto him. "I don't think I want to know."

Liz moved beside her chair and gripped her hand. "It's actually pretty cool if you look at it with an open mind." With her other hand, she offered Ryanne the glass of whisky. "Here. Do this shot first."

He rose and moved to the large potted palm in the corner of his office. He waited until Ryanne consumed her drink and carefully set her glass on his desk. When she nodded in his direction, Nash channeled his power, pulling the magic from his cells and pushing it out toward his fingertips as he touched the trunk of the palm tree. The stalk of the palm grew a good six inches as leaves sprouted and elongated to fill out the foliage.

Part of him feared looking in her direction. Feared what he might see in her eyes. When his cousin Autumn had told her boyfriend about her gifts, the guy had freaked right the hell out. Nash didn't want Ryanne to be afraid of him.

But he need not have worried. When Nash faced Ryanne, her eyes were huge in her face, but her expression was one of fascination.

She dropped Liz's hand and jumped up from her seat to join him. "Can you do that again?"

Keeping his gaze locked on her expressive face, he repeated his parlor trick.

When she laughed and clapped her hands, she threw him for a loop. He'd expected disbelief or terror, not excited acceptance.

"What else can you do?"

"What else do you want me to do?" he asked with a relieved smile.

"I don't know. I've never met a warlock before. Or have I?" Realization dawned, and Ryanne whipped her head around to stare at Liz. "Can you do things like this, too?"

Liz turned her hands palm up and lifted them toward the ceiling. All the items on Nash's desk rose three inches before carefully settling back in place.

"Ohmygod!" Ryanne's hands flew to cover her mouth, and she turned wondrous eyes to Nash. "I can't believe this. I feel like I'm dreaming."

"You're not dreaming, babe."

"I want to know everything. Is your entire family gifted? Can anyone learn how to do this, or do you have to be born this way? Does it drain you to perform magic? Ohmygod," she repeated. "I can't process this."

Nash laughed and brushed a wayward strand of her dark hair from her cheek. "Yes, my entire family is 'gifted.' No, anyone cannot do this because, yes, you have to be born with your gifts. No, magic isn't draining. If done properly, it's invigorating."

Her dark gaze traveled his features as she judged his sincerity. She studied him as if she'd never seen anything like him before. And in all likelihood, she hadn't—or at least hadn't realized she had.

A frown formed on her face. "Can you make people do things against their will?"

Nash should've anticipated her thoughts would eventually circle around to the dark side. Ryanne had a deep sense of right and wrong. But she also had an innate sense of fairness. She had the ability to view a problem from all sides, which made her the perfect assistant.

He cast a sharp glance in Liz's direction. She gnawed her lip. Liz, too, understood that if he answered honestly, if he said he could indeed make people do things against their will, then Ryanne might start wondering if they implemented shady dealings in their business practices.

And while sometimes the line between black and white was shaded with gray and Nash and Liz were forced to cross that line from time to time, they would never do anything to hurt another living soul if they could help it. That was the Goddess's rule; do as you will, and it harm none.

Ryanne read the answer in Nash's worried jade eyes. For a

moment, his irises darkened to a mossy green as he turned her question over in his mind. The color change had to be a trick of the light.

"Never mind. I can see that you can." She screwed up her courage to ask, "Have you ever done that to me?"

Again, the answer was written in his eyes. They turned a dark gray-green as his outrage flared to life. It startled her to realize that Nash's irises changed with his emotions. How had she never noticed before?

"What the hell kind of question is that, Ryanne?" His hand fisted, but he didn't raise it in any type of threatening manner. "Do you think so little of me that I would force you to do something against your will?"

Color leached from the palm beside him, and the leaves curled and browned.

"I..." What could she say? Trust had always been an issue for her. Due to her own crappy past with men, she found it difficult to believe that anyone else wouldn't set out to take advantage of her.

He slashed his hand in a dismissive gesture. "Forget it. Your thoughts are obvious. Take time to process what we've shown you. Tomorrow morning, we'll meet again." He ran a hand over the palm tree to restore its vitality. The cold-eyed stare he turned her way made Ryanne cringe. "I ask that you don't tell anyone what we revealed to you today. But it's *your choice* to do so or not."

Before she could comment, he disappeared. *Like totally vanished.* One second, he was standing before her, and the next, he was gone.

The muscles in Ryanne's legs chose that moment to weaken, and she leaned against his desk. She turned incredulous eyes on Liz. "Where did he go?"

Liz watched her warily. "If you reveal what we are, you can cause serious harm. If Nash showed you what he is, then he trusts you implicitly. You understand that, right?"

The weight of the revelation floored Ryanne. Liz was correct. Nash was an exceedingly private person—*and now she knew why.*

For him to tell the truth about his abilities meant he'd put his faith in her silence.

"I do," she finally said. "I won't tell a soul. Who would believe me anyway? I'm not sure I believe this myself."

"I'm sure you have questions. What do you want to know?"

"Is it like the movies? Are you all-powerful? Do you require spells for most things? Is this type of disappearing act normal?"

Liz poured them each another dram of whisky before she locked up the cabinet. She settled in a chair and lifted her glass in a silent toast before downing the contents. As Ryanne looked on, more liquid filled the glass.

"Holy shit!"

"That's called conjuring. We can all conjure our basic needs without a spell."

"Basic needs as in food and clothing?"

"Yes. And shelter."

"And whisky is a basic need?"

Liz flashed a sphinxlike smile. "Sometimes."

"The way Nash left, can you do the same thing?"

"Teleporting. Yes."

"Is there a limit to what you can do?"

"Mostly. But some witches and warlocks are stronger than others. With the Thorne line being the strongest."

"Your last name is Thorne. Are you as… powerful as Nash?"

"We've never pitted our skills against one another, but maybe. Nash's father, Alastair, is one of the most powerful warlocks in existence. It stands to reason that Nash would inherit some of that power through his bloodline. His direct line has never married or mated other than with another witch or warlock. Nash's mother was a witch, too."

Ryanne paused in her list of questions to process what she'd learned so far.

The one thing her mind circled around was her attraction to

Nash. Was she attracted to the man? Or was she drawn to the power she hadn't known existed?

"Liz, can I ask you one more thing?"

"Of course."

"You're beautiful, and Nash is, for lack of a better word, breathtaking. Are all witches and warlocks so gorgeous? The attraction I feel for him, is that the magic?"

Liz laughed long and loud, not bothering to disguise her amusement.

"What?" Ryanne snapped.

"You and Nash," Liz choked out as she wiped tears from her eyes. "Each of you dancing around the other, sending covert, longing glances at one another, and hoping the other doesn't notice."

"I don't send 'covert, longing glances' at anyone," Ryanne argued hotly.

Liz stood and patted her shoulder. "Ah, but you do, my dear friend. You absolutely do. And to answer your question, your attraction to one another has nothing to do with magic. I wish you two would do the dirty and get it over with. It might ease the constant tension in the room."

Heat flared in Ryanne's cheeks, and her heart pounded faster at the idea of doing "the dirty" with Nash. In her mind, she could picture his large, muscular frame atop hers as he drove into her with slow, steady strokes. The passionate look on his face would rival the one he'd worn two nights before in her apartment when he'd kissed her. He'd be as consumed with desire as she would be.

Ryanne found it difficult to meet Liz's knowing eyes. Wordlessly, she left Nash's office to return to her own.

CHAPTER 3

"You can come out now. She's gone," Liz called.

Nash stepped from his office's *en suite* bathroom. "You've got a mean streak, you know that?"

"I was being honest. You two are crazy about each other. The kiss I walked in on proved you have chemistry. Make a damned move on her already. Tell her you love her."

"It's not that simple, cousin."

Liz went to him and gave him a quick hug around his middle. "It is if you want it to be, Nash. You don't need to keep everyone at a distance, you know."

She referred to his rocky family relationships. As the bastard of the great Alastair Thorne, Nash was reviled by many of the others in their family. The exceptions were Liz, his sisters Summer and Holly, and a handful of others he'd helped along the way. Mostly, people feared him.

It was why he found it difficult to reveal to Ryanne exactly who and what he was. "Do you think she's okay with it?"

Liz understood his meaning. "Surprisingly, yes. On a deeper

level, I think she finds you fascinating. It might be the scientific bend to her thinking. That works in your favor."

"We need to get her on board—*soon*. If we don't get the Scorpion from Salinger, we're all screwed."

"I know. But you *do* understand by doing this, you are putting her in grave danger, right?"

"I can't think about that now, Liz. You only have to take one look at the pulse of the nation and see Salinger has already influenced the political climate on a global scale. People are at each other's throats on a daily basis through every media over every topic, and they don't know why. You hear it on the radio, see it on television, and read it on social media. Tell me you don't feel it; the weight of oppression. That's to say nothing of the financial markets. If we don't get that necklace out of Victor's clutches, the world as we know it is over."

Nash felt a twinge in his conscience, and the little voice in his head screamed at him to keep Ryanne as far away from this mess as humanly possible. But the truth was, the Red Scorpion necklace was the most powerful magical artifact in existence. It had the ability to ignite wars if it fell into the wrong hands. And Victor Salinger's were definitely the wrong hands. That money-hungry, power-grabbing bastard intended to be the only player left on the board.

"Nash, tread lightly. You know the family legend. If you do something to inadvertently harm Ryanne, you'll never be able to live with yourself."

His temper took hold. "What do you want me to do, Liz? Let Salinger run wild? Ryanne is the identical twin to his arm candy. With the wards Victor has in place, Ryanne is the only one with a chance of getting close to the necklace."

"For someone with such a high IQ, you can be an idiot, you know that?" Liz snapped. "You've loved her since the moment you saw her. Just try to deny it. Go ahead, and I'll call you a damned liar."

"So what? I should throw her down on my desk and ravish her like an animal?" Never mind that he'd thought the same thing right before Liz walked into his office. "Nothing can come of it, Liz. My business for the Witches' Council would put her in the path of unsavory characters if it were known she was anything other than my assistant. As a non-magical human, she'd be a sitting duck." Nash shook his head and moved to stare out his office window. "No. I can't do that to her."

"Oh, but you can put her in Victor's path?"

"That's different."

"How?"

"Stop plaguing me, woman! Don't you have work to do?"

"You know damned well that I can snap my fingers and have a week's worth of projects done. Now answer the question, Nash. How is it different?"

Nash spun and stalked to where Liz stood with her hands on her hips. "It's the *Red Scorpion*, Liz. How much more clear do I need to make it?"

The air crackled around them, and they both froze.

"Incoming," Nash muttered.

A knock sounded at his office door before it opened. Ryanne peeked her head in. She seemed startled to see him. "Your father is here, Nash."

Her dark, troubled gaze settled on him for a few seconds before she backed out of the door to make room for Alastair, who took one look at both their faces and sighed.

"Well, aren't you Gloom and Doom." Alastair flicked his wrist to close the door. "What's going on?"

"Nothing," Nash lied as he strode to his desk and shuffled papers there. "What do you want, Alastair?"

His father ignored him to nod at Liz. "Nice to see you again, child."

"Alastair."

"How is your mother? We haven't touched base in a while."

"She's well. Thank you."

"Good. Do you mind if I speak to my son alone?"

Liz shot Nash a questioning glance. He nodded and settled into his chair.

When the door closed behind her, he looked at his father. "Have a seat."

If one were so inclined, they'd have to admire Alastair's casual grace. Every gesture was done with minimal fuss or expended energy. He had an old Hollywood elegance about him. Since Nash's sister Summer had forced Alastair to come into the current decade with clothing and hairstyle, it was impossible to tell the man's age. He appeared only a year or two older than Nash himself. Not a single living soul would guess Alastair was older than thirty-five, or that he was really forty years older than he looked. *Ah, the blessed genetics of a warlock.*

"What do you want?" Nash asked again.

Alastair straightened his cuffs before he spoke. "Victor Salinger."

Inside, Nash swore a blue streak. Leave it to his father to scry and spy on him. Looked like reinforcement of the wards that protected his office was the next item on Nash's to-do list. "What about him?"

Amusement colored Alastair's bright blue eyes. "Do you really think I'm as dumb as all that, son?"

Nash lifted a brow.

Alastair barked out a laugh.

"How many times can I ask 'what do you want' before I get a straight answer?"

His father steepled his fingers and attempted to hide his smile behind his hands. He failed.

"Look, *Dad*, I'm not here for your personal amusement. I have work to do. If you can't get to the point of your little impromptu visit, then I'm going to ask that you leave."

"I want to help you retrieve the artifact."

Nash snorted. "I don't need your help."

"According to Isis, you do," Alastair said silkily.

"Fuck." *Achoo!*

Alastair had anticipated Nash's reaction and fisted his hand to prevent the influx of animals. It happened every time he swore. His two sisters were cursed with the same affliction. If someone didn't react quickly with a magical assist, things could get out of control.

"Thanks," Nash grumbled.

"See how well we work together?" Alastair grinned his amusement.

A whole list of swearwords danced on Nash's tongue. He curbed the impulse to utter them. He didn't need an invasion of crazed raccoons scratching at the windows or frightening his employees.

"Since when have you wanted to work for the Council?"

His father gave a nonchalant shrug. "Since never, but if it will help you…" Alastair let his words trail off. "Truthfully, Victor Salinger is not someone to be trifled with, as you are well aware. As you also know, he was Zhu Lin's right hand for many years." Alastair toyed with his cuff links. "I'll be honest with you, son, Victor was the man who delighted in carrying out the various forms of torture Lin had devised for me. He's sadistic and shouldn't be underestimated. You saw him shoot his own sister in Athens. Imagine what he could do to someone you care about."

While Alastair had never gone into the specifics of his imprisonment by the Désorcelers Society, on rare occasions, he'd let slip a tidbit of information such as the one he'd just revealed.

"Are you worried about me, Alastair?" Nash asked, curious despite himself. He and Alastair had been at odds for nearly two decades. Their father-son relationship went to hell right about the time Nash discovered Alastair had never truly loved his mother and had another family. The two of them had failed to see eye to eye on any one subject since, or if they did, it was grudgingly on Nash's part.

"You're my son." A simple statement, but one that held a wealth of meaning. Alastair took care of all things Thorne. Or at least all people with the last name Thorne. Lately, he'd extended his watchful eye to the Carlyle clan.

"I'm only a Thorne because you insisted my mother put the name on my birth certificate. So let's call a spade a spade, *Dad*. I'm your bastard."

"You are my *son*," Alastair repeated stubbornly, as if by being a relation—an unwanted one at that—solved everything.

"I don't want your help," Nash stated coldly. Of course, Alastair would ignore his wants, but the words needed to be said all the same.

"Duly noted." His father snapped his fingers, and a folder appeared in his hands. With an unconcerned air, he tossed it on the desk between them. "This is everything I have on Salinger. Do with it what you will." He rose with his usual grace. "Might I suggest you leave the lovely Ryanne out of your quest for the necklace? She's not of our world and can easily become a casualty of your war with Victor."

Nash stood so fast his chair slammed into the credenza behind him. "Ryanne is mine to do with as I please!"

Unfortunately, the woman in question chose that precise moment to enter the office.

"Excuse me?" she asked. Fury dripped from her tone, and her face was an icy mask.

"I…" What could he say? His words were damning. "It wasn't meant that way, Ryanne. I swear." Nash didn't dare look at Alastair. He knew what he'd see—a knowing smirk.

"Let's get one thing clear, *Mr*. Thorne. I am not now, nor will I ever be, *yours* to do with as you *please*. I work for you, which I can quickly remedy by taking a job elsewhere."

Nash's heart hiccuped, and his breathing halted in his chest. The idea of not seeing Ryanne every day almost drove him to his knees to beg her forgiveness. But he couldn't let her know the power she held over him. If he did, then she'd spend the rest of their lives walking all over his feelings. "Do whatever you—" His remaining words came out garbled and incoherent.

Had he suffered a stroke?

Nash cast a frantic glance in Alastair's direction, but his father wasn't looking at him. Instead, he'd focussed all his charm on Ryanne. But the telltale sign that Alastair had stopped Nash's stupid statement was the hand clenched behind his father's back.

"Don't mind him, my dear. Nash is a bit hot-tempered at times. Half of what he says, he doesn't mean."

Nash opened his mouth to deny Alastair's claim, but those words came out as mangled as all the others. He glared his rage at the back of Alastair's perfectly coiffed blond head.

A speculative gleam entered Ryanne's dark eyes, and she angled her head slightly to study him as she strode farther into the room. Her full lips curled into a smug half-smile. "I think I adore your father, Nash. He's been able to shut you up long enough for someone else to get the last word." She patted his cheek in a condescending manner.

Nash glared down at her but kept his lips sealed. It was embarrassing enough that his father had stolen his speech. To continue to attempt to talk would humiliate him all the more.

"Liz wanted me to remind you that Rafe Xuereb has arrived for your meeting. She refuses to start without you. Hopefully, your affliction will pass long enough for you to discuss any relevant issues."

Ryanne sashayed her perfect, round ass out the door, pausing only long enough to blow Alastair a kiss over her shoulder. The older man crossed his arms over his massive chest and grinned for all he was worth.

"That's one heck of a woman, son. Don't let her get away."

Ryanne heard Alastair's statement and Nash's answering "Fuck off, old man!" She fought to hold back her laugh. Having only met Alastair a few times, she maintained a healthy respect for the dangerous, off-putting air about him, but he also reminded her enough of Nash to put her at ease.

Without a doubt, Nash shared his father's arrogance. Like that stupid comment when she'd entered his office. She snorted her disbelief that something so idiotic could leave his mouth. The guy was brilliant, and yet he could be extremely clueless at times.

Ryanne was certain Alastair had used magic to halt Nash's comeback. The gesture endeared the older man to her. He'd saved her job and her pride. Deep inside, she knew Nash intended to draw a line in the sand and say, "Do whatever you feel you need to."

She'd have been forced to dig in her heels and quit. Because while she would take—and had taken—a lot of crap from Nash over the last couple of years, she wouldn't stand to be disrespected. She knew her worth. It had taken a lot of years to build up her self-esteem. One man would not lay waste to it with his momentary stupidity.

She wasn't at her desk long before Nash showed up. In his hands, he held an enormous bouquet of the palest pink roses she'd ever seen. The picture of contrition, he set the vase next to her computer.

"I'm sorry."

"Don't you have a meeting or something to get to?" She wasn't beyond being petty.

"I do, but not before I apologize for my behavior. And definitely not before you accept." His intense gaze bored into her. "What you overheard, it wasn't how it sounded. My father brings out the worst in me. I'm more reactive than I should be."

"And what would you have done if I'd quit?"

"I'd have come after you and doubled your salary," he said with a cheeky grin.

"Then I quit."

Nash urged Ryanne to her feet. With one arm around her waist, he pulled her close and cupped her jaw. "You'll see a pay raise in your next check."

"And?"

"An extra week of vacation."

"I don't take vacation as it is," she reminded him.

"True, but it's there should you want it."

He dipped his head and nuzzled her neck. "Do you forgive me, babe?"

"Yes," she whispered on a rush of breath. She moaned softly as he took her earlobe between his teeth. "This is a bad idea, Nash."

"What?"

"Any type of relationship that isn't work related."

He trailed light kisses along her jaw on his journey to her mouth. "I beg to differ. I think this is the best idea I've ever had where you're concerned."

"Personally, I think you're buttering me up for whatever hidden agenda you have planned."

Nash froze and drew back. Troubled green eyes stared down at her. "I'll always be honest with you, Ryanne."

A chill took her. Rarely did she see Nash this serious or worried. "What is it, Nash?"

"We'll talk more later. Have dinner with me tonight."

Her gaze dropped to his mouth. The one able to bring such pleasure with the simplest and lightest of kisses. "I feel like you've cast a spell over me," she said softly. "Since the day you showed up in my apartment, all I can think about is this." She placed her fingers over his lips and gasped when he sucked in the tips.

"Is that so terrible?"

"If it ends badly, I'll be out on my ass, looking for another job."

"Why would it end badly? You want me, and without question, I want you."

"All things end, Nash. It's the way of life."

He frowned as he studied her face. "You're cynical about love. I wouldn't have guessed that."

"I've not had much of it in my life."

"Take your time to decide about dinner. This thing between us, it's on your terms, Ryanne. I'll abide by whatever you decide."

"Will you?" Did she want him to? A large part of her yearned for him to take charge. To chase away her fears and exorcise her ghosts.

To show her what could be instead of leaving her to wonder "what if."

Nash flashed her a wry smile. "I can promise to try. Does that work? In the meantime, I'll have Liz draw up a contract. It will contain your new raise. It will also have the clause that with any termination of employment—on either side—you'll receive a severance equal to your existing salary until you find another job you love." He paused and smoothed a wild strand of her hair. "But know I will never fire you. You're much too valuable to me."

As he walked away, Ryanne experienced an insane urge to chase after him. She wanted to tell him she'd go out to dinner with him tonight and every night for the rest of their lives. Her sudden neediness bothered her. She toyed with the idea of taking a real vacation to get her head on straight. Somehow, she doubted Nash would allow her to be gone that long. Their work schedule wouldn't permit it.

When Nash reached the bank of elevators, he glanced back to where she stood in her office doorway. Across the distance, their eyes met and held. She imagined she could feel the pull of his power like a tractor beam. Whatever was inside of him called to her. It had from the moment they'd met. Now that Nash wanted to explore that connection, Ryanne had misgivings. But she wasn't a coward. She faced up to her fears, and because she did, she gave Nash a single nod.

His wide, happy smile told her he understood she'd agreed to dinner—had probably agreed to much more. Because he rarely displayed emotion, many passing employees halted to stare in wonder. Their gazes ping-ponged between Ryanne and Nash, pausing overly long on their boss. He was simply that beautiful.

It was Ryanne's turn to smile. Nash had no clue how attractive he was to the opposite sex. She hoped he never found out.

CHAPTER 4

"Are you about ready?"

Ryanne's nerves jumped when the deep baritone of Nash's voice wrapped around her. She nodded and logged out of her computer. "Where are you taking me for dinner?"

"Are you in the mood for the best that money can buy, or do you prefer a down-home meal?"

"If I say down-home, do you plan to cook for me?"

He laughed and shook his head. "You've already got me as your sex slave if you so desire. Do you want me as your domestic manservant as well?"

"Mmm, I like the sound of that. Would you do all the cooking and cleaning?"

"With a simple snap of my fingers," he agreed.

"Show-off."

"It comes with the territory."

He referred to his magical powers as casually as if he were referring to his morning coffee. Ryanne didn't know if she'd ever wrap her head around what he and Liz could do, but she did admit to a wild curiosity.

"Will you tell me more about what your abilities allow?"

"Does it frighten you?"

She mentally tossed about the things she'd learned today. By rights, she should be terrified, yet she wasn't. Her curiosity on the matter was too strong.

"No. I don't think so. If someone told me yesterday that magic like yours existed, I'd have laughed in their face. Now, having witnessed it first-hand, I don't know what to think. Whatever I feel, it isn't fear of you." She picked up her purse and walked to where he waited, his shoulder against the doorjamb. Trailing a finger along his angular jaw, she said, "I don't think you'd ever intentionally hurt me. Mainly, I find it incredible that I've known you for all this time and had no clue as to what you could do."

"There's something I've been meaning to ask you."

Because his tone sounded serious, she became guarded. "What?"

She suspected Nash's intelligent eyes missed nothing: not her stillness, not her discomfort with personal questions, and not her hesitation to answer those questions about herself. His watchfulness made her twitchier by the second.

"The other day, at your apartment… did you feel or hear anything strange?"

"The whole thing was strange in my opinion. How fast you —*wait!* You teleported that morning, didn't you? Like you did earlier. That's how you got to my place so quickly after I sent the email, wasn't it?"

He shrugged as if embarrassed. "I was worried. You never call in sick."

His confession triggered Ryanne's smile, and she let him off the hook and decided not to press the issue. "In answer to your question, yes. It started with an odd dream about goddesses and a cursed neck-lace. Then you showed up—suddenly, I might add. When you kissed me, it was like the ground shook."

"Did you hear the laughter?"

"Laughter?"

"Yes, a woman's laughter."

"Right, you mentioned that before." She frowned her confusion. "No. Should I have?"

"I don't know. I'm not an expert on all things goddess related." Some unnamed emotion flashed behind his eyes, indicating he wasn't telling the full truth.

Ryanne shoved aside her misgivings, although she was a bit concerned he believed in gods and goddesses. She struggled to keep the skepticism from her voice when she asked, "You think the laughter was a goddess?"

"I don't think; I know." He sighed and rolled his eyes at her wide-eyed stare. "I descend from Isis. It's how my family obtained their powers. I've been tracing your ancestry today, and I believe you descend from one of Isis's sisters. If I'm right, you may have latent powers you had no idea you possessed."

"How could I not know if I have magical abilities?"

"Many reasons. The top two I can think of? You may have been bound at a young age, or your family line may have been cursed or bound as a whole many years ago."

Ryanne couldn't wrap her mind around what he was telling her.

"Come with me." Nash took her by the elbow and guided her toward his office. When they arrived, he locked the door behind them and strode to a wall on the far side of the room. With one final glance in her direction, he waved his hand.

A feather could've knocked her over when the wall shimmered and disappeared. Beyond the new opening was an extensive library filled with what looked to be rare, leather-bound books and tomes. It went on forever and brought to mind images of the Trinity College library in Dublin. She'd seen it once in a magazine and itched to visit ever since.

Nash took her hand, and they entered what appeared to be the top floor of multi-levels of floor-to-ceiling bookshelves. She gasped as she stopped on the balcony overlooking the room.

"What is this?" Legs frozen in place, all she could do was gape.

The twinkle in his jade gaze mocked her. "My research center."

"I'm still dreaming, aren't I? I never woke up the other night." She scrubbed her hands over her face. "When I *do* wake, I'll find out this has all been some type of elaborate dream."

He tilted his head and pursed his lips. Having seen that look before, she could tell he was holding back.

"What?" she asked irritably.

Nash's brows flew skyward, and a smile played on his lips. "I'm wondering if I should kiss you again. You know, show you exactly how real all this is."

Her knees went weak at the same time a fire started within. That damned man knew what to say and when to say it to make her a big gooey pile of mush. She might've even squeaked in her surprise. If she'd have known that was his "I'm wondering if I should kiss you" look, she'd have jumped all over that two years ago.

Amusement lit Nash's handsome visage, and Ryanne swore under her breath. Yeah, he had more than just magical skills in his bag of tricks. Based on his smug attitude, he knew exactly how to use them.

"You and your sister were adopted after your parents died, if I'm not mistaken."

The about-face threw her. "Y-yes."

"Right. Come here."

On wooden legs, she walked to the top of the staircase and took the hand he offered. He drew her down the stairs and into his room of books.

"I can't believe this exists," she whispered her awe.

"Believe it."

"It explains why you're protective of your old, dusty tomes," she muttered.

"You can't begin to understand the problems I've had with women drooling on my books."

She yanked her hand from his. "You're an ass."

Nash laughed and hugged her from behind. "If it makes you feel any better, I'll let you drool on my papers anytime."

She caught him in the ribs with her elbow.

He dropped a light kiss on the shell of her ear before he released her. "Does anything here call to you?"

You, she wanted to say. "Do you mean one of the books or objects on the shelves?"

He cast her a sharp glance. "Objects? You can see them in addition to the books?"

Her brows drew together in her bewilderment. "You can't?"

"No, I definitely *can*. But *you* shouldn't be able to as a non-magical human. They are spelled."

"You're confusing me, Nash." Was he saying she was like him?

"This proves my theory."

"That I should possess magical abilities?"

"Yes. Let's see if we can do something about getting your powers back, shall we?"

Nash pulled back a carpet from the center of the room and exposed a pentagram. Next, he placed a candle on each of the five points. When Nash touched a fingertip to each of the wicks to light them, Ryanne plopped down on the nearest chair. How had she never known he could do these things? It worried her that she'd misread him.

"Are you all right?"

His concerned voice brought her head up. Unable to express exactly how overwhelmed she was, she remained mute.

"I know it's a lot to take in, Ryanne. But bear with me a bit longer, okay?"

After ten heartbeats of consideration, she nodded.

"Step into the center of the pentagram with me. I need to cast a circle."

Her curiosity got the better of her. "What does it mean to cast a circle?"

"Whenever a deeper magic is needed, such as spell casting, scrying, or the like, a protective ring needs to be created around the person using magic. It's a little more in depth, but that's all you need to learn right now."

"Why am I in the circle? How can I perform magic?"

"With my help. Hold my hand."

She gripped his hand and felt an immediate pulse of energy. Her eyes widened. "What's that?"

His pleased smile resembled the Cheshire Cat's. "That, my darling woman, is magic. I sent out a feeler."

"Do it again." When she felt the pulse a second time, she laughed. "I felt it down to my toes!"

"Do you want me to attempt an unbinding spell?"

"You're certain I have magical abilities?"

"I am. Some non-magical humans can feel the power pulse, but not to the extreme you did."

One thing troubled her. "You said *attempt*. Is there a possibility it's irreversible?"

"Most times it requires the person who bound you to remove the spell. If it was your mother or father who cast it, then it should've been broken when they passed away."

Ryanne's heart picked up its pace. "You think someone else did this."

"I don't know what I believe. But your parents died when you were a small child. Unless it was a super-charged spell they cast, you should've regained your powers at that time. I can only assume an aunt, uncle, or grandparent cast the spell."

"I don't have any other relatives besides my sister, Rylee."

Ryanne's words bothered Nash. Someone had removed her powers. To what end was the mystery. But it meant somebody other than family had to know she was a witch.

"What I am about to do might be met with resistance if the original spell caster is living. Either way, it shouldn't harm you. If you're willing, I'll try it."

Ryanne worried her lip, and Nash fought the urge to kiss her cares away. Now wasn't the time for distractions. If he could restore any abilities she was born with, he might be able to train her and utilize her skills to retrieve the Red Scorpion necklace from Victor.

"Okay," she said decisively. "Let's do this."

He smiled his approval, relieved she was open to the experience. "Stand here." He placed her in the center of the pentagram and strode to his grimoire. When he found the page he was looking for, he joined her in the circle. "Ready?"

"As I'll ever be," she muttered with an apprehensive glance at the book in his hand.

"You shouldn't feel anything but an influx of energy if this works. Don't worry."

"I'm not sure how I'm going to feel if it doesn't. You've built up my hopes."

"Keep in mind, I'm a warlock, not a miracle worker."

"Gee, thanks."

Nash laughed and gave in to his desire to kiss her. It seemed once he'd broken the hands-off rule, he couldn't get enough of touching her. He took it as a good sign that she didn't mind and was quick to reach for him in return.

As he read the spell from the book, he felt the slight atmospheric change that indicated the gathering energy and building power. He repeated the spell a second time and watched Ryanne closely. Except for the slight widening of her eyes, she didn't act any differently.

Eyes closed, he conjured a thick leather strip to rest over his shoulder. Next, he concentrated and called on his familiar. Within minutes, a hawk swooped down and landed on the leather perch he'd created.

"What the hell?"

Her reaction amused him. "This is Captain. He's what is known as a familiar. He'll give me a magical boost for this spell."

"Does that mean what you've done so far isn't working?"

"It's trying to. I imagine you can feel the magic building."

"I feel something, yes."

"I have one other ace up my sleeve, but I don't want to use that yet if I don't have to."

She nodded and clasped his hand again. "I'm ready when you are."

This time when Nash spoke the words, a crack rent the air and energy sizzled around them. The resistance concerned him. It was as if someone was working on the other side in an attempt to prevent him from succeeding.

"It's not going to work, is it?" Ryanne asked.

"Not this way." He stroked Captain's chest and gave him a silent nod in thanks. "You can go, boy. I appreciate your help."

After the bird had flown from the room, he pulled out his smart-phone. He scrolled through his contacts until he found the one number he always refused to call. Torn, he stared at the screen. If he called his father, Nash would feel indebted to him. All the years spent trying to become independent would be null and void.

Ryanne touched his arm and startled him from his tortured thoughts. She glanced down at the screen and immediately under-stood his dilemma. "Nash, you don't have to do this."

"You deserve to regain your gifts."

"We can find another way."

"Alastair knows more about this type of thing than anyone else alive. He's helped others throughout the years."

"Would it be better if I'm the one to ask him for the favor?" She spoke the question hesitantly as if she, too, were scared to be indebted to Alastair.

That she was willing to take the burden from him encouraged Nash to press the send button and call his father.

"Son."

"Sperm Donor."

"Probably not the best way to start the conversation," Ryanne muttered.

Nash heard Alastair's heavy sigh. "It must be dire if you're calling, especially so soon after my visit. What do you need?"

"Can you come to my office?"

The connection ended.

Within seconds, Alastair appeared in the doorway of the secret study. His father didn't enter without an invitation, but his eyes missed nothing from where he rested against the doorjamb. "Interesting place you have here. Is that a fifteenth-century conjuring stone?"

"It is."

"Nice. I haven't seen one of those in about thirty-five years or more."

"I didn't call you here to discuss artifacts," Nash snapped.

Alastair's blue gaze narrowed on him. "Then why don't you tell me why I'm here."

"I think Ryanne's a witch whose powers were bound. I can't seem to lift the binding."

His father straightened and dropped his folded arms to his sides. "May I?"

Nash granted permission to enter with a single nod.

Alastair came downstairs and approached Ryanne as if she were a new type of species that had yet to be discovered. His curiosity blazed brightly. When he reached her side, he held out his hand.

She tentatively placed her palm in his.

Alastair turned her hand over and arched a red light from between them. Nash assumed it was to test the strength of her magic, similar to what he'd done earlier.

"She's definitely a witch. This is eerily similar to the Carlyles." To Ryanne, Alastair explained. "My future son-in-law, Cooper, had his powers bound when he and his brother were toddlers. It leaves a subtle echo of the original magic that another witch or warlock can detect. You have that echo."

"That means she had powers once, correct?"

Alastair spared a quick glance for Nash. "I believe so."

Ryanne shifted her attention nervously between the two of them. "How do we unlock them?"

"That's the question of the hour, isn't it?" Alastair dropped her hand and strode to the table with the scrying mirror. A simple hand gesture, and he was lost to whatever he was witnessing.

"What's he doing?" Ryanne asked.

"Scrying," Nash replied. "It's a way to divine the truth of the past and see the present."

"But I thought you said he needed a circle."

"He's Alastair Thorne. He does what he wants."

"I'm not sure, but I think that terrifies me."

He squeezed her hand. "You aren't the only one."

They waited in silence as Alastair searched the mirror for the mysterious images he was looking for. Finally, it seemed he'd seen enough. When he turned in their direction, his expression was dark.

Ryanne shifted beside Nash, her nervous energy palpable. She, too, had picked up on Alastair's grimness.

"What did you see?" Nash asked.

"Nothing good." Alastair stared hard at Ryanne. "Are you sure you wish to know?"

Nash searched her face for the slightest indication she might not be agreeable to hearing the truth. "Ryanne?"

"Yes. Yes, I want to know," she answered after a long pause.

CHAPTER 5

Alastair Thorne had made it a point to study the interactions between his son and Ryanne Caldwell for some time. Nash needed a strong partner who would keep him in check, and his sassy assistant might be the woman to do it.

Of course, there was the fact that throughout history, Thornes fell in love only once in their lifetime. It wasn't a common occurrence, but there had been times when a Thorne's significant other had not been the most stellar character on the planet. Alastair doubted Ryanne fell into that category. Her relatives, on the other hand, *defined* said category.

He had met Ryanne's mother and father once, and a worse pair of role models would've been difficult to find. Because she'd been a small child at the time, Ryanne's memory might be vague. In addition to being horrific parents, it seemed Paul and Marsha Caldwell had been con artists intent on using their twin girls in their larcenous pursuits.

Yes, it had been a blessed day for Ryanne and Rylee when their parents died. But how did one reveal such a thing? *They didn't.* The other problem, as Alastair saw it, was explaining that sometimes the apple didn't fall far from the tree. He only hoped Nash moved forward in his relationship with caution and common sense.

"Your parents didn't block your powers. The Witches' Council is responsible for the action against you," Alastair revealed.

Ryanne's shocked face mirrored Nash's.

His son's response was understandable. He worked for the Council, and Alastair doubted that Nash had heard tell of the Caldwell scandal of years past.

"Why?" Nash demanded, ever Ryanne's champion.

"Years ago, Paul and Marsha manipulated the girls into using magic to break into depositories and safes for their personal gain and to amass their fortune."

"I don't understand." Ryanne looked between him and Nash. "Why don't I recall that part of my childhood? I remember my parents well enough."

"The Council wiped your memory clean at the same time they bound your powers."

She wrapped her hands around her stomach as if to comfort herself. "I was a thief?"

"No, child. Your parents were thieves. You and your sister were their tools."

A sheen of tears coated her eyes, and she dropped her gaze to the floor to hide her emotions.

"Ryanne." Nash drew her into his chest and kissed the crown of her shiny head. "Don't take this upon yourself. You were a small child." He looked to Alastair for confirmation.

"Indeed. This is not your fault, dear girl."

After she wiped a shaky hand beneath her eyes, she met Alastair's direct gaze. "Will I be bound for life?"

"Between Nash and myself, we can reverse the spell. But it means going against the Witches' Council, which my son is always hesitant to do."

Nash's stormy gaze snapped to him. "Don't presume to tell me what I will and won't do."

"Did I say you wouldn't do it?" Alastair shrugged. "I'm almost positive I didn't."

"I'm willing to help her regain her powers," Nash informed them.

Alastair studied him for a brief moment before he nodded. "All right. But I'd like a word in private before we continue."

"Anything you say to me, you can say to her."

Ah, young men in love. They were clueless at times. They were also quick to defend their women without ever having the facts. "Nevertheless, I will not reverse the spell without a few moments of your time, son. Your choice."

He imagined he could hear the grinding of his son's teeth. He was under no illusions that Nash held him in contempt. How it must have grated to call for his help.

Nash faced Ryanne. "Do you mind?"

"Of course not."

When they were alone, Nash turned to him and snapped, "What was that all about?"

"Are you certain this is the course of action you wish to take?" Alastair moved away to study a shelf of ancient artifacts. He noticed a few he might utilize, but knew his tight-assed son would never part with the items in his inventory. Not if it meant upsetting the Council. "Do you trust her?"

"What kind of question is that?" Nash scoffed. "Not three hours ago, you were encouraging me to go after her."

"True, but then I didn't fully know about her past."

"I trust her."

Alastair pivoted on his heel to face his son. "Then call her in and let's get started. But know this; if she hurts you, I will smite her from existence."

"Don't you dare threaten her!"

He cocked his head and smiled. "It does my heart good to see the fire in you. It's like you're a chip off the old block."

"Goddess forbid," Nash muttered.

Five minutes later, they merged their magic to remove the spell. For Alastair, who'd seen the original spell when he scried, it was a matter of reversing the process. When they were done, he lifted Ryanne's hand in his and sent a test arc from his fingertips. "Do you feel any different, child?"

"I feel strange."

"In what way?"

"Overly warm, as if I'm heating from the inside out. Does that make sense?"

"It does. That's the regeneration of the magic within your cells."

"Will this be a constant feeling?"

"No. Only when you conjure, teleport, or perform spells. Most times you will feel normal," he informed her.

A shimmer in the air around them caught his attention. "How strong are the wards protecting this room?"

Nash was by his side in an instant. "Why?"

"Someone's trying to spy on you."

"Shit! *Achoo!* Damn! *Achoo!*"

A laugh shook Alastair. "If you continue to swear, we will have the entire population of trash pandas from North Carolina on your doorstep in minutes, son."

"Don't you think I know that?" Nash growled.

"When you swear, you sneeze and raccoons appear?" Ryanne made an admirable attempt to contain her humor. "Is that normal?"

Nash shot a glare o'death in Alastair's direction, and he struggled to hold back his amusement.

"Yes, and no," Nash finally confessed. "It's a gift from my sperm donor to all his children. Remind us, Father, what is the result of *your* swearing?"

Alastair dusted his hands together. "Right. On that note, I will leave the two of you to carry on with your evening. But do remember to reinforce your wards, boy." He walked to the shelves containing the magical objects and selected one. "My payment for services rendered."

"You can't take that!"

"Can't I? Hmm." With a snap of his fingers, Alastair returned home. His manservant, Alfred, was there to greet him. "Here, my man. Stow this away for safekeeping, won't you?"

"Yes, sir. Right away."

"That sneaky sonofabitch! *Achoo!*" Nash clenched his hands into fists.

Ryanne shoved down the laughter threatening to erupt. "What was it he took?"

"A rare thirteenth-century Japanese jar."

"And what does it do? I mean, he didn't take it for its beauty, that's for sure."

"It can transform any liquid into a toxic poison. If you want to murder your dinner guests, you can serve wine from that particular decanter."

Her eyes widened in shock. She couldn't fathom desiring to murder anyone, much less guests. "Why would he want something like that?"

"Because he's Alastair Thorne and no one knows what the heck goes on in his head," Nash grumbled. "But he's right about one thing. I need to strengthen the wards protecting this room. He was able to teleport out. That shouldn't have been possible with one of the objects, even for him."

"Is there something I can do to help?"

"No. You have much to learn before that happens, babe. If you'll wait for me in my office, I'll wrap things up here and take you for that dinner."

Before he could step away, she latched on to his wrist. "What's the result when your father curses?"

She'd never seen such an evil grin in all her life, but Nash took great delight when he answered. "Locusts."

44

Thunder boomed and shook the building.

"Then you shouldn't have stolen my vase!" Nash yelled toward the ceiling.

Ryanne eyed him warily. What the hell had she gotten herself into? Was she buying into the belief she was a witch? Denying what she'd witnessed with her own eyes and felt within her own cells was difficult. A small part of her hoped she'd wake up and find it was all a dream. But a larger part of her was excited by the prospect of magical abilities. What were the limits to her powers?

While she waited on the white leather loveseat in Nash's office, her thoughts turned to her parents. *Larceny*. Wow! Just, wow! Who would use their six-year-old daughters in such a despicable manner? If she could get Rylee to return her phone calls, she'd ask her sister what she might or might not remember.

For certain, their adopted parents didn't know what they were, or that they'd had two witches in their midst. Chris and Hazel Jones had been two of the strictest, old-school, religious people on the planet.

Sadness crept in. Last year, a house fire took Chris's and Hazel's lives. Ryanne missed the steady love and support Hazel had always shown her. Maybe it was better that they'd passed. They would never discover what their daughters truly were.

Hot tears burned behind her lids, and she blinked to dispel the building moisture.

Despite their stringent, no-nonsense attitude, they had been good people, and she had loved them. The same couldn't be said for Rylee. Growing up, her sister had rebelled every chance she could. After Rylee took off for New York, all that the twins shared was a handful of phone calls and the occasional secretive visit.

Her sister returned after the Joneses' funeral. That was about the time Rylee went to work for Victor Salinger, claiming she needed to be close to family.

Ryanne snorted.

She still rarely saw her sister, and when she did, Rylee only talked about herself and how great her life was. Once or twice she tried to turn the conversation to Nash Thorne, but for whatever reason, Ryanne hadn't been willing to discuss him or what she did at Thorne Industries. Something was off about Rylee's obsession with Nash.

"Are you ready?" Nash's deep baritone voice pulled her from her musings.

"Yes, and absolutely starved."

"I could teach you how to conjure a meal." His mischievous grin tickled her insides.

"Conjure a meal?"

"Yep. It's something you'll have fun with in the coming days— conjuring whatever your heart desires."

"Like what?"

"What is your favorite food?"

She laughed. "Is this a trick question? I'm a woman. That would be wine and chocolate."

"Watch and learn." So saying, Nash held out his hands, and within seconds, a box of Swiss chocolates rested in one palm and he gripped a bottle of Krug Private Cuvee Champagne in the other.

Although both were out of her price range, even Ryanne knew expensive items when she saw them. "Holy crap! Is this for real?"

His deep laugh boomed. "It's for real."

One thing bothered her, and she voiced her concerns. "That is a private label Champagne, Nash. Did you steal that?"

"No. A good friend of mine works for Krug. She keeps me supplied. This was procured from my collection."

"She?" Jealousy curled in her belly, making her insides a jumbled mess.

With great care, Nash set aside the bottle and the box. He stepped in front of her and used one knuckle to tilt up her chin. "She. But *she* is simply someone I grew up with. Our mothers were best friends."

"So you never had a relationship with her?"

"Does spin the bottle count?"

Ryanne shoved his chest. "Why do I get the feeling you used your magic to always have the bottle land in your favor?"

Nash grinned and drew her close. "Maybe because you are starting to know me too well."

"Mmhmm."

"If it makes you feel any better, she is happily married with the two-point-five kids, a dog, and the white picket fence."

"It does."

"There you go."

"Fine. Now kiss me and feed me because I'm starving."

"Starving for the kiss or the food?" he asked in a silky, seductive voice.

"Both," she admitted.

Nash dipped his head and settled his mouth on hers. The soft, lingering touch of his lips made Ryanne hungrier still.

She curled her hands around his neck and wove her fingers in his soft, blond hair. This time when his lips came in contact with hers, she opened her mouth to allow him full access. The taste of him was more addictive than all the boxes of Swiss chocolate he could conjure.

Nash pulled back just as Ryanne would have taken things a step further.

"Let's get you fed and re-address this after dinner. I have something to propose to you, and I don't want you to feel I'm taking unfair advantage."

CHAPTER 6

"N o."

"What do you mean 'no'?" Nash wanted to smash something. "Ryanne, this is serious."

"I don't care. I'm not doing it." She held up a hand to stem his protests. "It's not like you're asking me to put on a French maid costume and play some sort of sex game. You are asking me to pretend to be my sister and seduce Victor Salinger into giving me a necklace."

She jabbed him in the chest with her index finger. Hard.

Nash winced. He caught her hand and drew her close. "Okay, we're going to get back to the French maid costume and sex games right after this, but I said *nothing* about seducing Victor. And for what it's worth, I'm highly *opposed* to that course of action." He sighed his frustration. "I know what I'm asking goes against your sense of right and wrong, but hear me out. Victor has a necklace dating back to the time of Isis. That one piece of jewelry has the power to topple dynasties and induce chaos throughout the world."

"That sounds a little extreme, don't you think?" She scoffed her disbelief.

"I have in my possession a journal that states otherwise."

"You have hundreds of journals. I'm not sure how you keep everything straight in that head of yours."

"I was gifted with a high IQ."

"Yeah, it goes right along with all those cool superpowers. So why can't you use magic to steal the necklace from Salinger?"

"It's not that simple."

"Look, Nash, I can't get my sister to return a phone call. It's doubtful she'll agree to this plan."

"Yeah, about that... I don't think we should ask her."

"What?"

Nash winced again for an entirely different reason. The ear-piercing octave of Ryanne's voice set his ears to ringing.

"You cannot be serious? What do you plan to do, kidnap her and put me in her place?"

He remained silent. Color crept up his neck due to her accurate guess. When she put it that way, it sounded a bit asinine.

"No! Not just no, but *hell no!*"

"Ryanne, babe, please be reasonable."

"I'll give you reasonable, you...you...you..."

Nash had done it. He'd officially broken Ryanne. Liz was going to kill him. "Look, it's not like she's going to come to any harm. We grab her, put her under a sleeping spell, and you take her place until we can swap the necklace."

"What happens when she wakes, goes back to Victor, and then has to face the music because it's discovered the real necklace is missing, Nash? Did you ever think of that? You're putting my sister's life in jeopardy."

"Okay, so maybe I didn't get that far in the planning stage of this little scheme."

"Gah!" She threw her hands up and headed for the door. When she reached it, she wrenched it open. "Get out!"

"Ryanne—"

"I said, *get out!* I mean it, Nash. I want you to leave."

"Please listen to me. This goes much deeper than you know. Let me show you."

Ryanne silently studied him. Nash could see the wheels turning in her brain. Inasmuch as she was pissed at him, she was also bright and logical. Eventually, she'd agree to the proper course of action. Or so he hoped.

She closed the door. "Show me how?"

"Be right back." Nash teleported to his study. When he returned, he brought with him the journal he'd mentioned a few minutes before. He opened it to one of several bookmarked pages and set it on her dining room table. "Here."

"I'm never going to get used to you disappearing into thin air," she muttered as she picked up the book. While Ryanne read, the frown line between her eyes deepened, as did the compression of her lips. Five minutes after she started, she looked up. "Holy hell!"

He knew what she'd read. He'd read it himself—many times. It discussed how influential the object was in the second World War when it fell into the hands of Adolf Hitler.

"And look here…" Nash brushed her shoulder as he reached past her to turn to another marked section. The resulting zing he experienced nearly caused him to chuck the book across the room and sweep her into his arms to make long, leisurely love. Shoving aside all thoughts of sex, he tapped the page for her to read. "Prior to that, Napoleon Bonaparte sent an unscrupulous character to Egypt in an attempt to acquire it. According to Lady Hester Tremayne, Napoleon had already escaped Elba at that point. His hired henchman stole the necklace from her in his quest to help Bonaparte defeat England."

When she turned toward him, he cupped her face between his palms to emphasize his urgency. "I'm not crazy, and I would never do anything to hurt you or Rylee, but you're the only one who stands a remote chance of getting that necklace from Victor."

"Why can't we bring Rylee into this? Why not tell her what's going on and get her help?"

How did he tell her that he didn't trust Rylee as far as he could throw her? Or that he secretly believed her sister was behind the fiery death of Ryanne's adopted parents?

He didn't need to. Ryanne guessed his reticence in mere seconds.

"You don't trust her," she stated flatly. "Why?"

"I don't know her enough to trust her." As far as evasions went, his answer was extremely lame, but Nash didn't wish to offend her any worse than he already had by not believing her sister was the be all, end all.

"You're lying."

His brows slammed together as he glared down at her. "You can't possibly know that!"

"I know *you*, Nash Thorne. And I certainly can tell when you aren't giving me the full truth."

He opened his mouth to swear, but she slapped her hand over his mouth.

"I also know you are about to curse up a storm and call North Carolina's entire population of raccoons to my apartment."

The wry twist of her lips struck him as funny. Yes, maybe she did know him better than he thought. He gave her a single nod, at which she slowly removed her hand. Had he imagined her regretful sigh and how her eyes had dropped to his lips?

"Fine." He sighed his frustration and ran a hand through his hair. It was imperative to get her on his side with this project before any romantic overtures because he didn't want her to believe he was only seducing her for his personal gain. "I don't trust your sister."

"Do you care to tell me why?"

"I don't want to, no."

"Then I can't help you."

"You'd put the fate of the world at risk simply because I don't like your sister?" he asked, incredulous and on the verge of a meltdown.

"You have the right to not like my sister. But what I find difficult to come to grips with is your refusal to tell me why."

She took a step forward, closing the short distance between them.

Her chest brushed his, and Nash sucked in his breath. She placed her hand over his rapidly pounding heart and smiled.

"Is this a ploy to get me to tell you? Touch me and make my mind go to sludge?"

Her smile widened. "Is it working?"

"Better than you can possibly know."

Ryanne sobered, and her face took on a look of soft pleading. "Tell me, Nash."

He closed his eyes and almost shook his head at how easily she could manipulate him without trying. "Your sister is not what she seems."

"Why would you say that?"

"When you first came to work for me, she tried to pass herself off as you."

"What?"

"You had left with Liz not ten minutes before when she sailed into the office in the exact outfit you'd had on. It meant she had been watching and waiting for you to leave. Unless I miss my guess, she used magic. How else could she have known what you were wearing?" He shook his head. "At the time, I thought maybe she had someone scrying for her. Now, I wonder if she found a way to revive her powers long before you."

Ryanne sank onto her coffee table and gripped the edges. "What happened?"

He didn't answer right away. Instead, he poured her a glass of water and brought it to her. He waited until she took a sip and put the glass down.

"Okay."

"She tried to seduce me."

"Ohmygod!" Disbelief gave way to her building rage. "I... how...what..."

Nash cupped her jaw and brushed his thumb back and forth along her cheekbone. "She came on to me, pretending to be you. I knew immediately that she wasn't."

"Why would she do that?"

"I let the scene play out, and—"

"Wait! What? *You let her seduce you?*" The fury in her tone couldn't be mistaken.

"No!" he denied quickly. "It never went past a few kisses."

Ryanne smacked his hand away. "Are you freaking kidding me right now? You kissed my sister? More than once?"

"Strictly to find out what she was after. I swear."

"I can't handle this right now." Once again, she stalked to the door. "I'll see you tomorrow at work."

His instincts were screaming at him to resolve this here and now, but the set expression on her face told him she'd already made up her mind. Nash moved toward the door but stopped inches away. "She made a mistake by approaching me."

Ryanne's head snapped up. "How so?"

"She isn't you." He let her see his sincerity. "She doesn't have your light."

"I don't know what that means."

"I think you do. Or I hope one day you will." He wanted nothing more than to lean down and kiss her doubts away, but he refrained. "Call or text me as soon as you're finished with the journal tonight. I'll return for it."

"I can bring it with me tomorrow."

"I know you'll need time to read it, but I'd prefer it not be out of my sight for that long. Since you don't want me here, you'll need to let me know when you're done. I'll come back when you're through with it for the night."

As he turned to leave, she grabbed his arm. "Nash?"

His silence encouraged her to continue.

"Did you really know the difference?" Her voice sounded small and uncertain.

His wide smile came unbidden. "Yeah, I really did. In my dreams, I've kissed you a million times, Ryanne. Rylee didn't even come close. You, on the other hand, put those dreams to shame."

The anger drained from her. "Come back in a half hour. Bring Häagan Dazs's Midnight Cookies and Cream from the Decadent Collection."

"Should I buy out the whole freezer section or only a few pints?"

"I'll leave that up to you in case you want any."

He lifted the hand clutching his forearm, and dropped a whisper-light kiss on her knuckles. "I'll see you in a bit."

CHAPTER 7

After Nash left, Ryanne sagged back against the wall. An unexpected rage had overcome her when she'd found out Nash and Rylee shared a kiss—more than one, according to him. That fury nearly set her hair on fire. Yet, the one thing she could and did believe was her sister's underhanded measures to get to Nash. It fit with Rylee's initial desperation to meet him. The question was why?

Now, with Nash gone, Ryanne could think clearly. It wasn't something she could do when he was close. This new sexual awareness between them had her too flustered to know up from down.

The idea of being party to kidnapping her sister and the subsequent identity swap disturbed her on every level. Although she and Rylee had shared a womb and still share an identical face, they were as different as night and day. Where Ryanne was staid and dependable, Rylee was impulsive and wild. Could she even hope to pull off a deception of that magnitude with someone who knew her sister as well as a lover? From all accounts, Victor Salinger wasn't someone to be trifled with.

What did it say about Nash's feelings for her if he was willing to throw her into the lion's den? Either he had a massive amount of confidence in her, *or* he was willing to sacrifice her to get what he wanted. Unfortunately, both scenarios could apply. Nash was difficult to read. Ryanne's one saving grace was that she was a damned good administrative assistant and Nash loved his routine. He might balk at having to replace her. Hadn't he doubled her salary today?

As she studied the journal he'd left behind, the air crackled around her, and she froze in place. Through what could only be considered a rift in space, Alastair Thorne stepped into her living room.

"Close your mouth, dear girl. We don't have much time."

She shut her mouth, but she couldn't do much about her stunned amazement.

"Listen carefully. Your sister is about to arrive. She's walking through the door of your building as we speak."

"Rylee?"

One of his arrogant brows shot skyward. "You have more than one sister?"

"For the love of all that is holy! You and Nash really are two peas in a pod, aren't you?"

His lips twitched, but otherwise, he didn't acknowledge her sarcastic comment. "Rylee has either tapped your place, or she was spying on you through a scrying mirror."

"That would mean she has access to magic."

"Precisely. But either way, she's out to cause trouble. I suggest you—"

A knock sounded on her front door. "Ryanne?"

"What should I do?" Ryanne asked him scarcely above a whisper.

"Why, answer the door, of course."

His wicked smile unnerved her. This man was far more dangerous than Nash on any given day.

As she walked toward the door, he waved a hand. When she looked over her shoulder, her jaw dropped to see the man she'd been kissing earlier that day. "Nash? No, wait. You…" What was it that Nash had said about a light? Hers was different than her sister's? How had she not noticed Alastair's light until she'd put a little distance between them?

"It's okay, child. Open the door, but make sure you play along with whatever I say," he ordered quietly.

Ryanne opened the door and prayed her face wasn't a dead give-away to the craziness happening in her apartment. Why Alastair felt the need to pose as Nash was beyond her, but when Nash finally showed up, it was going to be interesting.

"Leelee. What are you doing here?"

She noticed her sister's dark gaze zero in on Alastair. The expression on Rylee's face was nothing short of cunningly satisfied, and it sent a chill down Ryanne's spine. What the hell was her sister up to this time?

"Why, Nash Thorne, as I live and breathe," Rylee purred.

Even knowing Alastair was pretending to be Nash, Ryanne experienced a swift flash of jealousy unlike anything she'd ever known. What Rylee wanted, Rylee got—or at least she did ninety-nine-point-nine percent of the time. Her intent to add Nash to her string of men was obvious.

"What do you want, Rylee?" Ryanne ground out, this time forgoing the nickname.

Rylee's head whipped back around, and her mouth dropped open. Their entire lives, Ryanne had called her sister "Leelee" as part of their twin speak. But at the moment, any affection Ryanne held for her sister was sorely strained by her shenanigans.

Alastair shifted forward and dropped a casual arm across Ryanne's shoulders. "Rylee, we weren't expecting you."

It took every ounce of willpower she possessed not to do a double take. Alastair not only looked like Nash, he acted and sounded exactly like him, too. In a show of solidarity, she clasped his dangling hand, entwining their fingers. He gave her a subtle squeeze, and she assumed it was encouragement.

Rylee's gaze sharpened on Alastair before she smiled. "Do I need an excuse to pop in to see my sister?"

"Advance notice would be nice." His tone was brisk. "Ryanne and I were about to get busy."

Ryanne choked. Hearing the great Alastair Thorne try to be hip nearly did her in. If he pounded her a little too hard on the back, she probably deserved it for ruining his game.

"Sorry," she finally managed. "I swallowed my own spit."

"Drooling over the image of a naked Nash, I'm sure." Although Rylee thought she was being funny, her humor fell flat. "I've pictured him that way myself."

The green-eyed monster woke within Ryanne. The tips of her fingers started to burn, and when she looked down, she was horrified to see a flame spark to life from her fingertips.

Alastair leaned in close to murmur, "Pull it back." Pretending affection, he placed a light kiss on her temple. In a louder voice, he said, "It's rumored that you and Victor Salinger are an item."

A flash of some unnamed emotion came and went on Rylee's face. "Victor doesn't mind if I stray as long as I return to him."

"Enough!" Ryanne snapped. "You and Nash will not now, nor ever... ever..." She couldn't form the thought of them together, much less say it. She settled on a warning glare for Rylee. "Ever."

Wicked delight lit Rylee's coffee-colored eyes. "Oh, Ryanne, you're jealous! If I didn't know better, I'd think you were in love."

"Know better?" Alastair asked.

Because Rylee anticipated his question—and why wouldn't she, she'd set him up nicely for it—her smile widened. "My dear sister has never had more than a passing fling. Perhaps it was the loss of our beloved parents, or our sweet but starchy, adoptive parents, but Ryanne refuses to give her heart to anyone. Isn't that so, sister dear?"

Was it true? *Had* she refused to love another? Ryanne suspected her sister was correct. Black dots gathered behind Ryanne's eyelids, and she began to hyperventilate. In the blink of an eye, Alastair scooped her up and strode to the sofa. He placed her gently on the cool leather cushion and conjured a glass of water.

Rylee's gasp wasn't feigned.

He chose to ignore her and pressed the glass into Ryanne's hand. "Drink." When he seemed satisfied she wasn't going to pass out on him, he faced her sister. "Don't pretend you don't know about magic, Rylee. I've seen you in action."

With a wary look, Rylee sank into the armchair across from them. She opened her mouth to speak when the front door opened.

"Hey, babe, I got... *what the fuck? Achoo!*"

Faster than the speed of lightning, Alastair fisted his hand. A simple snap of his long, elegant fingers restored him to his natural visage. "Hello, son."

CHAPTER 8

Nash stared, speechless and more than a little confused. The weirdness meter was in the red zone. Why was his father pretending to be him? When had Rylee shown up to stir up her special brand of shit? And why was Ryanne looking like she wanted to toss her cookies at any second?

His primary concern was for Ryanne. Dropping the tubs of ice cream on the coffee table, he sat beside her in the space Alastair had vacated. "What's the matter? Why do you look so pale?"

Wordlessly, she rested her head on his shoulder, and he wrapped an arm around her to tuck her close against his side.

Nash looked to his father for answers.

"She was a little faint. I believe she finally realized she cares about you." Amusement was heavy in Alastair's tone. "Speaking from past experience, it's a shock when that happens."

A happy grin worked its way up from Nash's toes and took over his entire being. He couldn't contain his smile if he tried. His arm tightened reflexively around Ryanne.

Unfortunately, now was not the time to discuss love or relationships, certainly not with Rylee glaring at them with barely concealed hostility. She did a fantastic job of hiding her feelings, but one of Nash's special abilities was to discern other people's emotions. A simple magical probe of the air between them and he was able to read Rylee's angry energy as it carried across the short distance. It remained to be seen whether she was upset about a potential relationship between him and Ryanne, or some other unknown reason.

He'd need to revisit Rylee's motives later. In the meantime, the urge to ease Ryanne's upset was strong. "I didn't realize you were hosting a party without me and your Häagan Dazs's Midnight Cookies and Cream. I'd have hurried back."

Nash felt her smile against his neck. As she straightened and reached for the bag of goodies, he silently mourned the loss of her in his arms.

"Your timing is impeccable, as always. I could use this to cool down my temper."

"Who has you upset, my love? I'll tear the skin from their bones." He lifted her hand to drop a kiss on her knuckles. Those same knuckles rapped him on the side of his head.

"You're such a geek." She cast a hard look at the group. "Everyone, take a seat at the dining room table. We have things to discuss."

Because Ryanne looked so troubled, Nash felt compelled to tease her again. "You're sexy when you're bossy."

He grinned when she cast a glare in his direction. Try as she might, she couldn't stop the telling twitch of her lips. Her humor was one of the things he appreciated most about her. Well, after her smoking-hot body.

Nash followed her to the kitchen on the pretext of making coffee. A quick backward glance showed Alastair and Rylee giving each other the stink eye. Careful to keep his tone low, he asked, "When did your sister arrive?"

"Less than two minutes after your father—which was about twenty minutes after you left."

"I'm sorry, Ryanne. I wouldn't have left if I'd have known you had to deal with this mess."

"I don't even know what *this* mess is. And besides, I kicked you out, remember?"

"True dat." Nash dropped a quick kiss on her lips and conjured a pot of hot coffee. "We'd better get in there. Grab the cups."

"I'm never going to get used to you producing things out of thin air," she muttered as she rummaged through her cabinet for coffee mugs. "Or you saying things like 'true dat.'"

Once seated, Nash broached the subject of the enormous elephant in the room. "Rylee, we know you and Ryanne once had magical abilities. It appears an organization known as the Witches' Council bound your powers when you were younger and wiped the knowledge of magic from your minds." Casually, he took a sip of coffee then set his mug down. "What I want to know is when you got your powers back?"

He felt more than saw Ryanne's head whip in his direction. Not sparing her a glance, he kept his focus on her sister. "I'd also like to know how much you know about Victor Salinger's business and how deeply you are involved in his dealings."

From the corner of his eye, he noticed Ryanne stiffen and lean forward. Alastair remained the inscrutable statue he always appeared to be. Rylee, on the other hand, had a much more animalistic reaction. Her hands curled into claws, and she lunged across the distance.

With a quick sweep of his hand, Alastair threw up an invisible barrier designed to protect their group. Rylee crashed into it with a grunt and a few choice swear words.

"I'd say that gives you a good idea." Alastair's dry tone left no one in doubt of his thoughts on the matter. Nash was certain his father believed Rylee was complicit in Victor's schemes.

Alastair waved his hand and slammed it flat on the table, causing everyone to jump. *"Cohibeo."*

Nash understood the command and focused his attention on Ryanne. He could see the question forming on her lips and quickly shook his head. Taking his cue, she remained quiet and watchful. A glance showed Rylee understood her circumstances better than anyone. Fire blazed from her eyes as she squirmed in her chair and tried to break the magical hold Alastair had placed on her.

"You bastard! Let me go!"

"No." Alastair perched on the edge of the table and straightened his tie. "I'm inclined to let you sit there like a recalcitrant child. When you are ready to cooperate, perhaps we'll discuss your release."

Rylee sent a beseeching look toward her twin. "Ryanne, please help me."

Nash clasped Ryanne's hand and interwove their fingers. The gesture seemed to ease her concern because she squeezed tightly.

"No, Rylee, I don't think I will. Answer Nash's original question. When did you get your power back?"

Hatred blazed from Rylee's dark coffee-colored eyes. Nash felt the heat of her emotion, and he was left to wonder how it affected Ryanne. She had to be hurt by her sister's defection and animosity.

Inside, Ryanne wasn't as cool and collected as the other occupants of the room probably believed her to be. Wave after wave of dread for her sister's imagined transgressions crashed into her. If Rylee was here as a spy for Victor, then she'd just collected two powerful enemies. Neither Nash nor Alastair would forgive the perceived slight against their family, of that, Ryanne was certain. These men didn't strike her as the forgiving sort.

Following the dread was a profound sadness. When had her sister turned into such a devious person? Had she always been that way and Ryanne happened to miss this aspect of her sister's personality? Where had this hatred come from? If Rylee had hated her in the past, it had been hidden well.

"Answer the question, Rylee. I won't ask it again."

"Fine," Rylee spat. "Victor helped me regain my powers when I met him in New York."

"New York?" Disbelief warred with anger, and Ryanne didn't

know whether to cry or smack her sister silly. "Rylee, that was years ago. Why did you never tell me we were witches?"

"You? Miss Goody-Two-Shoes? I was supposed to tell you that our parents were thieves and used the two of us to get magical artifacts for the Dés—" Abruptly, she stopped speaking, as if she'd said too much. "It doesn't matter. Chris and Hazel had you wrapped up so deeply in their beliefs that you could scarcely breathe, and you didn't seem to want to change it. If Victor hadn't freed you, you'd still be under their influence. You'd never have met your beloved Nash Thorne." The sneer on Rylee's face was full of loathing, and each word she uttered dripped with acid.

Ryanne didn't realize how hard she gripped Nash until he raised their joined hands and dropped a kiss on her knuckles. Her throat closed at his gesture. In the course of a day, her world had turned upside down. What she thought she knew about her life had all been a lie. The closeness she believed she shared with her twin was nothing but a sham. And most startling of all? The man she had crushed on from afar appeared to have deep feelings for her.

Full of bemused wonder, she stared deeply into his green eyes. The silent understanding he offered brought tears to her eyes. She blinked the sting away.

"You said Victor freed her. How did he do that?"

Alastair's icy tone brought her up sharp. She whipped her head around to stare at Rylee.

Rylee laughed in the face of Alastair's rage. "He has connections. Isn't it ironic that the Joneses were always threatening fire and brimstone with each sermon, and then they themselves died in a fiery blaze?"

Ryanne's throat ceased to work. Although she swallowed air convulsively, she couldn't seem to get the necessary oxygen to her lungs. Jumping up, she raced for the bathroom. She managed to make it to the toilet in time to deposit the contents of her stomach in the bowl. Over and over, she retched until there was nothing left inside her. She sat back against the wall of the bathroom and took a ragged breath.

"Here, child."

Glancing up, she saw the washcloth Alastair held out to her. With a shaky hand, she accepted the offering and wiped her mouth.

"My son has a weak stomach when it comes to vomit. He calls himself a 'sympathetic yacker.' Otherwise, he'd have followed you." Amusement rested heavy in Alastair's tone. "Trust me, you don't want him to attend you at a time like this. You'd be cleaning two messes."

Ryanne was surprised she could laugh. "I'll keep that in mind for future stomach ailments."

"Do you want to talk about it?"

"Victor had my adoptive parents murdered, didn't he?"

"I have no doubt."

Hot tears escaped down her cheeks. She pressed the heels of her palms to her eyes. "How could she have a boyfriend as evil as him?"

"He's not her boyfriend."

Astonishment brought her head up.

"Victor isn't into women. He gets his kicks in other ways. If your sister is keeping company with him, it's for an entirely different reason."

"But she said he didn't mind if she strayed, and you said they were rumored to be together."

"I was curious as to how far she'd go with her advances toward my son." He held out his hand to help her up. "Get cleaned up and come out when you're ready. I'll prepare you a cup of peppermint tea to soothe your stomach."

"You're a kind man, Mr. Thorne."

"No, child. Never make the mistake of believing me kind."

"We can agree to disagree. Based on all you've done for me so far... well, let's say it's more than anyone else has done for me in the last ten years."

"Even Nash?"

"Until today, I assumed Nash had ulterior motives for doing the little things he's done. Lunch here or a coffee there. I firmly believed he wanted to keep me from finding another job."

Alastair's laugh was deep and full-bodied. "Thornes can be a selfish lot. We'll do for each other, but because of who and what we are, we stick to ourselves. It is written that a Thorne only loves once." He tucked a stray strand of hair behind her ear. The move, so similar to Nash's, made her wonder if mannerisms were genetic or learned. "If Nash did anything nice for you at all, it was his way of showing he cares for you. I think I know him well enough to say he has been struck by Cupid's arrow."

Ryanne rubbed the place over her heart.

"Dare I say that you've been struck too?" he asked gently.

"I think it's highly possible," she croaked.

He nodded his understanding and turned to leave.

"Mr. Thorne?"

"Yes?"

"Will you keep this conversation to yourself? I need time to process."

"Certainly, child. Come out when you're ready."

CHAPTER 9

Nash stopped pacing when his father entered the room. "Is she all right?"

"She's fine, son. I suspect she'll join us in a few minutes."

"Oh, aren't you the sweetest?" Rylee sneered. "Poor little Ryanne has an upset belly. You should go kiss her better."

"Shut your mouth," Nash snarled. "Your sister has had nothing but nice things to say about you until now. We…" He gestured to the three of them. "…all know better, don't we? You're nothing but a horrid wretch, out to cause trouble at every opportunity."

Something flashed in her eyes—possibly hurt or regret—but Nash wasn't buying whatever she was about to peddle. "I love my sister."

"Doubtful," murmured Alastair.

In this, father and son were in agreement. Nash didn't trust Rylee. She had trouble written all over her aura. It was funny how two women who were considered identical could be so different from one another. Ryanne's light was bold and beautiful, while her twin's was dark and twisted.

Misgivings assailed him. Would Victor spot Ryanne as a fake right away? Was she too good and pure of heart to fool him?

Ryanne stepped back into the living room, and it was impossible for Nash to keep his hands to himself. He wrapped her in his tight embrace and buried his face in her silky hair. She seemed to be desperate for the contact, too, because she clung to him for all she was worth.

He didn't care that the timing was shit. He couldn't let another second pass without telling her his feelings. "I love you, Ryanne."

Her hands fisted in his shirt, and she hugged him closer.

"You don't have to say it back, but I need you to know." He rubbed his cheek against hers and, in a low voice, said, "From the very moment we met, you've held my heart."

"So the drool comment was all an act?"

"Absolutely."

"Good to know." She lifted her head and met his steady gaze. "I'm not sure what I feel, Nash. It's definitely more than I ever have before, but this is all coming at me pretty fast."

He shoved aside his disappointment and tried not to be discouraged because she hadn't replied in kind. Not everyone loved as swiftly or as all-consumingly as a Thorne.

"Let's get back to the matter at hand, shall we?" Alastair asked.

There was a quality to his voice that made Nash take notice. What his father thought of all this was anyone's guess. Alastair usually held his cards close to the vest.

"Why are you here, Rylee? Here in Ryanne's apartment? Now that we know it isn't about sisterly love, the truth would be appreciated." Nash moved to stand before her as he asked the question. While he stared down at her, he experienced a wave of dizziness. He shook his head once to clear it. A wicked, self-satisfied smirk came and went on her face. She was up to something. Exactly what, was the question of the hour.

"I came for the journal."

Her eyes darted to the book, and she licked her lips.

In all likelihood, she spoke the truth. Not quite *all* of the truth, but enough to not set off Nash's BS alarm. He knew the answer to the next question, but he wanted to see how honest she would be. "What use is it to you?"

"It's not, other than to retrieve it for Victor. He needs it for the necklace."

"Is he expecting you back tonight?"

"No. Tomorrow morning at the earliest." She shot a resentful gaze toward Ryanne. "I told him that I needed to play the part of the loving sister."

Nash's heart ached for Ryanne. While he didn't necessarily place high in every family member's affections, he doubted they wanted to hurt him in the way Rylee wished to injure her own twin.

"Alastair, Ryanne, may I speak with you privately?"

They followed him into the kitchen but stopped where they could keep Rylee within their sights.

"What are you thinking, son?"

Taking a deep breath, he met Ryanne's worried gaze head-on. "I want to create a look-a-like journal to hand off to Victor, and I want you to pretend to be your sister."

Silence reigned. Disbelief and hurt were written all over her beautiful face. After a long pause, she spoke. "You would still put me in the path of that psycho, knowing he killed my adoptive parents?"

"We have to get our hands on the Red Scorpion, babe. We are out of options."

"What do you think, Mr. Thorne?"

It grated to see her seek Alastair's opinion, but Nash forcibly cooled his ire, hoping his father would persuade her to carry through with this plan.

Alastair turned his thoughtful gaze on Nash. It wasn't often they were in accord, but he could tell this was one of those times. Yet underlying Alastair's cool confidence was an uncertainty. About what or for whom, Nash couldn't say.

"We could use your help, child. Of course we will understand if you say no, but I have something that might make your decision easier."

"What would that be?" she asked.

"It's a tanzanite pendant. It acts as a communication device of sorts. You touch it, and it will psychically connect you to me."

"Only you? Not Nash, too?"

A soft understanding smile twisted Alastair's lips. "Would you prefer it be my son?"

"I..." She shook her head as if to clear it. "Is there a way to be connected to you both? I mean should I get into trouble, two heads are better than one, right?"

"I'll create a second tanzanite ring for Nash. In the meantime, have a bite to eat and get some rest, my dear. You too, son. I have the feeling tomorrow will take a lot out of us."

"What should we do about my sister?"

"My spell will hold her," Alastair assured her.

"Won't she be stiff in the morning after being magically tied to the chair all night?"

Nash shook his head and snorted. Leave it to Ryanne to care about someone else's comfort, even if that someone had set out to make her life a living hell.

"Before I leave, I'll alter it so that she will be able to recline on your sofa. Does that make you happy?"

"Thank you, Mr. Thorne."

"I'll go see to that now. You and my son have a few things to discuss before morning."

Ryanne waited until the elder Thorne left the room before facing Nash. "I seriously have a bad feeling about this whole thing."

"You are smart and quick on your feet, Ryanne. I have the utmost faith in you."

"No. You don't understand." She shook her head. How could she explain the alarm bells clanging inside her brain? This whole situation was a clusterfuck and likely to end with one of them dead. She'd only had this troubling sense of unease twice before: as a child, when her parents were in the accident, and again the night of the fire when Chris and Hazel died. "Nash, this is a horrible idea."

His large, warm palm cupped her cheek and made her want to lean into his hand like a kitten seeking attention. What did it say about her that she was starved for his affection? She curbed the impulse and looked him squarely in the eye. "I'm frightened."

His misgivings were clearly written upon his handsome features. The tightening of his full mouth, the narrowing of his beguiling eyes, and the tick of the firm muscle of his jaw all revealed his own struggle.

"I would never put you in danger if there was any other way, babe. You have to know that." When she remained silent, Nash continued. "Ryanne, tell me you know that. Tell me you understand you are more important to me than any other living soul on the planet."

His earnestness made her want to embrace him and all he offered. Yet trust wasn't always easy for her. In the back of her mind, a little doubt bomb detonated. What if he was using her for his own gains? Telling her exactly what she wanted to hear?

When he dropped his hand, she silently mourned the loss of his touch. His heavy sigh told her that he understood she wasn't going to be an easy sell.

"I'm sorry, Nash."

"You have nothing to be sorry for. We'll figure something else out."

"You're not mad at me?"

"No, Ryanne. You have the right to say no. No to this crazy mission. No to a relationship with me. No to whatever you find objectionable."

Right then and there, the feeling she was previously unsure of blossomed into something larger than her heart could contain. "I don't find you objectionable in the least. And I'm not saying no to a relationship with you."

His happy smile took her breath away.

"Good, because that offer was a little bit harder for me to put out there."

She laughed as he drew her close. "I love you, too, Nash."

He went still for a long moment before crushing her to him. It was difficult to take a deep breath because she feared he might crack her ribs.

"Can't... breathe..."

"Oh, crap! I'm sorry, Ryanne. I..." He had loosened his grip and was staring down into her smiling face. When Nash shook his head in wonder, Ryanne knew that he was for real. That he wasn't playing her to gain the necklace.

"I'll do it."

He frowned his confusion.

"Switch places with my sister—I'll do it."

"Don't do this because you think it's a condition of my feelings. It's not."

"No. I'm agreeing because it's *not* a condition of your love. You are the only person who doesn't expect anything of me, Nash. Do you know how rare that is in my world?" She shook her head and attempted to explain. "Not that I remembered their larcenous ways, but obviously my birth parents required me to be the perfect little thief. Then my adoptive parents expected me to always follow the religious path they envisioned for my life. Rylee used me and still expects me to fall in with her schemes." She caressed his hard jaw. "But you are giving me a choice. I can do or not do, and you are going to love me anyway, aren't you?"

"Yes. I will continue to love you whatever you choose to do. If you want to help retrieve the Red Scorpion, I'll be ecstatic, but if you don't, I'll understand. If you want to continue to be my assistant, I'll be delighted for you to continue by my side, and I'll be happy to finally be able to share the details of our dealings with the Council.

But if you decide you want to follow a different career path, I'll support that, too." He tilted her chin up and dropped a light, lingering kiss on her lips. "I love you for you, babe. Your happiness is my priority."

She blinked back the stinging prick of tears. "Thank you."

"Now, you decide what you'd like to eat, and I'll show you how to conjure it."

CHAPTER 10

Dinner was a quiet affair. Rylee's surly presence weighed heavily on Nash and Ryanne. At some point, they would need to find a way to deal with her, but for now, they sat and ate their meal under the resentful force of her glare.

Nash had offered to free the invisible ties binding her hands so that she might eat with them, but she sneered and stated she'd rather starve. He wasn't heartbroken or concerned in the least. It wouldn't hurt her to miss a meal. In fact, she needed to get used to the fact that her meal ticket, Victor, was going to be out of commission very soon.

"I'll dish up the ice cream. Do you want any?" Ryanne asked, eager to be away from the tension in the room.

"Just a scoop, please."

Her uncertain gaze darted to her twin. "Rylee?"

"Fuck off."

Disappointment darkened her eyes, and she quickly turned away to hide her hurt at Rylee's ugliness.

"You'd better offer your sister more respect, or I'll bind your tongue along with your body," Nash snapped once Ryanne had cleared the room.

74

A sly, come-hither expression settled over Rylee's features, and her mouth curled in sexual invitation. "Oh, come now, Nash. Surely, you realize my sister can't satisfy your needs. Not a virile man like you. If you help me, I'll make it worth your while. The things I can do make grown men blush and give their dicks a permanent hard on."

"Sounds uncomfortable." Instead of tempted, he was completely repulsed. "In case it's not clear, let me spell it out for you. I love Ryanne. Anything you offer? Yeah, that's going to be a hard pass."

Ryanne stood in the entryway between the rooms. The grateful look she gave him made his heart soar. While it bothered him to think prior to this moment she'd had such terrible relationships that she felt thankful for his simple statement, he also appreciated her unhappy past. It brought her to this moment and to him. He had no intention of ever letting her go.

She set the bowl in front of him with a butterfly-soft kiss on his cheek. "Thank you," she whispered.

"No thanks necessary. I don't want anyone else." He met her eyes, hoping his honesty shone through. "Ever. Only you, babe." He watched as her throat constricted, and he stroked the column of her neck with his fingertips to offer comfort. "You should know, I'm the grateful one. I'm sorry I never explored these feelings before now."

"Timing is everything. Maybe neither of us was ready."

"Perhaps. But I don't want to waste another second."

"Me either. Eat your ice cream." She leaned in until her lips touched the shell of his ear. "I'll make you forget Rylee's offer after you've finished your dessert."

The idea of making love to Ryanne had the blood surging from his brain to his dick. "What offer?" he managed through his dry throat.

Her husky laughter made him forget all about the ice cream on the table. In one smooth, swift motion, he rose and lifted her up. His hands cupped her ass as she wrapped her legs around him. "Is it bad form to have wild monkey sex while your sister is in the next room?"

"What sister?"

They shared a grin and ignored Rylee as he carried her to the master bedroom.

Nash cleared the door and kicked it closed with his heel while Ryanne gripped his face between both hands and fastened her mouth over his. With her positioned slightly above him, tilting his head back and taking the lead, the kiss was erotic as hell. Her tongue danced around his, and the taste of mint chocolate chip ice cream teased his senses.

He gave a low growl. "You snuck some ice cream in the kitchen."

"I wanted fresh breath for this."

He nipped her lower lip. "You knew this was going to happen, did you?"

A pink flush brightened her cheeks. "I'd hoped."

He laughed and carried her to the bed. "Clothes off the old-fashioned way or the magical way?"

"Magical way?"

He shot her a grin filled with wicked intent and snapped his fingers. Dropping his eyes to her bared breasts, he said, "Magical."

"Oh!"

Pivoting, he sat on the edge of the mattress and drew her down to straddle his lap. The action brought his erect dick in direct contact with her wet warmth. The heat emanating from her made him want to thrust into her and remain sheathed there for the rest of his life.

His cock twitched in reaction to his thoughts.

Ryanne released a small meep.

Hiding his smile, he buried his face against her neck.

The creamy skin begged to be sampled. He ran the tip of his tongue along the column of her throat, lingering over her wildly beating pulse point. Nash scraped his teeth over the area and sucked.

She inhaled sharply and dropped her head to the side to allow him greater access. Her hands drifted up from his shoulders to cup the back of his head, even as her fingers wound their way into his hair.

When she shifted to rub herself against the length of him, he nearly became unglued. "Again," he murmured as he dropped his hands to her hips.

She guided his mouth to her breast and gasped his name when he bit down lightly.

"I said, again."

Ryanne pressed herself to him and shifted her pelvis oh-so-slowly upward.

Each rub of her slick core against his straining erection almost sent him over the edge. He halted the motion of her hips and took a deep breath.

"You are the most beautiful woman I've ever seen."

When she moaned, Nash sucked harder on the tip of her pebbled nipple.

Her gasps of pleasure thrilled him, and he turned his attention to her left breast and devoted the same treatment to it because he believed in equality in all things. He cupped her full breasts and kneaded, delighting in the softness.

Ryanne's passionate cries spurred him on. Nash became more aggressive in his sucking and was rewarded with another throaty groan as she dug her fingers into the back of his head to hold him close.

Burying his face in the valley of her breasts, he inhaled the fresh pear scent of her skin. Goddess, it was a fragrance he loved, in addition to the smell of her arousal. Nash trailed his fingertips down the smoothness of her abdomen. He paused to circle her belly button then traced a line around her side and down to the slope of her hip. Bringing up his other hand, he cupped the fullness of her ass.

With an achingly slow rub of his dick along her wet folds, he took her mouth in his in a long, drugging kiss.

"Please," she panted when she drew away. "Please, Nash, touch me."

He knew what she was asking. She wanted him to prepare her for his entry. To engage in the foreplay that would allow her body to readily accept his. Giving in to her desires, he trailed his fingers along the slick opening before sinking a finger deep inside. He made sure to caress the wall of her vagina as his thumb teased the nub of her clit.

He lightly kissed his way along her jaw to draw the lobe of her ear between his teeth. "Tell me what you want," he murmured. "Exactly what you want."

"Your mouth on me. Your tongue... ah!" She sucked in her breath as he inserted another finger and gave a pump of his hand. "That too!"

With one arm, he pulled her to him and rolled onto the mattress. As he looked down at her, he noted the feverish glow in her dark eyes and knew he'd never tire of seeing her in the height of passion.

"I'm going to taste you now."

She whimpered and opened her thighs wider to accommodate his shoulders.

His tongue swept across her opening. On and on, he tasted and teased as she voiced her encouragement. Only when she cried out and gripped the sheets in her orgasm did he stop.

"I want you in me. Now."

"Isn't it amazing how both our desires align?" he laughed.

As he started to ease into her, she held up a hand. "Condom."

"No need. Witches and warlocks cannot catch diseases like regular mortals. Have you noticed you've never had a cold?"

She rose on her elbows, her mouth hanging open in amazement. "I never thought about it other than to believe I had a good immune system."

He smiled as he filled her. "You do."

Ryanne inhaled sharply and ran her hands over the contours of his chest. When she pinched one nipple, he bit back a moan. Slowly, he withdrew, and inch-by-inch, he entered her again, savoring the exquisite torture.

Her hands gripped his ass, and as she urged him deeper, he clenched his teeth against the pleasure. It wouldn't do to embarrass himself and come too soon.

"I never thought this moment would ever happen," she said, as she raked her nails along his back. "I thought you weren't interested in me that way."

He twitched inside her. "Does this feel like I'm not interested?"

She laughed, and the sound was pure joy. "Nope. But to make sure I'm not mistaken, could you do that again?"

He complied, adding a deep thrust.

On the next thrust, she raised her hips to meet his. "God, yes!"

Before long, they were both incapable of words. Each met the other with a fierce desperation, striving to reach climax. She crested seconds before him and clutched him to her as she shuddered her release. The spasms of her vagina walls milked him and heightened his own pleasure.

He collapsed onto his back, arms spread wide. "Dear Goddess, I think you've killed me," he moaned. "At the very least, taken me out of commission for days on end."

"You only need be taken off the market. I want you in full commission."

He sighed and patted her shapely leg. "Consider me yours and yours alone, babe. But you have to promise I get more of that."

Her delighted giggle triggered his grin. It occurred to him that Ryanne hadn't laughed nearly enough in the time he'd known her. He hoped to change that going forward. The sound of her merriment was something he wanted to hear for the rest of their natural-born days.

"I don't want to be the one to bring up your sister at this delicate time, but should we make her comfortable in the guest room? It's going to be a long night."

"I suppose we should, although I'm inclined to make her suffer a bit more."

He rolled atop her and buried his nose in her neck. The scent of spiced pears greeted him. "Is it bad how crazy turned on I get when you become bitchy?"

"You need therapy."

"Most likely. Want to pretend you're my doctor and I'm your sex-addict patient? I can tell you all my deepest, darkest fantasies."

"Mmm, your role playing has merit, but only if we get to act out those fantasies."

He might have whimpered. Not a good sound to prove his masculinity, but the fact that he'd found the one woman who was game for anything made him weak at the knees.

"I'll tell you what. You go do whatever magic is necessary to secure my sister while I run a bath. You can join me when you're done, and we can discuss what's next on your sexual checklist."

"Yeah, we may need to take the bath first. I'm not sure I can walk out of this room with a raging hard-on and still keep my head up."

She stroked the firm length of him. "I'd say you have plenty to be proud of, but I agree, I don't want anyone else catching sight of what you're packing. Let's get a shower and take care of your needs first."

"Marry me."

Her happy laugh rang out.

"You think I'm kidding, babe, but I'm not."

"Let's discuss this again after the retrieval of the necklace, okay?"

"All right, but don't be surprised if I ask you every few hours on the off chance you've changed your mind." He was dead serious. He'd marry her this minute if she was willing. But he also under-stood he needed to give her time to process all that had gone down today.

CHAPTER 11

L ater that evening, as Nash lay sleeping, Ryanne studied his face, half hidden in the shadows of the night. She memorized every pore, every soft whisker, but more importantly, all the planes and angles that made up his handsome visage. She could no longer deny how deeply her feelings for him ran. In the time she'd known him, he'd become vital to her happiness. Seeing him sit across the desk from her, engrossed in his books, or witnessing him finagle a deal over the phone as he shot her a wink and a wicked grin, had become the highlight of her day.

Liz had been correct. Ryanne *had* been casting covert glances his way. She only hoped she hadn't given him full-blown cow eyes.

"What has you thinking so hard?"

The deep rumble of his voice in the silence startled her.

"Good grief, you nearly gave me a heart attack! I thought you were sleeping."

His sleepy chuckle warmed her. "Come snuggle with me. My arms feel empty without you."

"Who knew you were so poetic?" she murmured as she snuggled close.

"You inspire me."

"Pfft."

Nash raised his head and squinted down at her. "You don't believe me?"

"I believe you're full of crap. How 'bout that?"

"You've wounded me," he moaned as he flopped back against the pillows. "A barb straight to the heart."

"Fine. I'll say I believe you if you stop being a drama-llama."

"You didn't just go there."

"I believe I did."

"Be prepared to pay the price, woman."

With an alligator roll, he managed to touch every part of her naked form. Her arousal followed fast on the heels of their playfulness. How was it possible that everything he did excited her? From teasing to serious discussions, he was electric. Was their combined magic responsible for the attraction? Had she been this overwhelmed before Alastair unleashed her power?

Nash lifted his head from where he'd been paying marked attention to her left breast. "What has you troubled, babe?"

"How do you know I'm troubled?"

He cast one last regretful look at her dampened nipple and sighed. "Mainly because you aren't producing the moans of pleasure I'd hoped to elicit. What gives?"

"I've been attracted to you from the moment we met. But now... now, I'm overwhelmed and a bit stunned. I feel like I've been smacked in the head with a frying pan. Is it all because of magic, Nash?"

"Thornes seem to know our soul mates straight away. You were that for me, Ryanne. When I walked into that conference room and saw you for the first time, I was gobsmacked. Liz saw it and teased me unmercifully after you'd left that day." He traced one finger along her brow line and cheekbone before he tapped her on the nose. "You're it for me. But know that I would never use magic to attract or bind you. I want you to be with me of your own free will."

"No, I don't mean that. I know you would never do something so underhanded. What I'm wondering is if the magic attracts other magic? Does it amplify our feelings?"

"No, not based on any of the texts I've ever read, and believe me, I've read plenty. What we feel for each other has been building since the instant we met. I think this moment was always inevitable for us."

"Okay. Then take me."

"Excellent!"

His delighted grin brought an answering smile to her lips. When Nash latched on to her breast, Ryanne gave over to the pleasure.

Morning came all too soon, and Ryanne found it difficult to crawl out of bed. Nash had made love to her two more times throughout the night, and as energized as the sex made her, she was currently worn out. As the sun's rays beamed through the curtains, she pulled the covers higher to block out the light.

She felt the mattress sink on her side of the bed, and she scooted a little to the right to allow Nash more room. The distinct whiff of roses tickled her nose seconds before the petal-soft touch of the flower caressed her forehead and moved to her cheek.

"Wake up, sleepyhead," Nash cajoled. "We have a lot to accomplish today, my love."

She cracked open a lid and squinted in his direction. "Go away. I need sleep. My new lover wore me out last night."

The rose left her face, and within seconds, a single petal teased her lips. "New lover, hmm? I'd prefer new boyfriend, but I get it if you are a little reticent to label our relationship."

"I'm not sure how you can call it a relationship when nothing's been defined," she retorted as she rolled onto her back and tucked the bedspread under her arms.

"I thought we made things pretty clear last night." Nash transferred the rose and the petals in his hand to the nightstand, then placed a fist on the pillow on either side of her head. "How about we define it now? Ryanne Caldwell, will you go steady with me?"

She fought a happy grin and lost. "Steady? As in I get to wear your letterman sweater and class ring?"

"I'll conjure them both this instant if that's what you want."

"No need. It's good enough that you're mine. Now I can tell all those letter-opener-wielding bitches to cool their jets."

"What am I missing here?"

"Never you mind, boyfriend."

"So that's a yes?"

"That's definitely a yes," she growled as she wound her fingers into his thick blond hair and dragged his face to hers.

He didn't let her down and immediately captured her lips for a possessive kiss that curled her toes. Or maybe it was her kiss that was possessive. It didn't matter; he was hers.

When he moved away, Ryanne released a frustrated sigh.

"I must not have satisfied you as well as I could have last night."

She bit the pad of the thumb brushing her lower lip. "You satisfied me plenty. I'm simply a glutton. It's been a bit of a dry spell."

"For me, too," he murmured as he bent to kiss her again.

Her hand flew up and stopped him on his downward descent. "Wait, what? Guys don't have dry spells. Especially not guys who look like you."

"I haven't touched another woman since the day you walked into my life. I haven't wanted to."

"Fuck me, that's sweet," she whispered, awed and a little emotional that he'd abstained from a random hook up.

"You think so?" He frowned and gave a slight shake of his head. "I hadn't thought about it." He released a heavy sigh. "Regardless, babe, playtime is over for today. We have to decide what we are doing about Victor and your sister."

"Way to spoil the mood," she muttered as she allowed him to pull her into a sitting position. "I need coffee and a shower before I can even dream of dealing with those two."

"Go get your shower. I'll make your coffee. I need to check on Rylee anyway."

"One cream, one—"

"Sugar. Yes, I know. I also know you treat yourself once a month to a caramel latte, with whipped cream and caramel drizzle. You're strict about it being the first Friday of the month."

"As a woman, I have to watch what I consume."

His hot gaze swept her naked form, lingering on all her lady bits. "No need to calorie count for my benefit. I prefer a woman with curves, and you have the perfect amount."

Her skin tightened with yearning, and she almost tackled him onto the mattress then and there. When Nash leaned in and licked the hollow of her throat, Ryanne whimpered.

"Want me to share a little secret?"

"Okay," she breathed. She didn't care what he shared as long as he continued those little love nips along her neck.

"With the return of your powers came an amped-up metabolism. You'll have a hard time gaining weight, even if you try. Oh, and your aging has pretty much slowed to a crawl. You'll look like this for the next fifty or sixty years of your life."

It was like being doused in cold water. The shock of his words brought on a gasp, and she shoved him back. *"Are you for real?"*

Nash laughed. "You've seen my father. Tell me, did you think he had plastic surgery?"

"I admit to being curious, but I had no idea it was anything as fantastical as not aging at the rate of non-magical humans." She shook her head in wonder. "I have so many questions."

"And I have the answers, but first, you shower while I make your coffee. Or would you prefer that latte?" he asked with a wicked grin.

"Definitely the latte with a double shot of espresso. Oh, and extra whipped cream!"

He laughed on his way to the door. Right before placing his hand on the knob, he snapped his fingers, effectively clothing himself. It was the first time Ryanne had seen him dress casually, and she liked the look of a worn Henley and the faded jeans that outlined his butt, showing it off to perfection. Still, she sighed that he had to cover up that fine-ass body at all. If it were up to her, she'd keep him naked and in bed forever.

As if sensing her thoughts, he shot her a wink and pulled open the door. When it closed behind him, Ryanne waited five seconds then waved her hands in the air and wiggled her ass in a happy dance.

"Nice."

His deep baritone from behind her evoked a bloodcurdling scream. As he doubled over in laughter, she smacked the top of his head.

"You're a jerk! You scared me half to death."

"Sorry." He didn't look sorry in the least. "I popped back in to see if you wanted any breakfast with that latte."

She scoffed and shoved past him. "You couldn't come back in the way you left?"

"Where's the fun in that?"

Stopping in the doorway of the bathroom, she tossed her hair back over her shoulder and shot him a glare. It was impossible to stay angry when faced with his devilishly handsome smile. Her lips twitched in response. "Do witches face health issues like clogged arteries?"

"Nope."

"Good. I'll take biscuits and gravy with a side of scrambled eggs, but not runny."

"It will be waiting for you when you are done."

As Ryanne shampooed her hair, trepidation for what had to happen today crept in. Without a doubt, they couldn't release Rylee, not before getting their hands on that cursed necklace. It was doubtful that Victor would take the extended disappearance of Rylee lightly. No, Ryanne would need to become her sister, sarcastic attitude and all.

Doubts assailed her. This was what Nash had suggested yesterday before Alastair arrived. Had last night and this morning been manipulation on his part? Seducing her into doing his bidding? She didn't care for the direction her thoughts had taken. Regardless, she was in the game now.

CHAPTER 12

Ryanne was quiet where she sat across from Nash. Misgivings plagued his thoughts. Liz's and Alastair's warnings about putting Ryanne in harm's way rose up in his mind and haunted him with what-ifs. What if Victor discovered she wasn't Rylee? What if something terrible were to happen to her and Nash couldn't get to her in time to save her?

"Are you all right, babe?" he asked in a low tone.

Her head whipped up, and she met his gaze. Her obvious anxiety bothered him.

"Talk to me, Ryanne. What has you troubled about all this?"

Her dark gaze shot to where her surly sister sat in the living room. "Everything about this disturbs me. I can't put my finger on what's wrong, but I have this churning in my gut, and it's getting stronger by the minute."

"You don't have to do this."

Her expression softened when she met his serious gaze. "I know, and yet I feel as if I do. My sister is neck-deep in this crap, and ultimately she came here to, at the very least, steal the journal. At most, to brew up her special brand of mischief."

She set down her fork with a heavy sigh. "Yeah, I need to do this."

"I'll text my father, and we can figure out how to get you in place." He abandoned his own food, unable to drum up his appetite now that the subject of Victor was on the table.

As if the mention of Alastair sent out a cosmic bat signal, the air around them shifted and a rip in the fabric of space opened for the man himself. Similar to a wild animal scanning its surroundings for danger, Alastair cast a quick glance about the room. His nostrils flared, and he narrowed his eyes at Rylee. His shudder was subtle, and had Nash not been watching his father, he'd have missed it. Alastair seemed to sense things were not as they appeared.

Odd, but Nash had had the same feeling earlier when he left Ryanne to her shower. It was as if evil were gathering in the room. A malevolent vibe of sorts. Yet the dynamics hadn't changed all that much. It was still the four of them, three of whom were on the same team. Perturbed, he studied Rylee.

Her eyes had taken on a wild look, darting back and forth before touching on their group, only to start the action all over again.

"What's going on?"

Ryanne's question nearly made Nash come out of his skin. Goddess, he was getting jumpy.

"I'm not sure." He tried to relay his caution with a quick glance in her direction. "I think we need to adjourn to somewhere with stronger wards," he murmured to his father.

"I agree, son. I'm not comfortable here. Something is off about this whole thing. The longer it goes on, the surer I am."

"Thorne Industries?"

"My old offices."

Alastair referred to when he was CEO of the company, before Aurora Gillespie-Thorne, in her state of stasis, had required his full attention and he had relinquished the reins to Nash. At the time, Nash hadn't wanted anything to do with the company his father's family had founded, but the Witches' Council had strongly encouraged him to seize control and turn it into a tool for their benefit. Not wanting to move into the same space Alastair previously occupied, Nash had constructed his current office and hidden treasure room.

"Wouldn't the wards on my offices be stronger after all this time?" Nash asked.

"It's humorous you believe so," Alastair returned. "My old office was built on sacred ground, son. Isis herself blessed that spot."

Nash grunted. He should've done his homework, or at the very least, questioned why his father found it amusing that Nash had conjured up the new office building.

"I'll bring our reluctant guest." From inside his suit jacket, he withdrew the journal. "Here. Gather your lovely young woman and whatever else you need, then meet me at my offices. The wards will be lowered for you for exactly five minutes from the time I teleport, son." Alastair graced him with a stern warning look. "Don't be late. You don't want to crash into the magical barrier. The shock will knock you on your backside."

"Understood."

As Alastair gripped Rylee's arm, he cast Nash one last long look. "Five minutes."

After his father disappeared, Nash waved an arm and restored the kitchen and dining area to rights.

An awe-inspired smile lit up Ryanne's face. "I'll never get tired of that."

"When this is over, I'll show you how to do that and more." He picked up the journal from the granite countertop and held out a hand to her. "I can't believe he smuggled this out last night. How did we miss that?"

"Maybe because we were distracted with other matters?"

"Most likely," he agreed as he caressed her cheek. "Are you ready to go?"

"As ready as I'll ever be."

They arrived with two minutes to spare.

"Prompt, as always." Alastair's tone bordered on snide. He was surprised by his own malice if the expression on his face was any indication. "I'm sorry, son. I'm not sure why I said it that way."

"It doesn't matter. Let's come up with a game plan. The sooner this is over and Ryanne is back home, the better I'll feel."

"I have a question," Ryanne said, hand raised to gain attention. "If I understand this warding thing correctly, no one can enter a space that is magically protected unless they've been granted access, is that correct?"

Nash gave her a brief nod.

"If that's the case, surely Victor will have warded his place, no? How will I be able to simply stroll in without consequences? And even if I *can* do that, how do I convey to both of you that I've gotten what I went for? I'm assuming one of you will need to get me out since I don't know how to teleport."

Nash wanted to swear a blue streak. His entire life had been filled with magic, and he'd gone on the assumption that he could simply spell Ryanne to look like her sister. But the reality was much more complicated than that. Ryanne was correct in assuming that Victor would have wards in place. He'd have a whole helluva lot more than that to detect intruders.

"We have to proceed as if magic doesn't exist," Alastair informed them. "Ryanne is correct. Anything more, charmed jewelry for communication, spells to alter her appearance, all of it will set off alarms. We have to assume Victor is prepared for anything."

"Without magic?" Nash was highly doubtful they could pull this off without their standard powers. "How are we supposed to do that?"

"We alter her appearance with scissors and makeup, then send her in through the front door with a wire."

The unease brewing in the back of his mind turned into a Category 5 hurricane of epic worrisome proportions. "I don't like it. I say we scrap this idea."

"Last night I did some light reading. We need to retrieve the Red

Scorpion from Victor. That kind of power, in his hands, is devastating."

In the privacy of his own mind, Nash let loose a string of curses a mile long. He'd known before his father spoke that this was a serious problem. Yet the idea of sending Ryanne into danger, as was his original plan, didn't sit right anymore. Not since last night. Not after what they'd shared.

A single glance showed she mirrored his misgivings, but even as Nash watched, resolve settled onto her features.

"I can do this, Nash. We don't have a choice."

Still, he didn't speak. *Couldn't* speak. If he gave the okay for her to step into Salinger's compound and something happened to her, there was no way on this green earth Nash could live with himself again. No way he wanted to. Not without Ryanne.

"I love you," he rasped.

Her face softened with her smile. "I love you, too."

Nash chewed the inside of his lip and nodded. "Are you sure you want to do this?"

"When did you become such a worrier?" she teased.

"He always has been. It's the bane of the Thorne family," Alastair inserted, his tone dry and his amusement obvious.

"Bite me, Sperm Donor."

Alastair laughed and clapped him on the back. "There's my disagreeable son. Welcome back. Now let's get started."

Anger welled up inside Nash, and the desire to knock his father's hand away overwhelmed him. As he lifted his arm to do so, he realized his rage was misplaced. Where had it come from? It couldn't simply be worry for Ryanne, could it? He shoved down the urge to snap.

"We need supplies. Do you have anything here, or do I need to make a supply run?" he asked.

"I can conjure scissors, and a simple phone call to your Uncle Ryker will get us a wire tap." Alastair cleared his throat. "But I'm no hairstylist, boy, as my overall look prior to your sister's makeover of my person should tell you."

Nash snorted. He remembered well that his father had looked like a Hollywood villain of old before Summer worked her magic. "Fair enough. How about we give her and the sisters a call?"

At Alastair's nod, Nash dialed Summer and explained their need. He then sent pictures of the inside of the office so she could form an image of the room and teleport freely.

CHAPTER 13

As with all the Thorne Witches stories, I have to honor the tradition of omitting this particular chapter for superstition's sake. Better safe than sorry, no?

CHAPTER 14

W ithin thirty minutes, Summer, Autumn, and Spring arrived.

"I feel like we are missing a few people," Nash joked.

"Winnie and the husbands are on baby duty. With the exception of Coop. He's doing sheriffy things," Summer informed him.

He placed a hand on her protruding belly. "How is little Olivia Rose today?"

"She's being a punkass, but I love her anyway."

As if on cue, Nash felt a forceful kick beneath his hand. "Should you be here this close to your time? If I'd have thought—"

"Pfft!" Autumn cut him off with a scoff and a simple wave of her hand. "She's not helpless. What's the plan? Whose ass are we kicking?" She frowned and glanced around as if confused. "I don't know where that came from. I didn't arrive all edgy."

Spring, the most quiet and reflective of all the sisters, walked around touching objects and books on the shelves closest to her. "There's great power here, isn't there? I can feel the vibrations from the earth, even through the concrete."

She said exactly what Nash had been feeling.

"Do you suppose the balance is off? Autumn isn't the only one to feel twitchy," he said.

"No. It's something else. I'm not sure yet." Like Nash, as an earth elemental, Spring would find it difficult to get a read on a place without plants to give off a vibration. She abruptly dropped her hand and faced them. "I suppose it will reveal itself in due time, but now I believe formal introductions are in order. We've been rude to your friend long enough."

Nash started and looked back at the other sisters in surprised wonder. How had he forgotten they'd never met Ryanne? Was it because she'd been such an integral part of his life for so long that he'd assumed everyone knew about her?

"I'm Ryanne." She held out her hand to Spring with a smile. "I'm Nash's… girlfriend."

Warmth flooded through him at Ryanne's words. A sort of possessiveness that made him want to shout *"Mine!"* He placed a hand on her hip and lightly squeezed.

"I'm Spring, and these are my sisters Summer and Autumn."

"Also known as the Weird Season Sisters in our one-horse town," Autumn quipped.

Summer rolled her eyes and hugged Ryanne as much as her belly would allow. "It's a pleasure to meet you. I thought Nash would never get his head out of his ass long enough to make a move."

Alastair laughed and wrapped an arm around Summer.

Another strong emotion—this one a burning jealousy—rose up and grabbed Nash by the throat. He envied their easy camaraderie. It was the very thing missing from his relationship with his father. The riot of emotions floored him. He had no idea why these long-suppressed feelings were surging to the surface, or even what he should do to get a handle on them. All he *did* know, was that this wasn't the place or time for his upset.

"Thanks for coming, ladies. Ryanne needs to be made over to look like her twin without the use of magic. There can't be any trace of power clinging to her or our game is up."

As one, the Thorne sisters turned to the pissed off woman sitting in the corner. If Rylee's fiery glare had the ability to set them ablaze, they'd all be on a spit overtop of a raging bonfire right about now, with an apple stuffed in their mouths.

"Why would Ryanne need to look like her sister?" Spring asked.

"Rylee is a confidante of Victor Salinger. Ryanne is going to take her place," Alastair informed them.

"Oh, *hell* no!" Autumn exploded. "You are not putting that girl in harm's way. No way, no how! I won't be party to such foolishness."

"It's my choice," Ryanne said as she moved closer to Nash and laced her fingers through his. "If you don't want to help, I understand and won't hold it against you, but I'm doing this. My understanding is that this necklace Nash needs has some bad juju attached to it. Victor can't be allowed to keep it."

"What is with this family and these damned scavenger hunts for magical items?" Autumn muttered. In a louder voice, she said, "If you're committed to this, have a seat. Spring will do your makeup, I'll do your hair, and Summer can conjure your outfit." She waved the men away. "Go find Uncle Ryker and Knox. Those two will be able to help think of all the little things you two have overlooked. They're more skilled at subterfuge than you are. Or at least Uncle Ryker is. But we could definitely use Knox for our magical muscle."

Spring smiled at her sister, and Nash assumed it was because she was more comfortable with her husband around. Spring had gone through a rough time at the hands of Victor Salinger's cohort, Zhu Lin, and she preferred to have Knox beside her when things got real. It didn't hurt that Knox was gifted with god-like powers, courtesy of the Goddess Isis herself.

As Nash saw it, Isis had been out to protect the bloodlines of herself and the Goddess Nephthys by providing Knox with the means to destroy enemies on any plane. His special ability to stop time had come in handy in the past, and probably would again in the near future. Nash pitied anyone who threatened Spring. Knox would destroy them without a second thought—and he had. Talk about your power couples.

Looking at Ryanne, Nash felt an affinity for Knox.

She caught his eye and smiled, but the normal sassy quality was missing. It was easy to see she was nervous. Yet he had no real way to comfort her. The mission she was about to embark on was as dangerous as it got for anyone associated with a Thorne.

"Son? You with me?"

Nash jolted and turned his head toward the sound of Alastair's voice. "Pardon?"

"I asked if you preferred me to fetch Knox while you remain here."

"That would be great, Dad," he agreed absently. Alastair's sharp intake of breath caught his attention. "What?"

"You haven't called me Dad and meant it since you were a teenager. I…" His father shook his head and graced him with a bittersweet smile. "I missed it."

A pang of some long-suppressed emotion struck Nash's heart. "Yeah, maybe when this is over, we should talk."

"I'd like that." Alastair cleared his throat and straightened his tie. "I'll be back soon."

After their father teleported away, Summer approached Nash. "He loves you. He always has."

"He has a funny way of showing it." But that wasn't true. Not really. Alastair was just… Alastair. The scary-ass patriarch of the Thorne Witches who would smite someone as soon as look at them. Or so he appeared anyway. For those he loved, he was indulgent. He'd also been known to go to the ends of the earth for his family. There was a time when he was unapproachable, and that time happened to be Nash's formative years when he needed a father figure. However, that too could be explained.

"He's changed. You should give him a chance to show you how much."

"Can we not talk about this now, sister? I have much more

important things on my plate to deal with." He couldn't prevent the edge to his tone. Speaking to his half-sister about his messed-up childhood when the retrieval of the Red Scorpion needed to be uppermost in his mind was out of the question.

Summer opened her mouth to retort but seemed to be caught on a wave of dizziness. She swayed toward him, with a deep frown marring her forehead. "I don't know what's wrong. I don't feel well suddenly."

"Sit down here." He led her to a nearby chair and squatted beside her to rub her wrists together. "What are you feeling?"

"I'm not sure. It was like a vicious wave of anger toward you, then it subsided as quickly. But it left me lightheaded."

He conjured her a glass of water and watched as she took small sips. "It's odd because I've been feeling bursts of the same thing for the last hour or so."

"Yeah, I didn't experience anything like it before we arrived."

"I wonder if our sperm donor knows anything about it. Could be the power of this room."

"Maybe." The disquiet in her tone spoke volumes. Summer didn't believe it was this place any more than Nash did. It left him to wonder what exactly *was* causing their amplified emotions.

"I think you should go, Summer. I appreciate that you want to help, but I'd feel better if you were safe at Thorne Manor or the Carlyle estate. As far away from Salinger and this mess as you can get."

Her ready agreement told him more than words that she was shaken by this whole incident. "I'm sorry, Nash."

"Nothing to be sorry for. We have more than enough witches and warlocks, should the need arise." He smiled to show he had no hard feelings on the matter. "Thank you for coming when I called."

"Anytime. You know that."

"I do."

They hugged, and a sense of belonging hit Nash. Before a year ago, he'd been a loner, protecting his twin sisters and cousins from afar. But they'd all developed a stronger bond after the crazy year they'd had, due in part to Alastair and the dangerous quests he'd sent them on in his determination to wake Aurora.

"I love you, brother."

He swallowed hard. "I love you, too." The words were rusty from disuse, but he meant them all the same. "Now go home."

A short while later, Alastair arrived with Ryker and Knox. Over Ryker's shoulder was a duffle bag of what Nash assumed was electronic equipment. The man had been a master spy. For years, Ryker had stayed under the radar in Zhu Lin's camp, feeding details to the Witches' Council and to Alastair, or so Nash suspected. As best friends, Ryker and Alastair had their own special language.

Another wave of irritation hit Nash. Surely he wasn't jealous of his uncle's relationship with Alastair? A sneaking suspicion developed that something more was brewing in the air around them. Before he spoke up, Nash wanted to get a better handle on the what and how.

"There. I think that about does it." Autumn stepped back and admired her hair-cutting handiwork. "We will need to apply dye to hide the purple streaks."

One of the things Nash loved about Ryanne had been her long dark hair with its wild purple highlights. He was saddened to see the bulk of that thick mane now sitting in a discarded pile on the floor. As Spring stepped back from applying the makeup, Nash looked back and forth at the twins. After they dyed her hair, a simple change of clothes would make the transition complete. A sliver of unease slithered along his spine. It was unpleasant and disturbing to see Ryanne now identical to her sister in every way.

It wasn't difficult for Ryanne to see the distaste on Nash's face. Oddly enough, it didn't bother her. Instead, Nash's expression bolstered her belief that he wasn't interested in Rylee in any way.

Ryanne's insecurity from the evening before, when he'd confessed that Rylee had come on to him, had vanished.

"I'll pick up some dark hair dye at the drugstore after we return home," Ryanne said aloud.

"Old Al here has already thought of that," Ryker assured her with a grin and a wink. In an economy of movements, he placed the duffle bag on the table, unzipped it, removed a box of Clairol, and tossed it to Nash.

"I'll give you 'Old Al,' you rotten SOB," Alastair muttered.

Ryker's devilish grin widened. "I'm trembling in my boots." In a flash, he turned serious and dug into his black bag of tricks. "I've brought a wire and listening device. Also, a few weapons for you to keep on your person. You should know, Victor will have Blockers in place. Teleporting in or out of his compound will be near impossible."

"What are Blockers?" Ryanne asked, suddenly terrified by the mission she was about to undertake. Really, who was she anyway? Certainly not Lara Croft, tomb raider, or the female equivalent of Jason Bourne. No, she was a damned administrative assistant.

"Blockers are witches and warlocks who specialize in stopping others from teleporting. The Désorcelers employ them when they target their enemies."

"Désorcelers?"

Ryker turned to glare at Nash and Alastair. "You didn't tell her what she was going up against?"

Alastair shrugged as if Ryker's pique was of little concern. "Mostly, yes. We didn't want to scare the poor thing."

"You're an asshole, Al. I can't believe you'd send her into this type of danger without the knowledge or means to protect herself."

"That's what you're here for, my friend. You'll take today to show her what she needs to know to defend herself."

"I should tell you to shove it. I would, too, if I didn't think you were going to send her anyway."

Ryanne studied her sister, who seemed to be enjoying the interchange between the two warlocks. Why was she so determined to cause discord between everyone? Rylee met her look with a defiant tilt of her chin. Tears built, burning Ryanne's eyes and nasal passages. Rapid blinking helped to dispel most of the moisture, but it could do nothing about the ache in her heart. There sat her last remaining relative, the person closest to her, and all her twin wanted to do was create havoc.

Turning away, Ryanne noticed Nash silently watching her. She gave him a tentative half-smile and grabbed the box of color from his hand. "Where's the ladies' room?"

"Come on, I'll show you."

He placed his large, warm hand on her lower back and led her out through the office doors. They hooked a left when they reached the main lobby and traveled partway down a long corridor. "I'm surprised your father didn't have an *en suite* bathroom for his office."

"He does. I thought maybe you needed a break from the oppressive air in there." Nash opened the door to the visitors' restroom and guided her inside. He pulled over a bench from the lounge area and gently urged her to sit. "I'll apply this for you."

As he moved to pass her, she reached for his hand. "Don't feel guilty or bad for sending me after the necklace, Nash. It's the only foreseeable way to get it from Victor."

"My uncle was right, Ryanne. This is dangerous for an experienced witch. For you, doubly so." He sighed heavily and straddled the bench beside her. "I'd be lying if I said I wasn't worried. All day, my nerves have been fighting to get the better of me. I'd be devastated if something were to happen to you."

"Now you're making me nervous." She cupped his jaw and stroked her thumb over his lower lip in an action similar to his new habit. "I can pull this off. Rylee and I used to make a game of imitating each other when we were growing up. We thought it was fun to fool our adoptive parents. Now, it's an easy matter of finding the necklace. I'm still hoping my sister might come through for me."

Nash bit down lightly on the soft pad of her thumb, then kissed the same spot. After a long moment, he met her gaze and said, "I think you're hoping in vain. She's resentful, and I dare say spiteful. Please don't be too trusting where she's concerned, okay?"

"I feel it too, ya know. That feeling of hostility in the air. It's almost as if it's trying to wrap around me and choke off my oxygen."

"Yes. That's it exactly. I don't feel it right now, though. It makes me think it's emanating from Alastair's office. Once we are done here, I'll talk to him about it." He rose and crossed to the sink. After a quick scan of the directions, Nash set about mixing the hair dye for application. He moved to her side and ran his hands through her hair, massaging her scalp in the process. "Tilt your head back, babe. Let's get this sacrilege over."

"You like the purple streaks?"

"I love the purple, just as I love everything about you."

She couldn't prevent the joyful smile taking over her face. As clueless as Nash sometimes seemed, there were moments like this, when he was perfect.

CHAPTER 15

Nash looked on as Ryker ran Ryanne through simple self-defense moves: the base of her palm to a nose, a heel to an instep, a knee to a groin. But it was the knife-wielding lesson that stirred Nash's protective instincts. Every time Ryker knocked the weapon from her hand and pinned her to the ground or against a wall, the beast in Nash rose up in its desire to defend his mate.

It didn't help that Ryker knew exactly what Nash was feeling—or he did if the smirk on his face was any indication. Finally, after what seemed like hours, Ryanne turned the tables in a stunningly fast move and held the blade tip to Ryker's jugular. A cheer welled up and out of Nash as he rushed across the room to sweep her into a hug.

"Well done, babe."

Her face flushed with pride, and she never looked more beautiful.

Ryker bowed his head in acknowledgment of her win. "You're as ready as you can be on such short notice. Remember to stay alert, and if all else fails, stab Salinger in the ball sack."

"I'd say that is a little vicious, Uncle."

One dark brow rose, and Ryker stared him down.

"I didn't say unwarranted, just vicious," Nash said with a laugh. "It's probably better to aim for Victor's balls since he's missing a heart."

"Any man who would murder his own sister is exceedingly dangerous," Alastair added as he strode toward their small group. He stopped in front of Ryanne and gave her a stern look. "Never forget that, child, and never hesitate."

"I'll remember," she promised.

Nash clasped her hand and squeezed. "As much as I hate to say it, it's past time for 'Rylee' to return."

"I could go with her," Ryker offered.

"You'd never get out alive, my friend." Alastair shook his head, expression grim. "His paranoia runs deeper than Zhu Lin's ever did."

"So the only thing left is to recreate a journal to look like the original," Ryanne stated. "How do we hide the magic of the journal?"

"We won't need to. He'll expect it to be spelled from the Council or from Nash. It's okay if trace amounts of magic are detected on it."

"Do you remember what we discussed for extraction? Once you find the necklace, you text Nash from Rylee's phone. We'll be waiting at the tree line on the edge of the compound. The Blockers can only maintain a perimeter of about fifteen yards beyond the building. The trees start at about thirty yards." Alastair's gaze bore into hers. "If you have to run for the trees, do not run in a straight line. It makes you an easy target."

"I understand."

"Good. Knox worked up a map from the GPS data. Victor's place shouldn't be hard to find." Alastair tilted his head toward his office. "There is a shower in the bathroom attached to my office. When you are done, Autumn or Spring will conjure clothes to match your sister's."

Nash lifted their joined hands and dropped a light kiss on her knuckles. "Have one of my cousins let me know when you are ready, and I'll attach the microphone. You won't be able to hear us, but we will be able to hear you and come for you if you get into trouble."

"Why do I need to text you if I'm wearing the wire? Won't you hear me if I tell you that I found the necklace?"

"It's assumed Victor will have video cameras everywhere. The signal interrupter only lasts a few minutes after it's activated, so you need to be fast when you search each room. When those cameras come back on, I don't want Victor to see you speaking into the wire." He shot a glance toward the other men and then looked back at her. "If you use Rylee's phone to text *your* phone, you can keep up a pretense of casual conversation. Ryker and Alastair have created a code of sorts. It will still appear like casual conversation. For example, type the words 'Do you still have that red dress?' and we will know you are in trouble. It's a code red."

"Fair enough. I'll assume you'll give me a rundown of these codes?"

"Yes. Are you sure you're okay with this, babe?" Nash wondered how she could be, when his own instincts were screaming so loudly that they practically drowned out the conversation around him.

"I feel as if you've asked me this a million times. I wouldn't have agreed in the first place if I didn't believe it was the right thing to do," she assured him.

A quick glance revealed his father's impassive expression. Ryker's countenance didn't show much more emotion than Alastair's. It seemed Nash was the only one freaking out. But then, he had the most to lose.

"Any last words of advice?" If his tone was gruff, it couldn't be helped.

"Yes," Ryker said as he placed a hand on Ryanne's shoulder. "Don't let your act slip. Not once. You have to assume someone is watching you at all times. You must *be* Rylee."

She nodded her understanding.

Nash crowded closer to her side. "If you two don't mind, I'd like a moment alone with Ryanne." After they left, he drew her into his arms. "I'm terrified for you," he confessed. "All along, I'd planned to ask for your help, but now that the moment's here to send you into Victor's compound, I can't seem to find it within me to let you do it."

She snuggled into his chest and sighed. "I'm taking the choice out of your hands, Nash. I'm doing this whether you want me to or not. I had a chance to read the journal a little this morning and again during my makeover. I don't need to tell you how dangerous that necklace can be in the wrong hands."

"No, you don't. But I feel like we should find another way." He kissed the top of her head and hugged her tighter. Part of him never wanted to let her go. Wanted to protect her from anything that could possibly hurt her. That same part urged him to battle anyone who might take her away from him.

Ryanne patted his chest. "If you can find a different solution while I'm in the shower, I'll be open to a new plan. Otherwise, this is all we have."

"How are you so calm about this?"

"I'm not. Not in the least. In fact, I'm downright terrified. But what choice do we have?"

He cupped her face between his hands and lowered his mouth to hers. Her lips opened under his, and he swept his tongue into her mouth. Into that kiss, he poured all the things he couldn't say. All the overwhelming love for her that he'd waited too long to act on. All his hopes and fears. And miracle of miracles, he felt her answering response. Nash never wanted this moment to end.

From the doorway behind Ryanne, Alastair cleared his throat. "Son, we have to get a move on."

A stinging started behind Nash's lids as deep, burning emotion clogged his throat and seized his vocal cords. All he could do was rest his forehead against Ryanne's as he cradled her face.

She lightly stroked his wrists. "It's going to be all right."

He nodded slightly, still unable to speak.

"We just connected. I'm not about to lose this," she whispered.

Her words gave him the strength to pull back and release her. "Go get your shower. I'll see you in a few minutes."

"I love you, Nash."

"I love you more," he said, casting her a teasing grin in an attempt to hide his distress.

She laughed, and it was sunshine to his soul. "Probably."

"Rylee, please help me."

When her sister remained stubbornly silent, Ryanne heaved an internal sigh. She'd been trying for the last fifteen minutes to get her twin to see reason and to provide any intel on Victor's compound she could.

"I don't understand why you would wish harm on me and Nash. What do you truly owe Victor?" Ryanne tried to reason. "He's done unspeakable things. He was responsible for killing his own sister. Do you truly believe he won't turn on you?"

"You love him more than me," Rylee whispered.

"Who? Nash?"

"Yes. You love him more than me."

"That's not true." Okay, it was a little true, but how did one tell their sister that they held very little affection for them anymore? Tell them that all the horrific things they'd done in the past had tainted that love and made it something ugly? Tell them that any love they felt now was a sense of obligation only? "I love you both in different ways, Leelee."

Rylee's eyes softened for a moment, but hardened back to cold jewel-like diamonds mere seconds later. "You're a liar! You've always been a liar!" she spat. Hatred flared to life in her dark eyes. Ryanne could see the flame of insanity deep in their depths, and a chill swept over her.

"When I return, we are going to get you help. Whatever spell Victor's cast over you, I intend to break, Rylee. Count on it."

Rylee snorted her derision. "You think he won't be able to tell you are posing as me the second you step into his office? You're a fool."

"Come away, Ryanne. You're wasting your time here." Nash stroked her back. "She's not going to help you."

"Yes, Ryanne. Run along. It's time to dance to the Great Nash Thorne's tune like the good little puppet you are."

Fury unlike any she'd ever experienced, pounded against her temples and made her want to smack the ever-loving shit out of her sister. The only thing that stilled her hand was the oddity of the sudden anger. Where had it come from? It wasn't like Rylee hadn't taken verbal pot-shots at her before. This blinding rage was so far from normal, it gave Ryanne pause. Was this another side effect of her revived magic, like the fire flaring from her fingertips last night?

When she returned from retrieving the Red Scorpion, she intended to get to the bottom of this. She couldn't go around raging at people or setting things on fire.

Because she refused to give in to hate, Ryanne leaned over and placed a soft kiss on her twin's forehead. "I'm sorry, Leelee. For whatever wrongs you think I've done to you, whatever affection you feel I've withheld, I'm sorry. I do love you, despite what you may believe."

Once again, Rylee's eyes softened and tears welled up. Their gazes locked in a moment of unity, as they had when they were young children before potential parents would interview them at the group home. But in a blink, their connection was lost, and Rylee turned her head to stare at the wall.

"Don't forget your fake journal, *Rylee*." Rylee gave a harsh laugh. "Like Victor will fall for that one."

Ryanne hurried away, unable to bear another second of the animosity. The very air around her sister was thick with hate and too stifling to breathe.

"You feel it too, don't you?" Nash asked her quietly.

"Feel what?" she asked, irritation heavy in her tone.

"That. Right there." He pointed. "The negative emotions bubbling up out of nowhere."

"It's been happening on and off since my sister showed up. I assumed it was my nerves getting the better of me."

"I think it's something else, although I'm not sure exactly what."

"Do you think anyone else feels it?"

"If I had to take a guess, yes. Autumn was snarkier than normal earlier. Spring definitely felt the pull of stronger magic. She mentioned as much before she introduced herself, remember?"

"Yes, but at the time, I didn't realize this...this...well, whatever *this* is, was what she was referring to." She waved a hand around her chest and head when the proper words failed her.

Ryker approached them. "It will be dark within two hours. If we want to find Salinger's compound, we need to get going." He faced Nash. "Your father and I were discussing it. We think you should stay here."

"No fucking way. *Achoo!*"

Alastair sauntered up, his clenched fist a clear indication he'd anticipated Nash's reaction. "You are too volatile where your young woman is concerned, son. Ryker, Knox, and I have this handled."

Ryanne looked at the tall blond man standing beside Alastair. He'd remained silent most of the day, only adding his two cents when asked directly. The guy was extraordinary in every way. His long hair begged females to run their fingers through the thick locks, while his intelligent blue eyes saw everything and made a woman feel overly warm if he spared them a glance. He was the perfect match for the breathtaking Spring, and appeared to only have eyes for her.

In his deep baritone, he now promised Nash he'd not let anything happen to Ryanne. "I owe you, man."

"I..." Nash pressed his lips together and turned to stare down at her.

Ryanne understood his reticence. She would never say it aloud, but she wanted him to wait for her outside the perimeter of Victor's reach, ready to step in should she need it. This man was highly capable when he set his mind to it. This new realization startled her, but she knew no one on the planet made her feel safer.

"Keep my sister out of trouble," she finally said, making the decision for him.

With one last hard hug, she left.

CHAPTER 16

As they traveled the long, winding road toward Victor Salinger's property, Alastair experienced misgivings. For certain, the overall energy of his office complex had been off, but he was at a loss as to understand why. He still wasn't convinced Ryanne had been completely in the dark regarding her sister's connection to Victor, but then again, Alastair had learned the hard way that loyalty meant different things to different people.

"My chances of getting out of Victor's compound are low, aren't they?" Ryanne asked from the backseat of Rylee's sporty Jeep.

Alastair shared a grim look with Ryker. Both of them had been in the enemy camp and lived to tell about it, but they'd both lost friends, fellow witches and warlocks who hadn't been so lucky.

He twisted in the seat to meet her steady gaze. She had courage, this mate to his son. And in that regard, he admired her. If Ryanne wasn't playing them false, Alastair would do whatever was in his power to help her return to Nash.

"I don't know, child. But what I can promise you, is that we will do whatever is necessary to get you out unharmed."

She nodded and turned to stare at the passing scenery.

Alastair twisted slightly to look at Knox. Spring's young man had been quiet since they commissioned his help earlier. "What's bothering you, boy?"

"I'm not entirely certain. I do know there is something off about this whole thing." He shot a glance at Ryanne. "I want to go in with her."

"You can't. We have to assume that Salinger has had us all under surveillance at one point or another. If that's the case, he'd recognize you in a second."

"I can glamour a disguise or cloak myself."

"He'd detect the magic. No, I'm afraid Ryanne has to go by herself."

"It goes against my nature to let her take all the risks. The Council won't care how we obtain the necklace, as long as we do. Maybe we should scrap this idea and try to get a plan of the building. Hell, you're skilled at picking locks. You could get us inside."

Alastair smiled wryly. "Son, you would charge in where angels fear to tread. Maybe it's the nature of your gift, but you're going to have to trust me on this one."

Knox's troubled expression weighed on Alastair. The man's instincts were sharper than any Alastair had ever seen, perhaps even his own. If Knox had a bad feeling about sending Ryanne inside to retrieve the necklace, chances were, he was right. Such had been the case when he and Spring went to Cartagena for the third magical artifact to revive Aurora. That trip hadn't gone as planned.

"Turn the vehicle around, Ryker." Three pair of eyes snapped in his direction. He smiled ruefully at the couple in the backseat. "We'll find another way."

"No. I promised Nash I'd get that necklace," Ryanne protested.

"And you will, child, only not today. Not like this. I've learned to trust this young man's feelings on certain things." He tilted his head toward Knox. "You mean more to my son than a piece of jewelry."

"A powerful piece of jewelry, Mr. Thorne. I couldn't live with myself if something terrible happens because Victor has it."

"He won't have it long, Ryanne. Never fear."

―――――――――

"If you continue to pace, cousin, you are going to wear a hole in the wood floor."

Nash halted in front of Autumn. The sardonic twist to her lips made him want to growl in response. "Why do you always have to be a sarcastic bitch?" He sneezed and balled his hand to forestall the onslaught of raccoons.

"Why do you always have to have a stick up your ass?"

"You—"

"Stop!" Spring commanded. The sharp edge was at direct odds with her usual melodic tone. "This is not like either of you." She paused for a second. "Okay, maybe it's somewhat like Autumn, but still." She stood and moved closer to Rylee, tilting her head as she studied the other woman. "What are you hiding?"

"Not a damned thing," Rylee snapped. "Who does a person have to kill around here to get a damned drink of water or to go to the bathroom?"

"Of course. You've been sitting for a while, haven't you?" Spring said, not unkindly. "I'll take you."

As Spring lifted her arm and spoke the words to undo Alastair's magical binds, a crafty, smug expression washed over Rylee's face. All Nash's nerve endings went on high alert.

"No, wait!"

In a stunningly swift move, Rylee was up and had the tip of a wicked-looking blade pressed to Spring's jugular.

"I will fucking rip you apart if you hurt my sister," Autumn snarled. "There won't be a place on this earth where you can hide from me or mine."

"I'm trembling in my stilettos, bitch," Rylee sneered. "Spring, in my pants pocket is a necklace. Reach in and get it—carefully I might add. You don't want to get stung by its tail."

"I'll get it," Autumn quickly volunteered.

"Not you. It will sense your anger and kill you immediately. It has to be someone in control of their emotions."

It was the only indication that Rylee didn't really want to harm Spring. Nash tried to force back his instinctive desire the rip out that treacherous bitch's throat as he channeled a calming energy. "I'll do it."

"No tricks, Nash. This blade is laced with poison lethal to witches. One nick and she's a goner."

"I get it, Rylee." What he didn't get was why none of them had thought to search her. For as smart as the Thorne family collective was, they tended to miscalculate the intelligence of others way too often. How she'd smuggled in a knife—and what Nash believed could very well be the Red Scorpion necklace—made him question his survival instincts. He sighed his disgust. "Which one?"

"Right."

He glanced down at her flowing palazzo pants and could have sworn he saw movement of the pocket in question. The bulge was obvious now that he looked closer. How had Alastair missed it? His father saw everything. Perhaps he thought she'd pocketed her keys?

"Invisibility spell."

His head whipped up to stare at her.

"It's the reason you didn't see it before now. Why none of you did. I'm assuming that's what you're thinking."

"Yes. Clever trick. We all underestimated you."

"People always do." Her look and tone hardened. "Now get the necklace."

Nash eased open the pocket of her pants. Again, there was movement inside. The sound of the shifting chain made the hair on the back of his neck stand at attention. Man, he so didn't want to reach in and touch that damned thing. The evil amusement in Rylee's mocking gaze made him doubly nervous.

"You don't have to do this, Nash. Not for me." Clear understanding shone in Spring's face, and she gave him a brave half-smile.

Keeping his eyes locked on Spring's, Nash asked, "What guarantee do I have that you won't hurt her?"

"None," Rylee snapped.

"Then why should he do as you ask?" Spring reasoned.

How the hell she could remain serene was beyond him, but Nash admired the hell out of her.

"Oh, fine. I'll let her go as soon as I'm free. Happy?" Rylee sneered.

Mentally taking his balls in hand, he reached into the pocket and grabbed the chain. Slowly, he withdrew it until it dangled in the air between them. He'd seen images of the necklace, but they hadn't done it justice. The piece was beautiful in a macabre way. The body was slender, fashioned of silver and rubies. One large stone made up the thorax; the deep red seemed to be illuminated from within, catching the light as it swung slightly. Miniature silver pinchers bit into the intricate silver chain. But it was the tail that drew the eye. Even as he watched, it stiffened and curled over the back as if to strike. The line of tiny rubies brightened to fire as the sharp barb whisked back and forth.

Goddess! He shouldn't fear the thing as much as he did, but he'd read the legend. One sting from that tail, and they'd be entombing him in the family mausoleum.

"Put it on," Rylee ordered.

"What?"

"I didn't stutter."

"You're a stone-cold bitch, you know that?" Autumn snarled, trembling in her rage and inability to take action.

Nash opened the clasp and reattached the ends at the back of his neck. Once again, the scorpion shifted. He could feel the sharp tips of the eight legs as they dug through his Henley shirt. His skin crawled, and he wanted nothing more than to tear the creepy thing off and fling it across the room, as far away from him as it could possibly get.

"Open the collar of your shirt."

Again, he did as Rylee commanded.

"Conpressi!"

He gasped and choked off a strangled scream as the necklace contracted around his neck and the scorpion dug into his skin. It was as if it wanted to burrow beneath his flesh. Unless Nash missed his guess, Rylee had sealed his fate.

"Now, my work here is done. Hand me that journal, and I'll be on my way."

On leaden feet, he walked to the table and lifted the leather-bound book. With a sense of *fait accompli,* he placed it in the outstretched hand across Spring's shoulder. Nash eyed the knife and wondered if he could wrench it from her grasp before Rylee could cut his cousin.

"I wouldn't try it, hero. Besides, you have enough problems of your own now." Rylee backed toward the door, using Spring as her shield. "Victor sends his regards to your father. He said it was a life for a life. Your father murdered someone Victor cared about deeply. This is his revenge." She paused by the door and eased the knife away from Spring's throat. "For what it's worth, I'm sorry it had to be you, Nash. My sister seems to really care about you."

With a hard shove to Spring's back, Rylee dashed through the door.

Autumn pivoted to go after her, but Nash placed a hand on her arm.

"No. Let her go."

"She took the journal, Nash! We need to get it back to get that thing off your neck!"

He reached up and parted the edges of his shirt. "It's too late. She sealed it on and accelerated the rate it merges with the wearer's body."

Twin horrified gasps from his cousins told him exactly what he expected based on the pain in his upper chest. The Red Scorpion had burrowed deeper and was about to claim another victim.

CHAPTER 17

Ryanne and her three warlock escorts walked in on Autumn's colorful tirade. From what little she'd heard, Ryanne could guess the anger was mainly directed at her missing sister. Spring's mournful expression and the pained, sickly look on Nash's face also spoke of the dire situation.

Knox took his wife aside and, in a low voice, asked, "What happened?"

Spring shot Ryanne an apologetic glance. "Rylee escaped, but not before sealing the cursed necklace around Nash's neck."

Ryanne slowly spun to look at Nash, who sat at Alastair's desk, his head resting in his hands. As if he sensed her regard, he lifted his head. The bleakness in his eyes nearly destroyed her. Never once in the two years she'd known him had she seen that look on his face. Her heart plummeted, and she rushed across the room to his side. When she would have embraced him, he held up a hand.

"No. It's alive. This necklace is somehow alive. I can't take the risk that it will sting you," he said hoarsely.

"Oh, Nash," she whispered, shoving down a sob. Even knowing her sister was responsible, she needed him to tell her it was a mistake. "Please tell me Rylee didn't knowingly do this to you. Please."

His grim look confirmed her worst fear.

"Why would she do such a thing?" she asked, dismayed.

Nash closed his eyes and pressed his lips together. One of his hands rose as if to touch his chest, but he balled it into a fist and slowly lowered it to his side.

She dropped her eyes to the base of his throat and blinked twice to clear her vision and to make sure what she saw was real. Even as she watched, the jeweled scorpion shifted and dug deeper into his skin.

"Ohmygod!"

Spring approached and laid a hand on Ryanne's shoulder. "I was about to go back to my workshop and find him something for the pain."

"Thank you," Ryanne said tearfully. "I…" There were no words. Nothing she could say to take away the horror of her sister's actions to one of the Thorne's own. How could Rylee have done this? And Nash, oh, dear God, poor Nash. He was showing remarkable control now, but soon enough, he'd be writhing in pain.

She checked the top of the desk for the journal and saw nothing. "Where's the journal? I'm almost positive I remember reading that there was a way to remove it from a person's neck. Where's the book?" Her tone had turned shrill, and she started opening and slamming drawers in her panic.

"Ryanne, stop." Spring gripped her hands. "Rylee took the book, too. But it wouldn't matter if she hadn't. She cast a spell on the necklace to seal it in place and to accelerate its merging with his body."

"I don't understand. I can't… I…" Sobs shook Ryanne, and she slid down the wall to sit on the floor.

"Leave us for a little bit, please." Nash's voice was coated in suffering, and yet he urged the others to go as he knelt beside her to offer comfort. "Babe, I need you to listen to me." He sucked in a breath and groaned. It took several heartbeats before he could continue. "None of this is your fault." His second long pause had Ryanne reaching for his hand. Although her fingers felt close to breaking under the pressure of his squeeze, she refused to make a sound. If he could endure the agony of the scorpion necklace, she could damned well tolerate his painful grip.

"I'm so sorry." The catch in her words said exactly how much.

"Victor's revenge on… my father," he panted. "It was never… about you."

"But he used my sister as his tool for that revenge. That *is* on me."

"No."

A low rumble started just as the floor shifted beneath her. Ryanne released an involuntary scream.

"Sorry. Me." Nash gritted his teeth and fell back into the wall. "You need… to… go. Can't hold… back… the magic."

Knox appeared and shoved the desk aside and hauled Ryanne to her feet. "We have to get out. Now!"

"No!" She violently shook her head. "I won't leave him!"

He gripped her chin and forced her gaze away from Nash. "Listen to me. We have to leave. He's an earth elemental, and he's only holding back for you. Soon he won't be able to. This whole place is going to sink into the earth. Do you understand what I'm telling you? You'll be buried alive."

Despite his steel-like grip, she inched her head sideways to stare down into Nash's tortured forest-green eyes. The truth was written there for her to see.

"I don't care," she choked out. "I'm not leaving him to die alone. I can't."

"He won't be alone, child. I'll be with him."

She whipped her head around to stare at Alastair.

"He's my son, and he's suffering because of me."

As Nash's father moved forward, the ground beneath them rolled. Everyone scrambled to stay upright.

"Get her out of here, Knox. My niece and Ryker, too."

"I'm not leaving, Mr. Thorne."

Where Ryanne got the backbone to stand up to this powerful man, she didn't know. Or maybe she did. Maybe love had infused her spine with steel. Either way, if they tried to drag her away, they wouldn't have to worry about the earthquakes Nash was causing because Ryanne would burn this stinking building down around their ears.

Alastair regarded her with exasperation clearly stamped on his features. "Fine." He met Knox's concerned gaze and nodded. "She stays with me and my son. The rest of you clear out."

As Autumn, Ryker, and Knox gathered together to teleport, Alastair had one last request. "Tell Rorie I love her. And Ryker, make sure that sonofabitch pays for this." A violent sneeze took Alastair, and he quickly clenched his hand.

The trio disappeared right as Spring returned. The floor buckled again, and Ryanne slammed into the ground, her knees coming in hard contact with the marble.

"I've arrived just in time," Spring said to no one in particular. She rushed to Nash and measured out a spoonful of liquid from the jar she carried. "Here, cousin. This should help with the pain." After a second helping, she placed the container on the desktop. "Where's Knox?"

"I made him take the others to safety. Nash was creating earthquakes," Alastair informed her.

"That man of mine is never around when I need him," she complained good-naturedly. She checked Nash's pulse and lifted one of his closed lids. "He's out. I think that medication should last for a while. I doubled the dose."

Ryanne cradled Nash's head in her lap, careful to stay as far away from the necklace as possible. "What did you give him?"

"It has an opium base. He's going to be in LaLa Land for a good bit of time. Hopefully, long enough for us to surgically extract that necklace. Aunt GiGi should be right behind me. She needed to collect her bag of tricks and my other sister."

"Do you really think you can remove it?"

"I'm not sure. If we can reverse the magical spell your sister used, we might be able to. Did either of you get a chance to read the journal?" The *before Rylee took it* was implied, or so it seemed to Ryanne who was feeling exceedingly guilty for her twin's actions.

Alastair gave a short nod and checked his son's pulse before parting the shirt. The ruby and silver scorpion's tail rippled, and the wicked point swiveled toward his hand. "In the journal, it states you must stroke the back of the scorpion three times in rapid succession. The trick is not to get stung. Otherwise, it's lights out."

"I didn't make it that far into the journal. Will it release its grip either way?" Ryanne asked. Was it her imagination or did Nash look grayer than normal? "I mean, if I stroke it and get stung, will the clasp still open?"

"It never stated as much." As Ryanne reached for the necklace, Alastair caught her hand. "No, child. I know my son; Nash would prefer to perish rather than have you hurt."

"I have to try."

"I'll do it. If it strikes me, it won't matter much."

"That's not true, Uncle," Spring protested. "You are loved by one and all. There isn't a one of us who wouldn't miss you."

"You'd miss those trips I finance," he teased with a wink. "Where are you and that young man off to next? Rome?"

She leaned in and kissed his cheek. "That's why you need to stick around. Who else gives me a limitless credit card for my travels?"

That same cheek flushed with pleasure but immediately paled when Nash arched his back and moaned.

"We can't wait for my sister," Alastair stated grimly. "We're out of time."

CHAPTER 18

As the words left Alastair's mouth, the Thornes appeared en masse with his beloved Rorie leading the charge.

"Hello, my love. How did I know you were going to show up?" he asked.

She stomped forward, full of fire and wrath. "Were you truly planning to go to your death without a goodbye? I could murder you, you bloody bastard."

He adored how her English accent thickened with her pique. "I thought I was limited on time."

"Foolish man." She knelt beside him and cradled his face, staring as if to memorize each of his features. "After we finally found each other again, it figures you'd do something to bugger it up. Is this your way of getting out of wedding me?" Aurora didn't give him a chance to answer, instead leaning over to check on Nash. "How is the dear boy?"

"Suffering," Alastair replied gruffly. He couldn't pretend with her. Couldn't hide his anguish upon seeing his firstborn at death's door. "I don't know how to help him other than to be here for him."

As she opened her mouth to answer, the ground shook beneath

them and another long crack appeared in the marble. Her worried blue eyes latched onto him. "He's doing this even in his unconscious state?"

"Yes. It's why I wanted our family clear of this place." He shot a glare at Knox. "It's why I entrusted the family to your care, boy."

"Sorry, sir." Knox held up his left hand to hide pointing at Autumn with his right. "*Someone* refused to listen. *Someone* told everyone what was going down. *Someone*—"

Autumn punched him in the shoulder. "I know what you're doing, you tool!"

Even as his lips twitched in response, Alastair cast them a stern warning look. "Now is *not* the time for horseplay."

"'Horseplay'?" Aurora snorted indelicately. "I thought our daughters brought you into this century, you old dinosaur. Who says 'horseplay' anymore?"

"*Et tu, Brute?*" He lowered his voice for her ears alone. "Remind me, if we get out of this, to show you how much of a dinosaur I am."

She grinned and winked.

"If Nash survives, I hope we are like the two of you years from now," Ryanne said tearfully.

Aurora stroked a hand down the young woman's glossy dark hair. "Not if. He will. Between all of us, we'll come up with a solution."

"Thank you," Ryanne croaked.

Any reservations Alastair had retained about Ryanne dissipated. He'd be a fool not to recognize the love she bore his son.

His sister stepped forward. "Alastair, the clearing behind your estate, do you think it would work to counteract Nash's magic? I have an idea." GiGi outlined her plan to utilize Knox's and his son-in-law Quentin's powers to manipulate time and throw Nash into a stasis state until a way to safely remove the necklace could be agreed upon.

The suggestion had merit, and Alastair mentally ran through the list of possible spells they might use. "I'm not sure the standing stones will help. In theory, they might give us an added boost for any spell we may cast, but I can't see it counterbalancing the earthquakes he's causing." As Alastair finished speaking, the floor beneath them rumbled. "Either way, we need to get out of this blasted building."

He tucked one arm beneath Nash's back to cradle his son to his chest. "Ryanne, take my free hand and don't let go. The rest of you, meet us in the clearing." He met Aurora's bright blue gaze and felt some of her confidence seep into him. "Grab on, my love."

He waited a moment until everyone vacated the premises before sending out a magical feeler to the glen. When he was certain he could teleport safely, he closed his eyes to concentrate and opened the rift between the two locations. It only took an extra push of his power to move his small group of four through the opening.

His son-in-law, Quentin, was on the other side with Knox to relieve him of the burden of Nash. "Place him on the stone altar," he directed them. "We need to call up the stones."

Previously, his brother, Preston, would have led the ceremony to raise the stone pillars, but since his passing, that job now fell to him or his sister as the most experienced witches. He went to GiGi and placed a hand on her shoulder. Sadness swamped him. It had only been six months, but he desperately missed his little brother.

Alastair cleared the emotion from his throat and said, "Would you care to do the honors, sister?"

She nodded, gestured to five Thorne sisters to assist, and positioned the group of seven into a circle.

As Ryanne moved forward to offer her assistance, Aurora clasped her hand. "No, dear. This is for the family. Come, wait with me over there." She gestured with one hand to the tree line beyond the clearing. "When the time is right, you can help Nash."

The two men who had followed them separated, with one moving to the path north of the clearing and the other heading south.

"What are they doing?" she asked Aurora.

"They are checking the wooded area around the estate. I like to call them the ceremony guardians. It would take an army to get by either of them, don't you think?"

Her eyes were drawn to the large dark-haired man as he strode away. The guy had to be at least six-six and was chock-full of lean muscle. "He's a beast."

"Ah, but a damned sexy beast, no?"

For the first time in what felt like days, Ryanne cracked a smile. How Nash's family retained a sense of humor when one of their own was in trouble was beyond her scope of comprehension. Yet, they did, and it was easy to fall in with their unwavering optimism. "I didn't think men like him existed outside of Hollywood."

Aurora placed an elegant arm over Ryanne's shoulder and gave a light squeeze. "As my daughter Autumn is fond of saying, he's the perfect eye candy."

Again, Ryanne's smile came unbidden. "I can't fault your daughter's eyesight."

The light, musical laugh from her companion drew Alastair's attention from across the clearing. If asked, Ryanne would have said the sound wouldn't have carried as far, but it was as if Nash's father was attuned to everything about the woman standing next to her. Even from this distance, his love for Aurora was obvious. His head turned in his sister's direction, but his eyes lingered for another second or two on his lover.

"I thought Mr. Thorne's sister mentioned utilizing their magic. Did I hear wrong?"

"No. Their usefulness will come in later, if we cannot remove that bloody piece of jewelry."

Ryanne simply nodded, unsure what to say or do to help.

"Watch," Aurora said quietly. "This is a sight to behold."

While Ryanne couldn't make out the words, each Thorne joined in a chant led by GiGi. This merging of voices was mesmerizing. The ground groaned and grumbled, then separated to reveal the tips of fourteen large rock formations. As one, the pillars rose from beneath the earth's surface, towering over the group and casting shadows around the circle. Oddly enough, all the shadows were directed outward, as if the main source of light came from the center of the stone ring.

The air crackled and became charged with electricity. Ryanne could feel the energy even from this distance. As tired as she was, the current gave her a boost and wiped away the bulk of her fatigue. In an instant, her senses sharpened, and she could smell the heavy scent of pine from the trees beyond them.

The stones were easily three times her height and had to be five feet in width. Moss decorated the rock formations, and symbols—not discernible from this distance—were etched into the hard surfaces of each stone. The setting reminded her of Stonehenge.

"Um, Aurora, these are eerily similar to the standing stones I've seen in the UK. Do people have ceremonies there too?"

"We do. We simply cloak the area and cast a spell to repel visitors."

"It's like pulling back the layers of an onion. I had no idea what lay in the center, no idea a magical community even existed."

"I have the feeling you'll take to it like a duck to water, dear. Your parents were gifted."

"You knew my parents?"

"I did. Your mother and I were school chums."

"You were friends? I got the impression from Mr. Thorne that she —they—my parents—were terrible people."

"I can't speak to what kind of person she was after she met your father, but when I knew her, she was lovely. Very much like you."

A chill swept through her. If her mother had been like her, which Ryanne doubted, what had been the catalyst for her change? Her father? If so, then what type of person allowed themselves to be swayed by another to the degree of using their children for financial gain?

Her gaze fell on Nash where he now lay still. Would she commit a criminal act for him? The answer was a resounding yes. Based on what little he'd told her, Ryanne had been prepared to steal the Red

Scorpion necklace. Only, to Nash's mind—and her own—the theft was justified. Had her mother thought the same? It begged the question, what items had they stolen? When this was all over, she intended to find out.

"I feel as if I need to find my sister and beat the hell out of her until she provides a reversal spell."

"That's one option. But I somehow doubt she knows how."

"What do you mean?"

"Knowing the type of person Victor Salinger is, I suspect he only provided her with the means to attach the necklace, not remove it." Aurora shrugged. "I also suspect your sister didn't have much of a choice in the matter."

"Bull. There's always a choice. She did this because she could and because she can't stand to see me happy."

"Or did she do it because he threatened her and gave her no choice? If faced with harm to you or your person, wouldn't she act in a manner to protect you?"

"I don't know anymore. I don't know if I ever did. My sister is a nutcase."

In the middle of the stone circle, the Thornes gathered and seemed to be discussing their options.

"Can we enter now?" Ryanne asked, unsure of the magical boundaries or how she was expected to deport herself.

"Certainly."

Before they could step forward, Nash's body arched up and a tortured cry escaped his lips. The earth buckled, starting from the altar and working out like a tsunami. The result tipped the stone formations.

Ryanne's fight-or-flight instincts kicked into high gear, and reacting on that instinct, she tackled Aurora, rolling them out of the way of the falling pillar.

The rock formations never toppled. Instead, every single one hung suspended at a forty-five-degree angle from the ground.

Aurora rose and pulled a gobsmacked Ryanne to her feet. "Thank you, dear girl. Now, I need to borrow a bit of your magic."

A warming sensation infused Ryanne's body, and she could literally feel the wave of heat sweep from her cells and transfer itself to Aurora. The winds around them kicked up to tropical storm force, except as far as Ryanne was able to tell, the direction of the air all flowed toward the standing stones. Even as she watched, the stones slowly straightened and settled back into their original upright positions.

Alastair closed the distance between them and swept Aurora into an all-encompassing hug. "Christ, that was close. Are you all right? Was that too much, too soon?"

"I'm fine, darling. Ryanne was lovely enough to lend me her power."

He released Aurora only to embrace, Ryanne. "Thank you, child. You're quickly becoming invaluable to my family."

"But who stopped the stones from falling in the first place?" Ryanne asked, dumbfounded by all that was happening and at the power these witches possessed.

"That would be Summer's or GiGi's instinctive response. Most likely both." He must have picked up on her confusion because he clarified, "They, along with Spring's husband, have the ability to halt time. It comes in handy now and again."

She shook her head at the wonder of it all. "Is this a thing? Like fifty percent of witches can do this? Can I do that?"

"Possibly, but doubtful. It's a gift from the Goddess. Few witches outside the Thorne line can achieve that level of skill."

While she was disappointed, she had other things to worry about right now. Like how the hell had Nash's pain killer worn off so fast? She asked as much and received a grimace from Alastair in return.

"What can we do to help ease his suffering?" She could hear the panic in her own voice, and while she wasn't one to overreact to situations, this one was more dire than most.

"We're working to figure it out, child. Be patient."

"I can't..." She paused to get her hysteria in check. "I can't be patient. Seeing him in such excruciating pain is killing me." The speed with which all this madness had taken place was astonishing. Was it only yesterday morning Nash had brought up the plan to steal the necklace? Ryanne had believed he and Liz were kidding. "Liz!" she cried. "Liz and Nash had been planning to get the necklace for a while, or at least that was the impression I got when we spoke yesterday. Is it possible that she has information we don't?"

"It's worth a try," Aurora agreed. "I'll get her and bring her back."

"Be careful, my love. Go straight there and come straight back. I don't trust Victor not to attack when everyone is distracted."

Ryanne got the impression there should be an "again" attached to his statement. It was more about the look the couple shared than any other reason, but she couldn't shake the feeling Victor had already used that technique to strike at the Thorne family.

After Aurora disappeared, Ryanne and Alastair strode to where Nash once again rested quietly. She stroked his sweat-dampened hair back from his face, and in his uneasy sleep, Nash turned toward her touch.

"Has Victor done something like this before?" she asked softly.

"Not this exact thing, but yes. He's part of a warring bloodline who has it out for our family."

She raised her gaze to meet Alastair's stare. "Anyone associated with you will never be safe, will they?"

"No."

Biting her lip against the flow of profanity rising up, she nodded and looked down at Nash. "He's collateral damage in this stupid-ass war of yours."

"Not if I can help it."

A viciousness welled in her chest and hate flooded her being. She whipped her head up and glared. "But you didn't help it, did you? Because of you, he's going to die. Tortured by some nasty piece of work who—"

Her ugly speech was cut off when hands jerked her back from the altar. All the fire inside was instantly banked. A dying ember. She looked around at all the faces staring in shock. "I'm sorry. I don't know what came over me."

Spring patted her arm. "I do. It's why I pulled you away. The scorpion was poisoning your thoughts."

"But I didn't touch it."

"You didn't need to. I noticed it early on at Thorne Industries. My sister and Nash were both acting out of character. With your sudden anger, well, let's say, it shouldn't have taken me that long to figure it out."

Ryanne focused her attention on Nash. Had she not been watching, she'd have missed the movement of the scorpion as it appeared to burrow deeper into his skin. "Dear God!" She grabbed Nash's hand and, acting on instinct, pulled the next wave of his power into her. The boost of energy knocked her flat on her back. She bit her lip and saw stars when her head slammed into the hard-packed earth. It felt as if all her blood and brain matter had pooled in that one spot in her skull.

Spring and GiGi got to her first. As Spring produced a handkerchief and dabbed at the blood on Ryanne's mouth, GiGi worked gentle fingers along the back of Ryanne's neck and palpated the bump forming on the back of her head.

A simple incantation by Nash's aunt took away Ryanne's headache and cleared her thoughts. "I need to get that thing off him. I don't care what I have to do."

With a determination and courage she didn't feel, she approached Nash's still form. As she grasped the edges of the shirt, the jewel-encrusted tail rose up to strike. "You can't have him," she said fiercely. "He's mine!"

CHAPTER 19

With a simple flick of a wrist, Alastair assisted Ryanne by splitting the material of the Henley in two. She didn't have time to admire the beauty of Nash's well-built chest. All her focus was on the little beast doing its damnedest to take the life of the man she loved.

"I read about you, ya know," she told it. "About why you were created and whose lives you were meant to destroy."

Ryanne inched her fingers closer and had to fight the desire to pull back as the tail surged higher and vibrated. The late afternoon sun reflected off the silver and illuminated the glow of the precious stones. There was no doubt that she'd get stung in the process of removing it. What had someone said? That the tail contained poison? A tear spilled on the back of her wrist. Nash's life was worth any price she had to pay.

"But I also read that Isis took pity on the couple. That she tried to remove the curse your mistress put on you. I don't believe you want to be evil. No creature does." What the hell was she saying? She was talking to a fucking piece of jewelry, for goodness's sake! "Please let him go. Please. He's a good man. He means so much to so many. He means so much to me."

From the corner of her eye, she noticed a type of light show, but she didn't dare divert her attention from the ruby arachnid for a second. She inched the tips of her fingers closer and managed a single stroke along its rippling back.

"I love him."

Stroke.

"If you need a sacrifice, take me."

The third stroke resulted in the tail plunging toward the vulnerable skin on the back of Ryanne's hand. The wicked-looking barb never pierced her flesh. It stopped mere centimeters away, but the intent was obvious.

She glanced around, expecting to see the other occupants of the clearing as stunned as she. Yet they all stood frozen in place. Had she done that? Was she one of the rare witches who could freeze time?

"It's beautiful, isn't it?" The silky, slightly menacing tones of another woman drifted to her from over her right shoulder. A stranger to this crowd, if Ryanne was to guess.

When she would have turned to see, her body refused to cooperate. Her paralyzed state only allowed a shudder of terror. "Who are you?"

Wild laughter tinged with insanity echoed across the glen. "I am the downfall of the Thorne Witches, girl."

"You're Serqet."

Ryanne wasn't sure how she knew, but she did. Perhaps she recognized the unhinged laughter from her dream earlier this week, or maybe she understood that only a goddess would have the ability to contain this powerful group in one fell swoop, but whichever it was, it was doubtful that she was mistaken.

"Smart. You get that from me."

"You?"

"You're a descendent of my line, girl. Did no one teach you about your history?" she snapped.

Another woman's voice entered into their conversation. "These newer generations of witches. They have no understanding or respect for the old gods and goddesses." Her tone of voice was slightly mocking and full of merriment.

Ryanne suspected she recognized this goddess, too. "Isis?"

"Yes, child."

Isis stepped into view.

Ryanne stared in wonder. The woman was freaking gorgeous. Black hair hung down her back with a wide gold band encircling her head. She was dressed all in white in a gossamer material that sparkled in the low light. Around her waist was a gold, braided rope-like belt that hung almost to the ground. High upon her arms were gold bangles shaped like asps.

"You're beautiful," Ryanne blurted.

Isis's lips twitched, but she held back the amused smile that was clearly gleaming from her eyes. "Thank you."

The hair on the back of Ryanne's neck lifted, and an uneasy feeling slithered down her spine seconds before she felt the hand of Serqet touch her back.

"What are you doing here, sister?" Serqet didn't bother to conceal her anger or loathing.

"It is a fine day for a stroll in the glen, don't you think?"

"What I think is that you are once again determined to ruin my plans."

Ryanne remained silent and watchful. Whatever war was playing out between these two, she wanted no part of it.

"What exactly would those plans entail, sister? Or do I need to guess?"

"No need to guess. I'm after the lives of your favorite toys."

Isis's mouth flattened into a thin white line. "And what is your idea to achieve this?"

A finger stroked Ryanne's hair. Fear kept her throat clogged and her mouth closed. Across the altar, she met Isis's watchful gaze.

"Do you know, this girl was the one born with all the power of past generations? Generations of my kin who were denied what should have been theirs by right. Who, because of you, lived their lives in the shadows." Serqet's temper had been building as she spoke. Her not-so-quiet rage frightened the area wildlife beyond the glen and sent them running.

Apparently, only the humans were frozen in place.

Serqet wasn't done with her tirade, but her voice was more controlled when she said, "She is of my line and of our brother's line. She and her sister, the first of their kind. The fire Ryanne contains inside is as powerful as a nuclear blast, and she would never feel the burn."

What the what? She was a walking Chernobyl? Was it only a matter of time before she decimated the area and people around her? Did Rylee have the same ability?

"What do you intend to do with your human bomb, sister?"

"I thought you'd never ask," Serqet laughed. "It's simple, really. Victor and Rylee so obligingly set this chess game in motion. Now, the queen will take the board."

Ryanne dug deep for the courage to speak. "What am I missing here?" she croaked.

"You can save yourself and destroy those in this clearing, or you can die. Excruciatingly slowly."

She closed her eyes and swallowed. "And Nash?"

"He's dead either way. My pet has pierced his heart."

A sob worked its way up from the deepest region of Ryanne's soul. She barely managed to contain it by biting the inside of her cheek. The metallic taste of blood filled her mouth, and she fought not to gag.

"How do I unleash my powers?" she whispered past her emotion-strangled throat.

"It starts as a single spark in your cells. You visualize it building, engulfing all the souls around you at once," Serqet instructed. The glee in her voice was unmistakable.

Was it possible to melt the necklace with her heat? If she'd have paid more attention in science, she might know what burning point could melt metal or destroy the jewels. Where was the power contained in the necklace? The head, the body, the tail? Any questions might arouse suspicion. She shot a furtive glance at Isis, looking for some type of help, but the goddess's attention was on the woman behind her.

"Why do you hate me so, sister? What did I do to wrong you?"

"You dare ask that?" Serqet stormed to Isis's side, her hands clenched to her breasts. "You took away my revenge. Because of your interference, I lost nearly everything."

"Your punishment by Ra was a result of your actions. Nothing more, nothing less."

Serqet pointed toward Spring. "You have protected her at every turn. And him!" For a split second, her eyes softened on the tall man with the shoulder-length blond hair moving toward them. "He loved me once."

"Maybe. But it was centuries ago, and you destroyed any affection he may have had for you with your continued attacks on his bride."

"Exalted Ones." Knox bowed his head slightly but never took his eyes from Serqet as he continued moving in an attempt to place himself between the goddess and Spring. He held one hand behind him, and from Ryanne's angle, Knox looked to be gathering elements into a glowing ball.

So as not to give away his actions, she glanced down. A second attempt to move her frozen body proved useless. Whatever spell that evil piece of work had cast on the clearing was still in effect. How was it that Knox could move?

Serqet addressed him now. "Months ago, I gave you the option to become my consort to save your woman. I am offering you the option again."

"I can't let you hurt her," he said softly. "I won't."

"You cannot stop *her*." Serqet nodded her head toward Ryanne.

"She has the power to destroy you, Knox Carlyle. I'll take great delight when she does."

Knox met Ryanne's frantic gaze. She had no desire to hurt anyone. That much was clear. How Serqet intended to use the poor woman was anyone's guess. Isis showed no concern, but then again, her standard enigmatic expression wasn't always easy to read.

When he had blocked Spring's body with his own, he breathed an internal sigh of relief. The second he'd noted the sounds of panicked animals fleeing the woods around the clearing, he hurried back to the standing stones. Across the distance, he saw Quentin's prone body and prayed for everyone's sake that the guy was okay.

It wasn't until Knox reached the inner circle of the stones that his mind connected the dots as to why everyone was locked in place. Of course, his first instinctive response was to get to Spring. To protect her at all costs.

"Not to be contrary, but Ryanne's a new witch who hasn't had training. I cannot see her taking on an experienced warlock and winning, Exalted One." He was careful to keep his tone neutral. Any inflection could be taken as antagonistic and might result in further hostilities.

"My sister has likened dear Ryanne to a nuclear bomb," Isis provided helpfully.

Knox went cold inside. Once again, his eyes darted to meet Ryanne's. He'd always been a decent judge of character, but he truly didn't know on which side she stood in all this mess.

"Is that right?" he asked casually, as if they were idly discussing the weather. "Interesting. I suppose she's the one who has frozen my friends?"

"Not me," she croaked. "Nope. I was totally going for the scorpion's removal when all this…" She rolled her eyes around. "… all this stopped."

He narrowed his eyes on the hand she had extended toward the necklace. No tremble or movement of any kind. She was as trapped as the others.

"How is it that you can move?" she asked in a low tone, confirming his suspicions.

"I'm special that way."

She glanced down at Nash, and Knox noted the tears building on the rims of her bottom lids. He hadn't meant to make her cry with his cutting comeback, but if she truly was Serqet's weapon of choice, he wasn't giving her any information to destroy him.

He studied the damned necklace Serqet had used to try to kill Spring during her first incarnation. It seemed he was to be forever plagued with that crazy-ass goddess and her attempts on their lives. Serqet would never stop. Not in this lifetime, or any other.

That knowledge put him in a bad situation. Isis had granted Knox the power of the gods on the off chance he would need it to fight her sister. He half suspected she'd only provided said powers because she knew he'd probably never use them against either of them. The threat of his retaliation should've been enough for Serqet. It seemed it wasn't.

Quentin was something like the thousand-times-over great-grandson of Zeus. That made him the only other formidable opponent Serqet might encounter. Unfortunately, while the guy possessed god-like powers, he was also human to a large degree, so whatever she'd knocked him out with was going to make him wake up fighting mad.

"Okay, how about this. You don't set off your human bomb, and I don't blast you into obscurity?" he suggested as a kind of truce.

Isis's dark brows flew skyward, and her mouth dropped open into a perfectly round oh. It could be that she'd never expected him to threaten a goddess, regardless of the magic contained within him. Her dark head swung in Serqet's direction, although she remained silent.

"You dare threaten *me*?" Serqet seethed.

Thunder rumbled overhead.

Christ, this was about to get ugly.

He moved forward, careful to keep himself as a shield between her and Spring. "It wouldn't have to come to a threat if you left my family alone. We just want to be able to live in peace. No Zhu Lin, no Victor Salinger, no Richard Knox or Marianne Carlyle, and no snipers waiting to take my wife out." He sighed heavily as he studied her set face. She was stunningly beautiful. Maybe more than Isis. He could see why they had been lovers in his previous life. Why he would have been attracted to her before he met Spring. "Don't do this, Serqet. For whatever we shared, don't make it ugly any longer. Know when to quit."

She gasped, and her rage kicked up a notch. *"I never quit."*

Okay, wrong thing for him to say. Obviously, she would take it as a challenge. He'd gone soft in the last few months he'd spent with Spring. He should've known Serqet would continue to send additional threats his way. With the hand tucked behind his back, Knox pulled more electrical energy from the air, gearing up for a lightning strike.

A blinding white light appeared in the space next to Isis. It was gone in an instant, and in its place stood a woman, similar in appearance to the two sisters, but thinner and standing about six inches taller. This woman he knew from dreams. This goddess was his ancestor, Nephthys.

He ducked his head. "Exalted One."

"Beloved One." She stepped around the altar and approached him from behind. With a gentle touch to his wrist, she dissolved his energy ball. "No need for that right now. Save your fight for another day, child."

She trailed a finger along his rigid jawline and smiled. "Are you sure you don't wish to become my consort?"

His eyes sought Isis. What was this? Had this been an option at some point? Why did all the goddesses want him as their consort when he was clearly in love with Spring?

"I…" Yeah, what could he say without offending the one goddess who might sway the outcome of this little skirmish? "I'm honored you should ask, but I'm in love with Spring."

"Yes, so my sister tells me," Nephthys said on a sigh. "Pity. You'd make my subjects stand up and take notice. I suspect you'd make the years ahead interesting for one and all."

"I'm boring. Truly," he demurred. "All I do is work with horses day in and day out. Certainly not worthy enough to grace your presence."

Her delighted laugh rang out. The sound made him want to chuckle in return, but he held back. There wasn't a thing about the current situation that was funny.

She sidled up to Ryanne and leaned over to study Nash's face, a canvas of pain. "Nasty business, this. A horrible death sentence, don't you think, child?"

Ryanne made a strangled sound but kept her opinions to herself.

In an unexpected move, Nephthys spun and perched on the lip of the stone holding Nash. She crossed her long, exposed legs and rested back on her palms. The pose screamed casual and playful.

"Well, sisters. It seems we all have a vested interest in today's outcome. All three bloodlines represented."

Isis lifted a brow and crossed her arms. "Personally, I feel this feud has gone on far too long. In recent years, the battle has cost too many casualties on all sides."

"I would have sacrifices from your line," Serqet told Isis. "Pick the three you choose to lose. There will be no reviving them this time."

"No. Three is too many. You have already cursed Nash. Let that be enough. Let it be done."

"It will never be done. Not until Alastair, Spring, and the mouthy redhead are gone," Serqet vowed.

The only mouthy redhead in the lot was Autumn. It seemed Serqet was after all the strongest Thornes. Knowing he had to derail this particular train of conversation, Knox stepped forward, still managing to keep Spring from Serqet's line of sight.

"You fail to realize one thing. Should anything happen to Spring, I will rain down hell on any and all involved. You can play your games and spin the wheel of destiny on the members of this poor family, but they've suffered enough." He warmed to his tirade and towered over Serqet. His rage at the unfairness of their fight, striking the match on his fury fire. "They've been subject to your whims for thousands of years. *Why?* Because of *me?* Have my life and be done with it. Let my death be the end. But know, if you do anything further to harm this family, I will come back from the Otherworld, and I will *destroy* you."

All three goddesses gaped.

Nephthys was the first to recover and clapped her hands. "He made my heart beat faster. No one has done that in years, not since... well, that doesn't matter." She waved a hand in dismissal. "But his speech was thrilling and so deliciously masculine, don't you agree, sisters? Such a worthy human. I vote he lives."

CHAPTER 20

Aslow anger began to brew in Ryanne's chest. With each nonchalant wave of a hand or casual mention of a Thorne family member's death, burning fury rolled through her. The longer she remained frozen, the more aware she'd been of the state of the others in the clearing. It took her long enough, but she recognized they were all aware of the happenings around them.

She met Alastair's eyes across the short distance. His gaze was steady, and no judgment or condemnation shone from his eyes. She tried to convey her apology for being manipulated, and somehow, she guessed he understood.

"Okay, new plan," she blurted.

Everyone's attention turned on her.

"First, I'm getting a cramp. This is uncomfortable as fuck, and I'm done. Release me at once."

"You—"

She cut off Serqet's predicted outrage. "If you expect me to do your bidding, you'll do as I ask."

From behind Serqet, Isis smiled her approval.

Ryanne was released so suddenly, she almost fell into the tail of the Red Scorpion and ended her impromptu plan before it began. The scorpion rippled and swished that shiny appendage as if it were an irritated cat denied its prey.

"I thought three strokes released the scorpion?" Granted she was pushing the limit of the goddess's tolerance, but Nash was the most important person in her universe. She'd do what she could to reverse the damage her sister had wrought.

"He'll stay suspended where he is until negotiations are settled," Serqet snapped.

"Can you repair the hole in his heart and save him or not?"

"I can do anything I so desire." The goddess stomped forward, the folds of her deep red dress billowing behind her as the winds increased their speed.

"So far, I'm not impressed," Ryanne growled. She had nothing to lose. Not anymore. "Remove this curse from him, and maybe I'll believe you."

"She's a horrid child. I'd smite her, sister," Isis said as she moved closer to the altar. "Teach her a lesson on how to talk to her betters."

If steam could come off the top of Serqet's head, it would. "I'm not smiting my prized weapon!"

"It was only a suggestion, my dear."

Nephthys scoffed her disbelief. "When has she ever listened to your suggestions, sister?"

"There is always a first time."

"Be quiet. A goddess can't hear the world hum with the two of you prattling on." Serqet gave her sisters one last glare before she settled her brooding gaze on Nash. "Do you love him, child?"

Ryanne held her breath and nodded. She refused to allow the small seed of hope she was feeling to take hold.

"More than your own life?"

"Yes."

The second she spoke the word aloud, the necklace retracted. The sharp silver legs released their grip on Nash's diaphragm and folded into the body of the scorpion. The tail relaxed its aggressive arch and curled into a ball.

When the clasp gave way and the chain fell from behind Nash's neck, Ryanne took her first deep inhale. Without waiting for the go-ahead, she grabbed the chain, whipped it back, and flung the necklace as far as she could. It hit one of the standing stones and sank into the dirt by the base.

"If you wish the hole in his heart to be repaired, you have to first agree to my terms," Serqet informed her.

Ryanne wanted to promise anything, but she refused to take a life other than her own. She'd never be able to live with herself, and if she *could* murder another, Nash would hate her. In that case, what would be the point in hurting one of his family?

"What is it you require?" she asked hoarsely.

"You will kill Spring Thorne." Serqet faced her sisters. "You will not interfere with her actions, whatever she chooses to do. You will not save the mortal."

Both goddesses gave a nod as affirmation.

The earth rumbled around them, and lightning flashed across the clearing. Knox was about to have a meltdown, if Ryanne had to guess. But she could no more hurt the lovely woman who had eased Nash's suffering than she could hurt Nash himself.

"You require a sacrifice?" she clarified.

"Yes."

Ryanne reached down to remove the knife Ryker had strapped to her ankle. "You agree, a life for a life, and then it's done?"

"No!" Knox yelled, surging forward.

"Yes, a life for a life, and then it's done." Serqet agreed. Her dark kohl-lined eyes glowed with an unholy light.

"Fine."

Knox gripped Ryanne's wrist in his meaty hand and whipped her around. An ever-expanding ball of bright white light brewed in his left hand. Sparks flew from the ball and shot in every direction. "I can't let you do that, Ryanne."

"You don't have a choice, Knox." She stared up into his hard, determined features. She allowed a small smile, and then she winked. It was enough of a surprise for his grip to lessen. She yanked her arm free and scored the vein of her opposite wrist with the tip of the blade. Pressing hard, she swiftly ran it the length of her forearm, trying not to scream from the excruciating pain.

"A life for a life," she gasped out and promptly dropped like a stone.

Nash's first conscious thought was that although his chest ached, the unbearable burning was gone. He cracked his eyes and took in the gold and red sky above him. Where was he? Inching his head to the left, he looked into the sky-blue eyes of one of the most beautiful women he'd ever seen.

Isis.

He swiped his swollen tongue over his parched lips and swallowed. His mouth felt like it had been stuffed with cotton and had absorbed all the available moisture. "Exalted One," he whispered.

Her slender fingers trailed across his exposed skin, creating heat wherever they touched. The warming sensation wasn't unpleasant, but he had to wonder why he was lying on a stone slab as she felt up his chest.

With a second swipe of his tongue along his dry lips, he asked the question of the hour, "Did my father decide to sacrifice me?"

Her light, amused laughter made him smile.

"No, dear boy. I'm healing your wounds."

He nodded his head and let his eyes close. "That's much appreciated. My chest aches like a four-hundred pound gorilla was using it as a bongo drum."

She chuckled again.

"How is he?"

His father's voice prompted him to open his eyes again.

"I'm going to go out on a limb and say I think I'll survive, Dad."

Alastair's large hand settled on his shoulder.

Nash could feel the tension in his father's grip. It was there in the lines around his eyes and mouth as well.

"What's going on?"

"We'll talk in a short while. Rest and let Isis work her magic."

He started to sit up, only to be shoved back down by both Alastair and Isis.

"Where's Ryanne?" Somehow, some way, Nash knew his father's grim expression had to do with Ryanne. "Where is she?"

Alastair looked over his head to a point beyond Nash's vision, his eyes questioning.

Nash lifted himself on his elbows and twisted his neck about to see what had caught his father's attention. Knox sat with a limp Ryanne cradled against his chest. She looked paler than Nash had ever seen her. GiGi was bent over Ryanne's wrist with a wand in hand. Purple light filled the space between the wand's tip and the skin of her arm. As he watched, the skin slowly knitted together.

In a flash, he was up and staggering toward her, his own healing forgotten. Nash crashed to his knees beside her and felt for a pulse. Her heartbeat was thready and barely detectable, but she was still alive.

"What the devil happened to her?" he demanded. His heart pounded double time to make up for her lagging rate.

"She traded her life for yours, son." Alastair's tone was somber. For once, the dry, mocking quality was gone.

"Why? Why would she do that?" he cried as he gently transferred her body from Knox's embrace to his own. "Why, Ryanne?" he whispered. "Why? Why? Why?" He swayed back and forth, his forehead on her cheek. The most precious thing in his life lay in his arms, knocking at death's door. "Don't leave me. Please."

"I've done all I can do," GiGi sat back and announced. "The next few hours will be the determining factor."

Nash lifted his gaze to Isis. "Help her."

Isis's expression was grave. "I cannot. It was the one promise I made to my sisters. Your mate knew what she was doing when she cut open her wrist. She entered into a bargain with Serqet. A life for a life."

"So you're saying she is going to die regardless?" he managed.

"I'm sorry, child."

"I don't accept that." He tore his gaze from her sympathetic blue eyes and desperately glanced around the clearing, hoping there was someone with a solution. "I've done everything any of you have ever asked. Even when it went against the Council or the Goddess. Help me now."

Spring moved to the front of the crowd and knelt beside him. "Of course we will. Take her back to her apartment. I'll see what I have in my storeroom and follow shortly."

"But the magic of the stones—" he started.

"Won't help," Isis quickly cut him off. "The stones are of the gods and goddesses. We cannot get involved in the saving of this human. The magic of the clearing cannot be utilized."

Resting his cheek on the silky softness of Ryanne's thick hair, Nash closed his eyes against an onslaught of emotions. Bitterness, anger, despair—they all attacked at once, fighting for dominance.

Visualizing the interior of Ryanne's apartment, Nash transitioned his cells and teleported to her bedroom. He carefully laid her on the bed and drew the covers up around her to keep her body warm. Like non-magical humans, witches were susceptible to shock. Exhaustion overtook him. He reclined beside her and gathered her close in the hope of keeping her warm.

"What happened to my sister?"

He jolted out of his sleepy state and jumped from the bed. He was halfway to Rylee, hands outstretched, when her ragged appearance registered.

"You have ten seconds to leave and never return, or I won't be responsible for what I do to you," he warned with a snarl. It took every ounce of self-control not to wring her scrawny neck.

"What can I do to help her?" she pleaded.

"*Help* her? You're the reason she's in that state!" His fists clenched and unclenched in his desire to harm.

"She was never supposed to be hurt. Victor promised."

"You're a fool if you believe anything that comes out of his mouth." He sighed heavily, all the rage evaporating. His energy levels were at an all-time low, and maintaining that type of fury was draining. "You need to leave, Rylee. You no longer have a sister. You forfeited that right."

"Please, Nash. Let me help her."

"How? How exactly do you think you can help?"

The air around them crackled, heralding the arrival of the Thorne family.

Rylee's skin turned a sickly shade of green when she saw Alastair and Autumn step through the bedroom doorway.

When Alastair lifted his hand in preparation for a magical strike, Nash stepped in his path. "No. No more violence. Let her go, Dad."

His knees buckled, but he never hit the floor. His father leapt forward and supported Nash's weight.

"I'm not leaving," Rylee stated firmly. Where she found the courage was anyone's guess because based on the trembling in her voice, the woman was terrified. Perhaps there was more of Ryanne in her than imagined. "I need to help her."

"What about a transfusion? Blood and magic."

Nash lifted his head to stare at Quentin Buchanan. "Pardon?"

"They are identical twins. Ryanne needs an infusion of both," Quentin said.

All eyes turned to Rylee.

She paled. "I'll do it."

"I wouldn't trust that she doesn't have poison in her veins and intends to finish off her poor sister," Alastair stated coldly. "She's a puppet."

Spring stepped forward. "We can test that. But first, empty your pockets, Rylee. No one is stepping within range of you until we see what you are packing. Fool me once, and all."

Rylee turned her pockets out, then lifted her shirt hem to the bottom of her bra and spun around.

"Lift your pants legs to the knee," Spring ordered.

Again, Rylee complied.

"Follow me to the living room. And know that if you pull anything, my husband will fry your ass without a second thought." Spring gave a side nod to Knox, who stood next to her with arms folded across his muscular chest.

"No tricks. I swear. I only want to save my sister."

"Quentin, you and Autumn ward this apartment. The strongest wards you can conjure," Alastair ordered. "Now everyone out. I want to speak to my son."

The family left, with Quentin closing the door behind him.

"Don't be angry with Isis, son. She did what she could, and she repaired the hole in your heart when Serqet went back on her word."

"Then why won't she help Ryanne?" Nash demanded. He wanted to shrug off the hand on his back.

"Because she doesn't go back on her promises. She did what she had to in order to protect our line."

"Our line," he scoffed. "That's what it always boils down to, doesn't it? The mighty Thornes. Who cares about the collateral damage to anyone else? I was cursed the day I was born into this family."

"I'm sorry you feel that way, boy. But know I am proud to call you my son." Alastair embraced him. "So proud. I'm sorry for all you've been subjected to as my kin, but somehow, we'll save Ryanne."

Nash hesitated for a moment. Of their own volition, his arms encircled his father. It was the first hug they'd shared since Nash was a child. Tears burned his eyes, and his nasal passages filled. He barely held back the weighty sobs threatening to crush his chest.

"I love you, Dad," he choked out.

The words were barely audible, but Alastair seemed to hear them all the same because his arms tightened.

"I love you, too, Nash. I always have, from the moment you opened your bright, intelligent eyes. You had a world of knowledge in them, even then." He cleared his throat and gave one final squeeze before releasing Nash. "Now, time is of the essence to save your girl."

CHAPTER 21

Ryanne cautiously approached the iron gate to her childhood home. Surely she was dreaming? She was amazed that nothing had changed. The old Victorian was still a charming shade of pale yellow with a bold royal-blue door. White scrollwork decorated the eaves, making the large wrap-around porch that much more inviting.

As she opened the gate, the front door swung wide, revealing her mother attired in a floral sundress. The wide welcoming smile on Marsha Caldwell's face filled Ryanne's heart to overflowing. "Mom?"

"Hello, my beautiful girl."

The embrace was real and warm and everything Ryanne suddenly remembered it could be. "How is this possible?"

A fleeting, sad look crossed her mother's face before it was replaced by a bright, happy grin. "You're with us now. In the Otherworld."

Heart pounding, Ryanne looked behind her at the way she'd come. Nothing but a row of homes greeted her. What had she hoped to see? Nash waiting for her at the gate? The Otherworld was what non-magical humans referred to as Heaven. Which, if this wasn't a crazy, vivid dream, meant she had crossed over.

"I'm sorry, baby."

Ryanne couldn't see her mother's expression through the blur of tears, but the pained sympathy was there in her tone. "Have you been here the whole time? In this house?"

"We reside here, yes. Similar to the living world, but we're on a different plane of existence."

"Is Dad here, too?"

"He is."

"I thought…" She didn't know how to broach the subject of their stealing, and she let the conversational ball drop. From behind her mother, Paul Caldwell appeared in the doorway, looking as hale and hearty as Ryanne remembered from her childhood. The beard and plaid shirt he sported reminded her of the character from a popular paper towel commercial. His look was like the quintessential lumber-jack. "Papa?"

His face scrunched up as if he was struggling not to cry. "Hello, muffin."

He swept her up and twirled her around. The past came crashing back. All the times he'd arrived home and swung her up in his arms this way. She'd search his pockets for her favorite candy, and he never failed to be fully stocked with treats.

When he set Ryanne down, she reached into the breast pocket of his flannel shirt. Sure enough, he had a small chocolate drop hidden inside. She laughed. "Still the same Papa."

"Always." He opened his mouth to speak, but his eyes caught something beyond her shoulder. Paul charged forward and stood toe-to-toe with a large auburn-haired man. Expression hard, he said, "What do you want?"

"Calm down. I simply want to speak with your daughter."

"You Thornes have done enough!" her mother spat.

"Thorne?" Ryanne pushed between her father and the newcomer. "You're a Thorne?"

The man with the mussy rich red hair smiled and held out his hand. In his smile, she saw the ghost of Nash's smile.

"I'm Preston Thorne."

"Preston? As in Alastair Thorne's brother?"

"Yes."

"You're not welcome here," Marsha warned.

Ryanne shushed her and faced Preston. "May we speak, sir?"

"I was hoping we might."

Her mother surged forward as if to stop this from happening, but her father gripped her arm. "Let them speak, darling."

"He'll fill her with hope, and she'll leave us," Marsha cried.

"She deserves to be happy, doesn't she?" he returned softly.

"I don't understand." Ryanne looked between the three of them. "What does a simple conversation have to do with anything?"

Paul's steely gaze met Preston's steady stare. "You should know, with a Thorne, anything is possible, muffin." Abruptly, her father turned and shuffled her mother away.

"What the hell was that all about?" she muttered.

"Your parents finally get to spend time with you again. They fear I'll take you away."

"Can that happen? Don't we determine where we want to be on this plane?"

He smiled, and there was a wealth of amusement in his eyes. "We do indeed."

"I assume you see and know all on this side?" At his quick nod, she said, "Your family, they're safe now. I can't promise it will last, but Serqet can no longer use me as a tool to harm them."

"I know. What you did was admirable, Ryanne." He glanced toward the house. "Walk with me a spell, won't you?"

She fell into step beside him, and they strolled an entire block in silence. When it seemed as if he was lost in thought, she spoke. "Mr. Thorne? What is it you wanted to tell me? I can't imagine you sought me out to stroll around the neighborhood."

He laughed. The sound was robust and contagious. "I can see

why my nephew loves you. Beautiful, smart, feisty—all things designed to bring a Thorne male to his knees."

"Nash was hardly on his knees. The idiot took two years to ask me out. And look where that went!"

"Oh, I agree that timing is everything. It wasn't until I passed over that I met the love of my life."

"Wait, what? How is that possible?"

"She doesn't know it, but she's destined to be my future bride."

"Isn't that a little arrogant?"

The big man laughed again. "Perhaps a little." He stopped walking and looked up toward the vibrant blue sky. "Tell me, if you could go back, would you?"

"Back? To the moment in the clearing? Would it undo what I've done to save Nash or Spring?"

"If it would?"

"I'd say no."

"Wise choice. But I'm offering you a different one this time. Your life for your sister's."

"Rylee?" Ryanne's knees felt weak, and she plopped down on the sidewalk's edge.

Preston tugged up his pant legs and squatted in front of her. "Yes. Rylee. Would you do it?"

The intensity in his stare made her squirm inside. She wanted to tell him yes. She'd do almost anything to return to Nash, but the reality was she couldn't trade her life for her sister's. "I won't do that to her."

"What if it is what she wished?"

"Pfft. You don't know my sister very well."

"Oh, I think I have a good idea what your sister is like." He rose and held out a hand to help her up. "Go spend time with your mother and father. I'll be back in two days' time. I'll need your answer by then."

On the short trek to her parent's home, Ryanne mulled over their conversation. What did any of it mean? Even if she was willing to swap places with Rylee, her sister was too selfish by far to risk her own neck. And did she really want to cut short her twin's life? Was that fair?

She paused at the gate and stared at the replica of the home in which she'd been born. Was her room the same as when she was a child? Did the banister still bear her name and Rylee's from where her sister had snuck their father's pocket knife to carve the jagged letters?

Melancholy struck her. As much as she wanted to be with her parents, she wanted to be with Nash more. She spun back to find Preston Thorne, but the landscape had changed. Across the street was a park-like setting with a single stone bench by the water's edge. Ryanne instantly recognized the woman sitting there. Isis.

Without a backward glance, she rushed across the distance, stopping only when she reached Isis's side. "Why didn't you help? Why did you let your horrible sister do what she did?" Ryanne demanded. "Why is all this such a game to you three?"

"Sit." Isis patted the space beside her. "Please."

Reluctantly, Ryanne perched on the edge of the cool stone seat.

"What do you think of the Otherworld, child?"

"I haven't been here long enough to think anything."

The goddess ignored the surliness behind her response. "True. But how do you feel about spending eternity with your parents?"

Because she sensed there was a reason for these questions, Ryanne replied as honestly as she could with as little attitude as she could manage. "They died when I was young. While it's great to see them, I don't truly know them anymore." She looked out over the sparkling water. "If I had a choice, I'd spend my life and my eternity with Nash."

"Good. That is what I had hoped you would say."

"Why?"

"I intend that you should spend your life with your young man. You are as deserving as Nash Thorne."

Hope swelled in her breast. "I don't understand. I'm dead."

"No, child. Your body is in stasis. It's a type of permanent sleep state until magic can be employed to restart the life cycle."

"I can go back?"

"That remains to be seen."

"On what?"

"Your sister."

The building hope died. "That will never happen."

"You would be surprised what one will sacrifice for another. Didn't you sacrifice for a relative stranger when you took your life?"

"No. I didn't do it for Spring. I did it for Nash. He loves his family and would hate to see them torn apart by that type of loss."

"And perhaps you did it for yourself as well?" Isis suggested with a knowing look.

"Maybe. I couldn't bear to live with his condemnation. How could he love me if I murdered another to be with him?"

The goddess reached out and patted Ryanne's forearm. "You are wise beyond your years, my dear. All will work out as it is intended. Spend these few days with your mother and father. Find out the truth of the past from them. It might lead you to understand the present."

Before Isis could leave, Ryanne had to know. "How is Nash? Is he well?"

"He is as well as can be expected. He's grief-stricken at the thought of losing you, child."

Deep emotion clogged her throat. There were many questions she wanted to ask, but Ryanne couldn't manage the words.

"Save your worry, dear girl. All will be well in due time. This moment will be a distant memory."

"It's not working." Nash dropped his hand and broke the ring of light flowing from palm to palm. "If we don't stop, we'll kill them both."

For the last forty minutes, they had worked to transfer blood and merge the magic of the twins in an effort to revive Ryanne. But the only thing they'd achieved was to place Rylee's life in peril. Her skin was practically translucent, it was so pale. Her breathing had become shallow and strained. Although he couldn't say he cared for the woman, he didn't want to kill her on a fool's mission to revive her sister.

Nash placed his palm above hers and sent out a spark to test her remaining power. Whatever magic she still retained was faint. He gently set her hand on the mattress beside her torso and moved to the other side of the bed to stare down at his beloved.

Ryanne hadn't responded to any of the spells they tried. It was time to face the fact that she was lost to him. He hung his head to hide his grief. He wanted to bawl like a small baby but would reserve that right for when he was alone with his pain.

"Nash—"

He held up a hand and shook his head. "Please don't. If you could all close the circle and go, I'd be grateful."

Words were spoken to end the ceremony, and the candles were extinguished. The family filed out of the bedroom to gather in Ryanne's tiny living room. Nash knew they wouldn't leave completely because they feared how he'd react, but still, he wished they'd leave him to mourn.

He perched on the edge of the mattress and picked up Ryanne's hand. Cool to the touch, it was a sickening reminder that she was clinging to life by a mere thread. Idly, he traced the blue veins on the back of her hand. The tip of his finger ran the length of the fragile bones, over the knuckle, and down her index finger to the tastefully polished nail. The French manicure had been an odd choice compared to the deep amethyst streaks she'd previously had in her hair.

But that was Ryanne. Everything about her was a complete contradiction. She came across as hard and matter-of-fact, yet inside, she was a marshmallow and always fought for the underdog. Her hair was wild and fun, but her mode of dress was always formal and business-like. She downplayed her beauty at every turn, and yet, she was insanely attractive. And unless a person took the time to know her, they would never know how intelligent she really was.

He held her palm to his cheek. "You should never have sacrificed for me, my love. I'm not half the person you are." He sniffed back the threatening moisture. "How am I supposed to go on without you there to brighten my day?"

He closed his eyes and swallowed against the building ache in his chest.

"Every single day, I watched you, just to catch a glimpse of your smile. You were so unreserved with Liz, allowing her to see a part of you not many did." Nash kissed her palm and placed it back on his cheek. "Now, you've sentenced me to wander around my big, lonely house like a wraith. A pale imitation of my father, who waited almost twenty years to resuscitate the love of his life. Is that going to be us, Ryanne?" His voice broke, and he sucked in a lungful of air. "Am I destined to search for artifacts to bring you back to me? Because I'll do it. I'll do whatever it takes. You're essential to my very existence."

He rested his head against her breast and allowed the tears to fall. "Is it crazy that I miss you already?" Nash inhaled her scent. "Every time I smell fresh pears, I'm going to be reminded of you." He hiccuped a ragged breath. "I love you. So much."

How long he stayed in that uncomfortable position, Nash never knew. It wasn't until a hand touched his shoulder, bringing him back to himself, that he straightened with a wince for his abused back.

"Nash?"

His head whipped up to stare at Ryanne. It took him a solid ten seconds to realize the voice was Rylee's. Without the underlying attitude, she sounded exactly like her sister.

"You're awake." A stupid observation for a man with a genius IQ, but still, he was at a loss as to what to say.

"I know what we have to do to save her."

His lungs ceased to function as he stared down into her sympathetic eyes. Dare he hope it wasn't a game?

"We need a spell from the *Book of Thoth*."

Definitely a game. His disappointment tasted like bile in his mouth. "I don't have the book anymore. Even if I did, I wouldn't let you anywhere near such a powerful tool."

"It's what Preston told me we needed. His exact words were, 'Spring will know the Transmutation Spell.'"

Transmutation. It meant to switch or alter the state of a being to another. "Did he say how it will help?"

"He did."

He couldn't keep the bite from his tone. "Care to share anytime today, or am I expected to guess?"

"I'm going to switch places with my sister."

CHAPTER 22

"Pardon? You are willing to swap bodies with Ryanne?"

Surely Nash hadn't heard Rylee correctly. He wasn't sure he wanted to. The idea of Ryanne inhabiting Rylee's body creeped him out to no end.

"Not bodies," she corrected. "Circumstances."

"You will take on the attributes that have placed her in stasis?" Was he understanding this correctly?

"Yes."

"Rylee, you might never recover. You could be in stasis for the remainder of your life." Why he felt the need to caution her was questionable. He should take the gift of her life in exchange for Ryanne's and be grateful.

Rylee's dark, troubled gaze shifted to her twin's still face. "She'd do it for me."

"Would she?" He wasn't so sure.

"In a second. It's who she is. Who she always was. My sister would give the shirt off her back. It's what made her an easy target for my machinations most times." Rylee closed her eyes, and a single tear escaped down her cheek. "She wanted to see the best in me. I am so undeserving of her."

"Yes, you are," he agreed. "We all are."

"Not you, Nash," she argued softly. "You are the one person who *is* worthy. You both deserve to be happy. Together."

Rylee touched his wrist, and it was all Nash could do not to snatch his arm away.

"Let me help. Please."

What choice did he have? Ignore Rylee's overture and let Ryanne waste away? Or let Rylee do a selfless act for once in her miserable life and possibly save Ryanne? There was no real choice to be made.

"I swear to you, if this is a trick, I will cut your heart out and drop it into a vat of maggots."

"A vat of maggots?" She laughed in disbelief. "Okay, tough guy."

Rylee's amused words were similar to something her twin would've said. Ryanne would have scoffed at him, too.

Nash felt a pang in the region of his heart. His eyes involuntarily shifted to Ryanne's still face, and he ran a thumb along the underside of her jaw.

"It's going to be all right, Nash," Rylee said softly. "I know my promises haven't been worth the paper I might write them on, but in this, I'm not lying."

"What else did my uncle say?"

"That in a place where she wasn't supposed to feel pain, Ryanne is walking about weighed down in sadness. He said time is different there. For us, it's been hours. For her, it's been a week, and she's in deep mourning for you. Despite what both he and Isis have told her."

"Isis?" he asked sharply. He focused all his attention on Rylee, looking for any sign she was playing him false. "Are you sure he said Isis?"

"Yes. He mentioned that she wasn't allowed to get involved. Something about giving her word to Serqet. It's why Preston is taking point on the transmutation from his plane."

"Why would you want to help now when you were the one to set this all in motion, Rylee?"

"Because Victor swore to me that my sister wouldn't be harmed. He said the plan was foolproof and only you would be hurt." She turned her face away to stare up at the ceiling. "I didn't know she loved you to the extreme that she'd take her life to save you. I suppose I should've guessed she'd do something like that, but I didn't see that far ahead."

Her ravaged face and halting words assured him, as nothing else could, that she now spoke the truth.

"I'll get Spring," he said. This time, he touched her wrist. "Are you sure you want to do this? You'll be forfeiting your life."

Her face softened with her smile. "Your uncle assures me that my parents are waiting for me on the other side. I'll be okay. Promise me you'll make my sister happy, Nash. Don't ever break her heart. She's had enough of that."

"I promise," he said gruffly. "She'll never want for a thing, and I'll love her until my dying day."

"That's good enough for me."

They shared a long look. Each in silent agreement.

"I'll get Spring." He had taken four steps when it occurred to him that she'd never mentioned talking to Ryanne. He pivoted back to see Rylee stroking her sister's face. Tears poured from her eyes, and the raw pain was there for all to see. "Rylee?"

She swiped at the moisture on her cheeks. "Yeah?"

"If you were in the Otherworld, why didn't you see Ryanne?"

"I went to a plane right before the final destination. Preston found me."

He nodded and left her to her goodbye.

Nash entered the living room and studied the haggard faces of its occupants. Turning to his father, he said, "Rylee's awake. She's still weak, but she said she talked to Uncle Preston during our spell."

His father noticeably paled. "Preston?"

Aurora reached for Alastair's hand. In a gesture of unity, he wove his fingers through hers with a light kiss to her knuckles.

"What did he have to say?"

"That Isis mentioned a spell from the *Book of Thoth* to save Ryanne." Nash shifted his gaze to Spring. "Apparently, you might be familiar with the spell? Transmutation."

She nodded slowly and glanced around with a frown. "Obviously, I've never performed it—we've never needed to—but I have it up here." She tapped her temple.

"Do we need to be in the clearing again, like with Mama?" Autumn asked from her position by the window. "You know, to light the stones?"

"No. We can perform it here. We will need a few items from my shop. If I'm not mistaken, the spell is also written in our family grimoire."

As if she'd be mistaken. Nash did a mental eye roll. Spring was the smartest person in their family, and she possessed a photographic memory that kept the Thorne clan in awe more often than not. She knew the spell book inside and out. If she believed there was a transmutation spell in the Thorne grimoire, there damned well was.

"Are there any special requirements? Time of year, phase of the moon, or anything like that?" He moved toward the kitchen with the intent of brewing a pot of coffee.

Quentin had anticipated his need and met him halfway with a steaming hot mug and a shrug when Nash raised his brows. Accepting the offering, he spun back to face the crowd. They all wore thoughtful expressions.

"How does the process work?" Knox asked.

"It's fairly straightforward. It's a simple spell, really." Spring stood and glided toward the bedroom door. "She's willing to trade her life for her sister's?"

Autumn joined her sister by the open doorway. "Pfft. I find that hard to believe."

"I believe her." Nash joined the sisters and stared at the twins on the bed. Rylee had fallen asleep and shifted positions, resting her forehead against Ryanne's shoulder, as if to seek a connection.

"Should we all trust your tendency to believe that chick, cousin? Because she's screwed you already. Or have you forgotten the knife to Spring's throat and the cursed necklace?" Autumn, although tall in her own right, grabbed him by the ear and jerked his head down to meet her burning gaze. "I promise you, if she tries anything else, I'm going to fry her ass. One wrong twitch of her hand, and it's a fireball to the head. You got it?" To emphasize her warning, she conjured a dancing ball of fire.

Irritation bordered on anger, and he shoved her arm away. "I have done everything this family has ever asked of me, Autumn. Every. Last. Thing. Despite going against the Council, despite the risks to myself or others, despite making enemies in the witch community at large, I've done whatever was required for the good of this family." Ryanne's houseplants wilted under the barely contained fury in his voice. "I'm asking you to trust in *me* now. You do this, and I'll never ask another thing of you. And before you answer, let me remind you that I was the one who saved *your* butt once upon a time."

The fireball snuffed out, and Autumn ducked her chagrined face. "I'm sorry, Nash. Truly. I'm still reactive where Spring is concerned, all things considered."

"I get it. And if this is too dangerous for the whole…" He paused and swallowed, shifting his gaze to Spring. It hadn't occurred to him that it might be. "Is it? Dangerous?"

"Not to any of us. To the two of them?" She compressed her lips and shrugged. "Like I said, it's a fairly simple spell, but the repercussions could be anyone's guess. Technically, we'll be altering Fate's timeline."

"Would Isis have suggested it if she saw a long-term problem?"

"Who knows with gods and goddesses?"

Autumn snorted. "And they call us volatile."

None of them dared contradict her. The woman had firebombed her husband's truck when they were fighting.

"What about the Chintamani Stone?" Autumn suggested. "I hadn't thought of it until right now, but didn't it give you the boost you needed to wake me?"

"Dad?" Nash redirected the question to Alastair. In this, his father was more knowledgeable.

"It couldn't hurt, I suppose. Spring, is there anything you can remember about the original spell that would indicate a magical artifact might muck it up?"

"No, but I'll grab our book just to be sure. Be back in a sec." With hardly a ripple of the air around them, Spring was gone.

"I'll retrieve the stone and return momentarily. Son, I don't need to remind you to keep an eye on that viper in there."

Nash turned his attention back on Rylee. "She seems regretful."

"She's a duplicitous bitch," Autumn argued. "You go get some rest. I'll keep an eye on her."

"I'll rest when this is over, but I will take a few minutes to shower, if that's all the same to you."

"Whatever you need, Nash. When you come out, we'll have something for you to eat."

"I don't want anything."

"Too bad. You're going to eat anyway. You need to keep up your strength for when we wake Ryanne."

Nash opened his arms to his cousin. "Thank you. I know your bossiness is your way of showing you care."

"You've become vital to all of us, and not for that incredible brain of yours. We love you, Nash. It kills everyone to see you suffer." She sniffed and squeezed him harder. "We'll bring her back because you deserve to be happy."

His high emotions wouldn't let him form a verbal response. Instead, he dropped a light kiss on her forehead and released her.

Alastair watched his son hurry away before anyone could catch a glimpse of the emotional tidal wave crashing over him. But Alastair saw. Could feel it, too. His son had empathic abilities and felt more than most. The flip side of that coin was that when he was hurting, Nash's feelings pulsed out and smacked at others, like him. Similar to the way the sea beats upon the shoreline on a stormy day. For that reason, Nash was always contained.

The exception was Ryanne. With her, his son had come alive. Deviltry and happiness frequently shined from Nash's bright jade eyes whenever Ryanne was near and giving him sass.

Alastair hated to see how dark his son's eyes had turned in his pain. If they couldn't pull off a resurrection, Nash would become a shell of his former self. That much was obvious.

With a side glance at his niece, Alastair placed an arm around her shoulder. "Whatever you want, whatever you need, if you help my son, it is yours."

"I'm not doing this for personal gain, Uncle."

"I know that, child. But I'm offering you a boon anyway."

"You've already paid a hundred times over." She turned away but then stopped and shot him a grin over her shoulder. "But if you *want* to set up a trust fund for my children, who am I to stop you, you rich old Midas."

His own laughter caught him by surprise. "What is it with you girls and my money?"

"If I have to answer that, you don't know women at all," she teased.

"Fair enough." His smile died out. "Nash likes his steak slightly seared with a faint touch of pink in the center. He'd most likely devour that and a baked potato with a pint of Guinness. Will you see that he eats? I have an errand to run before I pick up the Chintamani Stone."

"Yes."

He nodded his thanks, and visualized the clearing by the Thorne estate in Tennessee. Pausing for a second, he cast Aurora a concerned look. "Go back to our place and get some rest, Rorie. It's liable to be a long night, and you're still recovering. Will you do that for me?"

She smiled softly. "Of course. I'll have Alfred get the Chintamani Stone from your vault. It will be ready when you return home."

"I'll be there soon."

CHAPTER 23

When Nash walked into the dining room after his shower, he found the table set for five. "Where is everyone else?"

"Your dad had an errand to run before picking up the stone. The rest of the family went home to check on the kids. Spring and Knox went for a walk, but should be back any time."

"And the fifth plate?"

"For your girlfriend's sister. I thought maybe she should have a final meal and all."

"She might find it hard to digest the food if everyone is viewing her with disdain and anger."

"We'll keep it to a minimum."

He leaned over and kissed her cheek. "Thank you."

"No worries. Go get her and help her to the table. I imagine she's still a little weak. If she prefers, I can fix a plate and bring it to her."

Nash stepped into the master suite to find Rylee sitting with her back against the headboard and staring down at her sister.

"Hey."

"Hey."

"Any change?"

"No. But then, you didn't expect there would be, did you?"

"Not really." He sat on the edge of Ryanne's side of the bed and clasped her hand. "She died in that clearing today, Rylee. When she crossed to the Otherworld, she made it difficult to bring her back. The gods and goddesses don't like to give up their new souls without a fight."

"I gathered as much earlier."

"I suspect it's why my Uncle Preston suggested the *Book of Thoth*." He raised his gaze to meet hers. "When you remove a soul, you have to offer a trade. Isis likes to say, 'balance in all things.'"

"I get it, Nash, okay? I'm to be the trade."

"Only if you want to be. None of us will force this on you. This has to be your choice. Ryanne would never understand if I compelled you to do this."

The defiance fled from her features, and she looked as if she wanted to cry. "I know."

"I'm going to tell the others that you're going to sleep on it. If you're still willing in the morning, we'll do the ceremony then." He studied Ryanne's beautiful pale face for a long moment then turned back to Rylee. "Come on. Autumn made dinner for the family."

"I'm not your family, Nash."

"Yes, you are. You're Ryanne's beloved sister. That makes you family."

She did cry then. Big heartbreaking sobs that tugged at Nash's weary, aching heart. He reached across the body of Ryanne and gripped Rylee's hand.

"Please don't cry. I don't think I can handle it right now. If I break down..." He swallowed hard. "I can't go there."

She nodded but continued to cry, and Nash was helpless against her tears. Perhaps if she wasn't identical to Ryanne, he might have been able to hold out. Instead, he hurried around the bed and pulled her into his arms.

"Let it out."

He continued to rock her as she released her grief, all the while focusing his gaze on Ryanne's beloved countenance.

Spring entered the room and brushed a hand down Rylee's hair. "I can sit with her while you go eat, Nash."

"We'll only be a minute longer," he assured her.

With a pat to his shoulder, she left the way she'd come.

"I'm all right now." Rylee pulled away and pressed the heels of her palms to her swollen eyes. "I'll be out in a sec."

"Are you sure?"

"Yeah."

He was halfway to the door when she spoke again.

"Nash? I'm glad she has you. She couldn't find a better man in all the world."

Pressing his lips into a thin line, he nodded. Words were impossible.

After dinner, Rylee took a pad of paper and a pen, then disappeared into the guest room. Nash's cousins were hesitant to leave him, but he insisted they return home to their beds.

Because he was still wary of Rylee's intent, regardless of her remorseful display earlier, he cast a quick guarding spell on the bedroom door after he closed and locked it for the evening. If anyone entered the master bedroom tonight, they were in for the shock of their life.

Rest. Sleep. Yeah, no. He wouldn't get any of either. Not tonight. Not when Ryanne's life hung in the balance. Although they'd been lovers—albeit briefly—curling up next to her on the bed felt like an invasion of her privacy, of her right to lay untouched, so he moved the armchair closer to the bed and settled into it for the remainder of the evening.

Somewhere, on the other side of the veil between the living and the dead, did she sit, watching *him*? A large part of him hoped she did. Hoped she wanted to come back as badly as he wanted her back. Another huge part of him worried she didn't. Worried perhaps she had already moved on despite Rylee's assurances that

Ryanne was wandering around the Otherworld as distraught as Nash.

"When you wake up, I'm going to wring your neck for slicing through your vein. Really, it was a foolhardy thing to do. But it was also brave. You'll fit right in with my crazy relatives, babe." He leaned forward and rested his forearms on his knees, clasping his hands together. "Oh, the stories I could tell. Like you, they plunge into danger without thinking twice. If they feel it's right or just, they will fight to the death."

Resting his chin on his joined hands, he sighed. "I'm not sure I ever felt that strongly about anything before. Certainly nothing before you. Definitely nothing after you. If you leave me, I don't think I want to feel anything ever again." He swallowed and sat back. "It would hurt too much."

Nash awoke with a start. Heart pounding, he glanced wildly around the room. A quick check showed Ryanne's status was still the same. When all seemed in order, he inhaled a deep, cleansing breath and worked to calm his heart.

The bright morning sun mocked him as it peered through the cheerful purple curtains. He frowned at the material. Wispy and bright, with shimmering threads that caught the light. She loved purple, that much he knew. But those curtains brought to mind the decor of a child's room and were completely at odds with the rest of her room. Why? A pull from the past? Maybe a nod to her parents, but which ones? Birth or adopted?

A light knock sounded at the door.

"Nash? I'm about to make some breakfast. Are you hungry?"

"I'm good. Thanks." He was a bit hungry, but the idea of Rylee making breakfast while Ryanne lay in stasis was surreal. To a large degree, it angered him. He and Ryanne should be making breakfast together in her tiny kitchen.

A single second knock sounded, harder than the first. "Calm the fuck down. You're killing my sister's plants."

Ryanne's houseplants didn't deserve to suffer for his irritation. With a deep sigh, he sent a magical boost out to reverse the damage he'd done with his anger. He cast a defeated look at the stack of books he'd read last night and, with another wave of his hand, removed the ward and opened the bedroom door.

Exhaustion weighed heavily on Nash. He was only in his early thirties, and yet he felt like he was at least three times his age. If they couldn't pull off the transmutation spell, he didn't know what he was going to do. The idea of facing every day without Ryanne across the desk from him didn't bear thinking about.

"Did you sleep?"

Rylee's concerned voice startled him from his musings.

"Not really. A bit of a cat nap."

"You're not doing Ryanne any good by—"

"Stop mothering me, Rylee," he snapped, surging from the chair. "Just. Stop."

"I'm not—"

He slashed a hand through the air. "You are. I don't know if this is misplaced guilt on your part, but you can't make up for what you've done. Stop trying."

Her stricken look cut him to the quick. It wasn't in Nash's nature to be cruel, but he also couldn't tolerate her overly solicitous act. Not when she was the one ultimately responsible for Ryanne's stasis.

"I'll conjure food when I'm hungry. I have phone calls to make."

She nodded, cast one last remorseful look toward her twin, and fled.

The air around him altered, and a fizzing pop signaled an incoming group. His cousins Autumn and Spring arrived, bringing Aunt GiGi with them.

"Any change?" GiGi asked as she moved to Ryanne's bedside.

"Not that I can tell."

"Is the wonder twin still willing to fix her fuck-up?" Autumn asked.

"Yes, this wonder twin is still willing to fix her fuck-up," Rylee growled from behind them.

As one, they turned. She stood in the doorway with a plate of food, cutlery, and a napkin. Nash could only assume she intended to feed him regardless of his earlier surliness.

"She didn't mean anything by it, Rylee. Autumn is just that way."

"Don't apologize for me, cousin. I can do that on my own. When necessary," she added with an arched brow.

"Can we not fight today?" he asked wearily. "I can't handle any more of this strife. Rylee has already agreed to do what was necessary to help. This animosity isn't benefiting anyone."

The hard look on Autumn's face eased into chagrin. "I'm sorry." She faced Rylee. "To both of you."

Rylee took the three steps she needed to reach Nash and shoved the plate into his hands. "I made you something anyway. Eat."

Her words, actions, and attitude were all Ryanne's, and that familiarity slayed him. He sank onto the edge of the bed and stared down at the steaming eggs as he fought the gut-wrenching sobs wanting to rip through him.

"I didn't poison the damned thing," she snapped before she exited the room in a huff.

Nash set the food aside for two reasons; there was a small part of him that still didn't trust her *not* to poison him, and his appetite had effectively vanished with his worry about the upcoming ceremony.

Spring glanced toward the empty doorway and ran a hand overtop the plate. When she was done, the appearance was of a meal three-quarters of the way consumed. She met his eye and gave him an understanding smile.

"Okay, enough messing about. Let's get this show on the road." Autumn stepped forward, ready to take command. "Spring, will you let Rylee know we are ready?" She directed her next request to GiGi.

"Will you let Uncle Alastair know we are ready to proceed? Have everyone meet back here in ten minutes."

Autumn placed a hand on Nash's arm. "I want to talk to you a minute."

"What's up?"

"Are you sure you want to do this?"

"What now, Autumn?"

"Even if we somehow pull the rabbit out of the hat and bring her back, there may be a part of her that she leaves behind in the Otherworld. It happened to me, and it happened to my mother."

"And my father too, if I'm not mistaken."

"Yes."

"What's it like? Other than this hard edge it seems to give everyone?"

"It's like a small part of you can never be warm, no matter how hard you or the people around you try."

"Do you not feel things as deeply? Love any less?"

"Maybe. I don't know. I haven't thought to rate it." She turned her thoughtful gaze on Ryanne. "I love my family. Keaton, Chloe, and Jolyon are my world. I don't want to live without them. Yet there are moments when I look at them without feeling any emotion at all. It's like my emotions go on hiatus. It's fleeting, but it happens." She shook her head and met his steady gaze. "If we're being honest, it freaks me right the fuck out."

"Why?"

"What if those moments grow into minutes? Hours? Days? Keaton has a slight understanding, but what about the children? Do they sense that their mother doesn't care one way or another? And what might I do in one of these unfeeling moments?"

His big bad cousin looked more vulnerable and frightened than he'd ever witnessed. Without too much thought, he hauled her into an embrace. "You could never hurt anyone you loved, Tums. We all know that. You're worrying yourself needlessly."

"I'm not so sure."

"I am." He pulled back and framed her face. "When this is over, I'll do research and see if I can't find a solution, or at the very least, a way to set your mind at ease, okay?"

She nodded. The grateful smile curling her lips was at complete odds with her standard mocking grin.

"Do you need another minute?"

"No." She inhaled deeply. "I'm as ready as you are. Let's do this thing."

CHAPTER 24

T he ceremony was simple, according to Spring. It would take no more than the five Thornes to complete. The bed was pulled out from the wall, and a salt ring was created around it.

Alastair set white candles around the inside perimeter of the circle. Next, he directed Rylee to lie down next to Ryanne. "Is there anything you need to convey before we start, child?"

"I left a note for my sister in the guest bedroom. Will you see that she gets it?"

"Of course."

"Thank you, Mr. Thorne. And thank you for being kind despite what I did."

"Victor has a way of manipulating others to do his bidding, whether they want to or not. Because you are doing this for your sister, I'm going to give you the benefit of the doubt and believe you never truly wanted to hurt anyone."

A single tear trailed down from the outside corner of her eye to disappear into the dark hair at her temple. "I'm afraid," she whispered.

Nash started to reach for her hand, but his father beat him to it.

"No need, dear girl. I've spoken to Isis. Your welcome is assured."

Her tears came in earnest, and she graced him with a small smile.

From his pocket, Alastair withdrew the Chintamani Stone in its ugly setting and handed it to Nash. "Put this on Ryanne."

As soon as he did, he noticed a flush of color came into her skin. A good sign if memory served. "What's next?"

"We will need blood from both," Spring stated, producing an athame and a copper bowl. "Only a few drops. You can take it from the thumb."

Nash offered Rylee the knife. "I won't be able to cut her."

Her lips twisted in a wry smile, and she pricked the pad of her sister's thumb. When she got the few drops she needed, she gestured for him to come closer. "You might want to seal that up."

It was a simple matter to create a magical Band-Aid.

Rylee repeated the process to her own thumb and squeezed out the blood. She handed the athame and bowl back to Spring, who placed a handful of mixed herbs into the dish and set it at the foot of the bed, between the twins.

"Rylee, please join hands with your sister," Spring said. "Nash, take the point at Ryanne's left shoulder. Autumn, you take the point at Rylee's right shoulder." She positioned herself at Ryanne's feet and pointed to the place a few steps from her. "Aunt GiGi, here. Uncle Alastair, you will need to stand at the head of the bed."

Nash instantly realized they had formed a human pentagram.

Spring addressed Autumn. "Please light the candles."

A simple flick of Autumn's wrist lit all the wicks in one shot.

The action brought a smile to his face. Because they were more powerful than most, the Thornes took their magic for granted. But to him, as skilled a warlock as he was, he took delight in the energy around him. Not only did he feel the hum of his own cells firing up, but he experienced a contact high from the witches around him.

"What now?" he asked.

"Now we call on Ra."

Nash's heart nearly stopped. "Ra? As in the God of Egypt? Are you crazy? If Set doesn't kill us first, Ra will definitely finish the job."

Set was brother to the goddesses and known as the combatant, the primary protector of Ra.

"We have no sacrifice to offer."

"We don't need one. Trust me, cousin." Spring's smile was serene.

She held out her hands, palms forward, and they all repeated the action. "We ask that the God Ra hear us. We ask that you grant us—"

A deafening crack rent the air, cutting Spring off mid-spell. The retinal-searing gold light flooding the room forced the occupants to shield their faces or risk blinding.

As soon as the light eased to normal, Nash removed his arm. Black dots danced about his vision, and he blinked in a vain attempt to clear them.

"Who calls to Ra?"

Based on the sheer size of the newcomer, Nash assumed the guy was Set. The militant, no-nonsense attitude spoke of previous battle experience.

"I do, Exalted One." Spring bowed her head in deference to the god and gave a hand gesture behind her back for the others to do the same. As one, their group dropped to their knees.

"I know of you, Spring Thorne."

She simply smiled.

The god slowly raked his hot gaze down the length of Spring's perfection.

Nash ground his teeth together. He didn't relish fighting the guy, but if Set stepped across the line of proper etiquette, then he would have no choice.

"Why am I here?"

"We called on Ra to perform a transmutation spell. It appears he sent you instead."

"He no longer cares to help mortals. Your kind have desecrated the ways of old."

"Forgive us, Exalted One, but I thought I was performing the ceremony properly based on the writings of our people."

She was up to something, Nash could tell. His brilliant, beloved cousin was wrapping this god around her petite pinky finger.

"You did. What is it you wish?"

Spring waved a hand toward the twins on the bed. "Rylee, sister to Ryanne, wishes to take her place in the Otherworld."

"That is the business of Isis or Nephthys. Not Ra."

"Your sisters claim they cannot become involved due to a promise to Serqet, Exalted One. I had hoped the Great One could settle the issue."

Set shifted forward to tower over her. Nash had to wonder if Spring's neck hurt looking up at the guy.

The man's honey-gold eyes were lined with a thick streak of black kohl, which lent to the eeriness of his unwavering regard. Spring never broke Set's cold-eyed stare.

Nash was certain he was imagining things when the lines bracketing the god's eyes crinkled and a wide white grin took over Set's face.

"You are courageous, child. I will settle your issue with my sisters." He snapped his fingers, and an ancient-looking scroll appeared. As he handed it to Spring, he retained a firm grip and tugged when her fingers closed around the parchment. "What do you give in return?"

"My undying gratitude."

The Thornes all gasped at her audacity.

Set took no offense, instead laughing and releasing the scroll. "You shall be my favorite from this day forward, Spring Thorne." His interested gaze scanned her delicate features before dropping to her mouth. "But you still owe a gift. Balance must be kept in all things."

"My wife is not kissing you." Knox's voice came from behind

Nash. The dark menace in his tone couldn't be mistaken for anything other than the barely concealed fury it was.

"Who said anything about kissing? I require more than a mere kiss for trade."

"Over my dead body."

Unholy glee filled Set's eyes as they settled on Knox. "You are no match for me, boy."

The building shook, and the metal frame of the bed began to bend. "Try me."

Before a fight could erupt, Spring laughed. The musical sound turned all attention to her. "What is the gift you require, Exalted One? My husband will not stand in the way of the trade."

"Spring!" Knox growled. The floor shook again.

"Oh, hush. Set is too honorable to step across the boundaries of propriety. Aren't you, Exalted One? You would never prey on another man's wife, would you?"

Nash bit the inside of his cheek to contain his laughter. Spring had effectively boxed the god in, relying on his honor to stay his hand.

A slow, appreciative smile spread across his countenance. "Of course." He glanced between the couple. Deviltry lighting his face. "Your payment shall be to name your firstborn son for me."

"The hel—"

"It's done," Spring spoke over her husband, warning heavy in her tone. "Our firstborn son shall be called Seth, the modernized version of your name."

Knox threw up his hands and shook his head. "Un-fucking-believable."

"You may wish to shorten your lead rope around your husband's neck, girl. It will keep him from trouble," Set warned with a hard look in Knox's direction.

"Forgive him, Exalted One. He is but a dumb beast."

Nash did laugh then. Knox's IQ was as high as Spring's, if not higher. The outrage on his face was priceless.

Set released the scroll and backed from the circle. He was mighty, but Nash suspected the god wasn't stupid enough to turn his back on an enraged husband.

"Go in peace, Thorne family."

They all bowed their heads, and in another searing blast of light, Set was gone.

"Dumb beast?" Knox growled. *"Dumb beast?"*

Spring rolled her eyes as she unfolded the scroll. "Hush or I'll stuff your mouth with dirt."

"Woman, you try my patience."

"If you two would like to put aside your domestic squabble for a few minutes, we have Nash's young woman to retrieve," Alastair interrupted. He straightened the cuffs of his shirt and shot them a reproving look. "Time is of the essence. Every hour we delay is the equivalent of a day in the Otherworld. The longer a soul resides there, the more of that soul is lost."

"Apologies, Uncle Alastair. To you too, Nash," Spring said. "Would you care to finish the ceremony?"

"No. You read it. I can't be the one to send Rylee to the Otherworld."

Spring spoke the words written on the parchment. Some familiar to Nash, but most not. As he watched, the half-healed wound on Ryanne's arm knitted together. The gray leeched from her skin, resulting in a healthy glow. Her breathing deepened and filled her lungs with each new inhale.

Rylee's pained gasp drew his notice. A long, ugly gash split open the graying skin of her wrist. Blood pooled up and out. Her back arched up, and her mouth widened in a silent scream.

In spite of the trouble Rylee had wrought, Nash found it difficult to let this happen to her. When he would've moved to help her, Knox clamped a hand on his shoulder, staying him.

In another instant, it was over. Rylee's vacant stare was an indication her body hadn't survived the transition. The candle flames were all extinguished with a sweep of Autumn's hand.

A low moan escaped Ryanne's lips, and Nash shrugged off Knox's steely grip to rush to her side.

Nash didn't want the first thing she saw upon waking to be her sister's dead body, so he scooped her into his arms and teleported to the living room. He set her on the couch and grabbed the quilt from the sofa's back to bundle her chilly body.

A peculiar sense of déjà vu struck him. Was it really only a week since the last time he'd wrapped her in this blanket in his laughable attempt to protect his heart?

"Nash?"

"Welcome back, babe."

Her eyes widened and searched the living room. What she was looking for, he had no clue. "Was it all a dream?"

"Was what a dream?"

"The goddesses. The necklace. My sister," she ended on a whisper.

"No. It was all real."

Her wide, chocolaty eyes filled with moisture, and the beseeching look tormented Nash's soul. "She's gone then? Rylee?"

"She is. I'm sorry."

Her broken-hearted sobs ripped him to shreds. All he could do was hold her and rock her in an eerie repetition of Rylee's crying jag from last night. What must it be like for one identical twin to lose another? If it was even a fraction of the grief he'd experienced in losing Ryanne yesterday, then it had to be horrendous.

CHAPTER 25

R yanne didn't know how long she cried, and she didn't care. Her last surviving relative was gone. Now she was alone in the world. No one to call mother, father, or sister. Alone. The last one of her family left alive.

But she hadn't been, alive that was. No, she'd been dead, and Nash had brought her back. Had she wanted to come back? She wasn't sure. The days she spent in the Otherworld had seamlessly flowed one to the other, and her mortal desires had become murky the longer she spent there.

Preston Thorne had come by every day to remind her of Nash's existence and of the things that awaited her back here. The problem was, she didn't care anymore. Leaving paradise for the real world sucked more than she could ever articulate.

"You should have left me there, Nash."

The large hand rubbing Ryanne's back stilled, and she could feel him inhale in a deep breath. She'd wounded him with her words, but she didn't care. Why did the Thornes feel it was their right to alter the course of everyone's history? She hadn't realized she asked the question aloud until he eased back to stare down into her face.

Deep emotion burned brightly in his gaze, but he quickly banked it. He turned his head to look at his handful of family huddled in the bedroom doorway.

"Will someone stay with Ryanne, please? I have something to do."

He rose without looking at her and walked into her bedroom, shutting the door behind him.

Drawing her knees to her chest, she curled her arms around her legs and rested her chin on her knees.

"It's going to take you a while to readjust to normal life," Autumn said, not unkindly. "You have to give it some time."

"Thank you, Sherlock. I wasn't smart enough to figure that out for myself."

"You're ungrateful, you know that?" Autumn snapped.

The echo of Nash's words the night he'd first come to her apartment made Ryanne's heart ping. Where he'd meant them teasingly, his cousin's words were harsh and unforgiving. "What should I be grateful *for*, Autumn? That you all gathered together to restore my life? Did you ever think that in doing so, I wouldn't be so *grateful* for the fact Nash traded my sister's life in return?"

"Nash didn't. Your sister wanted to do this. He tried to talk her out of it a number of times." Autumn took a deep breath and stomped to where Ryanne sat. "It didn't matter that wasting an additional eight hours would cost you another week in the Otherworld or that even knowing you might lose more of yourself, he told Rylee to sleep on her decision. For *you*. Because he knew you would never want her to trade her life. Because he knew you would hate him if he was the one who made that trade." She warmed to her tirade. "You—"

"Autumn, stop!" Nash's words cut through the anger and tension building between Ryanne and Autumn.

"She needs to know the facts, Nash."

"Not that way. Go home." His hard expression softened. "I

appreciate all you did for us, but it's time to let Ryanne grieve for her sister. You'd feel the same."

Autumn's mouth compressed in a thin white line, but she nodded her agreement. Within seconds, she'd teleported away.

Nash came farther into the room. "The rest of you, too. Ryanne needs her space."

Spring peered into the bedroom, nodded, and kissed Nash's cheek. "Call us if you need anything." Then she grabbed Knox's hand and left.

"Is Rylee in my bedroom?" Ryanne choked out. "I want to see her."

"Yes," Nash said, "but first let Aunt GiGi check you out. I want to make sure you are okay."

As the older woman checked Ryanne's vitals, she noticed Alastair and Nash in an intense discussion across the room.

"What are they talking about?"

GiGi glanced over and shrugged. "It's anyone's guess. Most likely the effects of your stasis."

"Effects?"

"You cannot return to the living world without side effects, dear. It appears your anger is yours. Everyone reacts differently."

"Does it go away?" The idea of walking around pissed off all the time unnerved her.

"Mostly. You may be quicker to anger from here on out. You may not." GiGi opened a black bag and pulled out a sachet.

"What's that?"

"It's willow bark tea infused with chamomile. It should help with the headaches you'll have. Those are normal the first week and should go away. If they don't, have Nash call me." GiGi smoothed back a strand of Ryanne's hair. "Let him help you through this, dear. He loves you."

Irritation welled. "So because he loves me, everything should be all roses?"

"I didn't say that. But because he loves you, he'll find a way to help you get to a place of acceptance. He'll also find a way to temper your anger."

Ryanne shot a side glance toward Nash. His solemn expression made her shy away.

"Bear in mind that you are powerful in your own right, Ryanne," GiGi cautioned. "If you don't find a way to control your emotions, you'll end up doing exactly what Serqet wanted and taking out everyone around you with your power."

With a jerky nod to acknowledge GiGi's warning, Ryanne shoved back the blanket and stood on shaky legs. Closing her eyes, she visualized blood flow to her limbs and felt the resulting strengthening of her muscles.

"Well done, dear."

"Thanks." Ryanne headed for her bedroom but stopped when Nash held up his hand. "I want to see my sister."

"You will. Wait a minute."

He left her standing next to a silent, watchful Alastair.

"Why do I have the feeling you're judging me?" she asked.

"I'm not. However, I am still here to insure you don't become a threat to those I love."

Before she could comment, Nash had returned. In his hand, he held an envelope addressed to her. Seeing Rylee's handwriting caused Ryanne's heart to hammer.

"I think you should read this before you go in there," he told her quietly.

She placed her hands behind her back, unable to let herself accept the envelope. "What does it say?" she asked hoarsely.

"I don't know. I didn't want to intrude on what was between you two."

She frowned, incapable of removing her gaze from his. "Will you read it to me?"

His eyes searched hers, looking for what, she didn't know.

Finally, he withdrew the note and unfolded it.

He began to read. "Ryanne, if you are reading this, I grew a set of balls and went through with the transmutation spell. Please know, it was what I wanted. Know that although I was always a shit of a sister…" Nash sneezed and balled his free hand. Ryanne felt the push of power to ward off his curse. "…I wanted to do a selfless act on your behalf for once in my life."

A wry half-smile graced his features. "Nash is fine as hell…" Here he sneezed again. "…but more importantly, he's kind and thoughtful. Don't screw up your second chance to be happy." He grew serious and met her tearful gaze. "He loves you, Ry. I've never seen a love like that. It's in everything about him: the way he looks at you, the way he says your name, the way he will do anything for your happiness."

Nash's attention went back to the scribble on the note. Ryanne caught the final words and fought not to break down. "I love you, sister, but I'll be happy to see our parents again. I do this for both of us. Don't be sad. Peace out. Leelee."

He folded the paper and handed it to her.

"I've prepared her for your goodbye," he said softly.

Her anger didn't seep away as expected. Instead, it intensified, making her hands tremble and her fingertips warm. In a flash, Nash snatched the letter from her hands.

"Careful. If you light it on fire, you can never get it back."

"I'm so mad at her," she whispered. The fierce rage made her throat raw and her head hurt with all the words she couldn't say.

"Talk to me, Ryanne," Nash said achingly. "Let me help you."

Love, understanding, and need poured off of him, threatening to suffocate her on the spot. She couldn't handle his pain on top of her own.

"Leave me alone."

If she'd slapped him, she didn't think he could be more shocked. His mouth dropped open and his eyebrows rose, almost reaching his hairline.

When he would have reached for her, she tucked her hands

behind her and stepped back. "Don't touch me. I mean it. I want you to leave me alone."

As she watched, he paled and his irises darkened to a murky hazel.

"Sure."

She blinked, and he was gone.

"A little harsh, don't you think?"

"You need to go too, Mr. Thorne."

"Why? So you can wallow in your grief and pretend it's all Nash's fault?" He moved to within a foot of her. "Don't be a fool, girl."

"A fool? I was a fool to trust any of *you*."

"Need I remind you, it was your sister who set this whole thing in motion?" He leaned forward, his anger and menace rivaling her own twisted emotions. "*She* was the one who sentenced Nash to death without ever taking into account your relationship with him. She cared not if you loved him. Your sister systematically set out to seduce him, steal information, and murder him."

His tone was as icy as she'd ever heard, and he wasn't finished.

"On the other hand, he tried to find a way to save you without costing your sister her life. Last night, while your sister slept in a bed down the hall, while she was allowed to decide if she wanted to sacrifice her life for yours, he read through book after book, trying to find a spell to revive you without cost to your sister. For *you!*"

"I didn't ask him to bring me back," she screamed. Fire flared to life from the palms of her hands and continued to spread up her arms.

The overhead smoke detectors went into overdrive with their ear-piercing alarm.

GiGi rushed forward and flung open the windows to alleviate the building smoke. She stepped up beside her brother and clasped his hand. Lifting her opposite hand, she swirled it in a continuous circular pattern. The effect was like a high-powered fan, and the sulfuric-scented air blew out the open window.

GiGi reversed the motion of her hand, and damp air filled the room.

Alastair simply snapped his fingers, which pulled the moisture from the air and doused her arms.

Ryanne stared at her dripping hands in shocked wonder. What the hell had just happened? Her heart rate increased to such a level, she feared heart failure. Too terrified to look at either of these powerful beings, she closed her eyes.

"I'm sorry. I don't know where that came from."

"I do." The understanding in Alastair's voice floored her.

Opening her eyes, she locked onto his smiling face.

"You needed to release the rage, child. I helped you with that."

"I don't get it."

"You were holding back for my son. A small part of you didn't want to risk physically hurting him, so you drove him away. Now that you've released the initial fury, you can process what has happened and begin to heal."

"You experienced amplified stages of grief," GiGi explained with a hug. "Allow my brother to help you one more time, now."

"Help me how?"

"Al, care to share?" GiGi asked with a ghost of a smile.

"I can restore some of what was lost, if you'll allow me."

What was she missing here? She looked between the siblings and searched for the unspoken answer. Finally, it clicked. *Part of her lost soul.*

"Does it hurt?"

"A little."

"Okay."

Alastair placed one palm flat over the area of her heart and the other horizontally across her forehead. "Now breathe in. Feel your cells warm and let the magic flow through you. Pull it deep into yourself until you experience the burning. When you can stand no more, I'll know."

Taking a deep breath, Ryanne did as instructed. As her insides heated to what felt like molten lava, she cried out. Only then did Alastair drop his hands. Oddly, her body cooled almost instantaneously.

"That's crazy!"

He shrugged. "How do you feel?"

She took stock and realized the emotional distance she was experiencing had lessened. "Better, I think. Thank you."

GiGi moved forward with another hug. The lightest scent of gardenias permeated the air around them.

"That was my mother's favorite perfume," Ryanne told her.

"I know, dear. Go say goodbye to your sister. When you are ready, we will see she is entombed in your family's crypt."

"That sounds ominous," she muttered with a shiver.

Alastair smiled slightly. "Shall I retrieve Nash?"

"I need a little time with my sister first." As they turned to leave, she called out. "Thank you. Both of you."

They gave her matching nods and left.

The silence in her apartment was disturbing after the noise of the last twenty-four hours. Although she didn't want to, she stepped through the door of her bedroom. The sight brought her up short. Deep red rose petals covered the mattress Rylee rested upon. Surrounding her body were cheerful white daisies. Nash had conjured her sister a long lavender robe, and a circlet of flowers crowned her head. Her hands were joined and resting below her breasts. She looked peaceful, as if she were sleeping in a meadow.

Ryanne raised a hand to her throat and fought to hold back the sobs. Nash's thoughtfulness tore at her heart. She'd wronged him when she sent him away. Kneeling by the bed, she gave way to her anguish.

CHAPTER 26

Twenty minutes. It was all the time Nash could stand to wait after his father left. Alastair had explained away Ryanne's reaction but had also cautioned Nash to give her time to herself to process all that had gone down that morning.

Because teleporting into Ryanne's space seemed arrogant and assuming, Nash took the time to drive from his home to hers. He spent the next seven minutes in his car, drumming his fingers on the steering wheel and staring at Ryanne's lighted bedroom window, like some crazy-ass stalker.

A sharp rap on the window startled a yelp from him.

When he got out of the car, it was to find Quentin not trying too hard to fight back a grin.

"What the hell are you doing here, man?" Nash sneezed and grunted his thanks when Quentin balled his hand into a fist to stave off the closest raccoons.

"Your father asked me to hang out and watch over Ryanne."

"Thank you."

"You were there when we needed you. This is a small repayment."

"Still, I'm grateful. How are you feeling from yesterday's little nap in the glen?"

"GiGi patched me up, right as rain." He gestured to the apartment with a thumb over his shoulder. "I just saw your girl cross from the bedroom to the kitchen. I think it's safe for you to go up."

"You heading home to Holly?"

"Yep."

"Give my sister a hug for me."

"Will do. Take care of yourself, too, Nash. You need rest."

"Yes, mother."

Quentin flipped him a bird as he mounted his Harley. "Later, loser." He gunned the throaty beast and headed out of the parking lot with a wave. Although it didn't chase away the worry in the pit of his stomach, Nash's lips quirked upward at Quentin's well-hidden concern. A few months ago, he never would've imaged his sister's happy-go-lucky husband caring if he lived or died.

He turned toward Ryanne's apartment building and stopped short. The woman herself stood at the main door, looking like hell. She was still the most beautiful thing he'd ever seen.

"Am I welcome?" he asked roughly.

"Always."

He ate up the distance between them and lifted her as she jumped. He held her tightly against him with her legs wrapped around his waist and her arms firmly locked around his neck.

"I'm sorry," they gushed simultaneously.

They parted to look at one another.

"I should never have dragged you into this stinking mess."

"It wasn't your fault, Nash. None of it. I know that. *Knew* that, but it was like—"

He stopped her apology with a gentle kiss. "All I care about is that you are okay. Right now, in this moment. I need to know you are okay."

She gave him a tearful nod. "For the most part."

"That's good enough." He kissed her again. "Want me to be romantic and carry you up the stairs?"

"Three flights?" she asked skeptically.

He leaned in to whisper in her ear, "I do have a spell that can make you light as a feather."

"If you're calling me fat, Nash, we're done."

"Pfft. It's more along the lines that I'm a book nerd who seldom works out."

"I'm going to call you a liar. I've seen you naked." She sighed and released him. "I can walk."

He clasped her hand and tugged her into the building. As they made their way upstairs, he thought about all the things he wanted to say. All the promises he wanted to make. There would be time for all of that, thanks to her twin's sacrifice. For now, she needed to heal. To be given the space a thoughtful partner would allow.

"I can take care of your sister for you if you'd like."

"Your aunt already said she could make arrangements for the crypt." She tugged him to a halt on the last landing. "How does the death certificate thing work? I assume we need documentation. How do we… hide what happened?"

He raised his brows and waited.

"Oh, yeah, never mind. I suppose it's a simple matter for people like us."

"Simple enough," he agreed. He didn't care to have this type of conversation in the hall where anyone within hearing distance could listen in. He could cloak the sound, but he'd prefer to discuss this topic later. "Come on."

"I'm not sure I can stay here tonight."

"Okay. Let's get a few of your things and head back to my place. I—"

A sixth sense had him spinning and tucking Ryanne against his chest. A bullet ricocheted off the wall by his head. When a hail of bullets began to pepper the hallway walls, Nash quickly shoved her up the stairs toward the top of the building.

Victor! It had to be.

Already he knew that teleporting was out of the question. Victor would have Blockers surrounding the building, but Nash had a plan in his back pocket. They only needed to make it to the roof, and they'd be golden.

When they reached Ryanne's floor, she tried to bolt toward her door, but he dragged her onward. "Up. Keep going," he urged.

"We'll be trapped!"

"Shh, keep your voice down and move your ass." He sneezed but didn't have time to worry about his particular trash panda curse.

They made one more flight before Ryanne started to show signs of weakness. Looked like he would need his feather-light spell after all. "Climb on and don't let go, no matter what." With each step, he grunted out the words to the spell until she weighed next to nothing upon his back.

Just as he thought his heart would pound out of his chest and his lungs would cease to work, he burst through the rooftop exit. "Hop… off." He pointed to the Rebar pole to his left even as he reached for the one to his right. With her help, he slid them into two-inch-thick steel brackets he'd had installed on either side of the door.

"How did you know?"

"My family has enemies." He paused for a deep breath. "As my employee and the love of my life, you fall under my protection." He grinned and grabbed her hand. "Better to be prepared, no?"

They ran toward the westernmost side of the building.

"Who is after us, or shouldn't I ask?"

"Victor. He wants the necklace."

"But we don't have it."

He snorted.

"We do?"

"It's in my pocket. All your anger tonight wasn't your own."

"I'm confused."

"The explanation can wait. Put this on."

She was dumbfounded when he dragged out a set of harnesses.

"We are ten stories up. If you think I'm putting that thing on and scaling down this building, you've lost your mind."

"Scaling, no. Zip lining, yes." He tested all the fastenings and kissed her hard. "You've got this, babe."

"Did you take into account the men on the ground with automatic weapons?" she screeched.

"I did. We aren't going down. We're going across. They'll think we trapped ourselves up here to wait for assistance. Which reminds me…" He held up a finger and dug out his phone. No signal. "That bastard jammed the signal. *Fuck!*"

A strangled scream came from below. Nash peered over the edge and laughed. *"Fuck, fuck, fuck!"*

A second scream echoed up to them.

"The raccoons!" she exclaimed, peering over the edge. "Good God, you really are brilliant."

He grinned and swore longer and louder.

"Fall back! Fall back!"

More strangled screams mirrored the first.

"Shoot them! Shoot them!"

The distinct chirp of locusts echoed around them. Nash lifted his head from the scene below to check the surrounding buildings.

His father leaned back against the wall of an adjacent apartment complex, arms crossed over his chest. Laughter shook his frame when someone else screamed, *"What the fuck?"*

A low whistle caught Nash's attention.

"Move away from the edge," Knox called.

Nash hustled Ryanne about ten feet from the lip of the building. As they watched, Knox spread his arms, closed his eyes, and clapped. A low rumble started, and the building swayed beneath them.

"What is he doing?" she yelled.

"Earthquake is my best guess."

The cries of the injured men below drowned out Nash's affirmative response.

"We need to move." He grabbed Ryanne's hand and pulled her toward the zip line. Miraculously, it still held. "This is going to be a tandem ride, babe. Don't freak out when our weight causes a major dip in the line."

"What about the light-as-a-feather thing?"

"We need the weight to carry us faster."

"No spell for that?" she muttered.

He dropped a kiss on the shell of her ear and double-checked the straps securing them together. "I won't let anything happen to you. Try not to scream. We don't want to alert them to our getaway plan."

Ryanne squeezed her eyes tightly shut and managed to keep her mouth closed as well although that particular feat was a little more difficult. If asked before tonight, she probably would have said she wasn't afraid of heights. Zip lining to another rooftop from ten stories up had her reevaluating her fears.

How had Nash found time to retrieve the Red Scorpion? The thought of it this close to their bodies made her shudder. If she never saw that creepy freaking thing again as long as she lived, she'd consider herself fortunate.

She also wondered why Victor's men hadn't made an attempt to kill them while they were in the parking lot? Had the soldiers figured the chance of escape was greater on the ground floor?

She shrugged off the questions as she extended her arms to Knox. He pulled them to safety and glanced over the edge. "They are regrouping. Hold on, kids."

Before she had a chance to blink, Ryanne's cells were heating to burning. Within seconds, the three of them were in a place she'd never seen before. She glanced around the glen and looked to Nash for an explanation.

"This stretch of land is protected on all four sides. Thorne Manor lies there in the center of that land." Her eyes followed the path of his finger. "The Carlyle lands run adjacent. This is the middle ground and is sacred. Blessed by Isis herself."

"We're safe here?"

"As safe as we can be for now."

Knox stepped forward and steadied her as she stripped her harness off. "There was a breach once, but the wards were strengthened since then. We've also added some high-tech gadgets. You're safe."

"Incoming."

The air crackled, and Alastair stepped through a rift in space.

"I still don't understand how you can do that," Ryanne said to Nash. His abilities left her in awe.

"I feel a temperature change in the air." He stepped away to hug his father. "Thanks for the locusts. I'm not sure how you knew to come back, but it's appreciated."

"Call it a feeling, and I simply followed your lead with the bloody trash pandas, son. The swearing was inspired."

"I feel bad for unleashing a hundred raccoons on the town."

"They'll find their way home soon enough."

Nash cast his father a worried look. "Salinger isn't going to stop until he has the necklace."

"The necklace?" Surprise lit Alastair's face. "I thought he was targeting you because you're my son."

"Maybe that, too," Nash agreed. "But Spring made a point of retrieving the Red Scorpion before she left the standing stones. She handed it off for safekeeping."

Alastair scrubbed his hands up and down his face then ran his fingers through his hair. Ryanne couldn't remember a time when she'd seen him so disturbed. It was concerning.

"He won't stop, son. We have to find a way to keep you and Ryanne safe."

"I only hatched an escape plan. I'm not sure where to go from here."

The men locked eyes.

Alastair grimaced. "I think you do."

Ryanne suspected the only way to stop Victor was death and that they all knew it. "How do we eliminate him?" She was proud her voice only shook slightly.

"Good question, child." An admiring light flared in Alastair's sapphire gaze when he looked down at her. "That's what we all need to figure out together."

His kind regard warmed her. Alastair Thorne didn't tolerate incompetence, as she now well knew. Any type of praise from him meant a lot.

"It's been a long few days. Let's get everyone back to Thorne Manor to rest," Knox suggested. "It's safe for the time being."

They all concurred with this plan. Ryanne especially because she felt like the walking dead. Could witches turn into zombies? She'd have to ask if that was a thing. At this point, she couldn't even think about her sister and the fact Rylee's body needed to be left behind in the apartment. If she did, she'd lose her mind. Better to allow the numbness to take hold.

The silence around Ryanne registered, and she glanced up to find three sets of concerned eyes focused solely on her.

"I'm sorry. What did I miss?"

"We were discussing Rylee." Nash squeezed her hand. "Dad intends to send a team of men to your place to move her to a safer location and to gather anything you can't live without. Are you okay with that?"

Tears burned her eyes, and she pressed her lips together. A single nod was all she could manage.

While she could feel the intensity of Nash's gaze, she avoided looking at him, preferring to devote all her attention to the blades of grass at her feet.

"You go ahead," she heard him tell the others. "Ryanne and I will be along shortly."

Once the others were gone, he led her to a spot under an ancient oak tree. He took a seat and gently drew her down into his lap. "Want to talk?"

"No." She heard the catch in her throat, and she feared saying another word.

"Then let me just hold you for a bit, okay?"

She nodded and folded into him, her face buried against his neck. The warmth of his embrace eased a fraction of the coldness invading her mind and soul. And it was there, in that precise moment, that she understood what selfless love was. Nash's silent consideration was the perfect example of what true love should be.

"I love you, Nash," she whispered fiercely, gripping his face to stare into the depths of his beloved jade eyes. "I love you so damned much."

His grin was slow to form and transformed his entire face. The wink he shot her should have made light of the moment, but it only emphasized the fact that he was perfect for her. She snorted, an aborted laugh, and wrapped her arms around his neck to hug him tight.

"I love you, too, Ryanne." He rested his cheek against her temple. "You make me a better person in every way."

They sat in silence for a while, each digesting their feelings for the other and maybe what that meant going forward. As Nash cuddled Ryanne close, she allowed her fingers to play with the thick hair at the base of his neck.

"I never want to go back," she told him. "If I could stay like this with you forever, I'd die happy."

"Let's not talk of dying today. It's still too raw for me." He shifted marginally. His beautiful eyes left no inch of her face unexplored. "I don't know what I would have done if I lost you—to either death or to indifference."

"I feel the same." She frowned and glanced down at the pocket containing the necklace. "Why do I feel so at peace here? Why isn't that horrid little thing upsetting the balance?"

"I can only guess it's because we are on sacred land. Or perhaps it's done all it can do to us."

Sacred land.

"Nash? Do you think if we buried the Red Scorpion here, it might neutralize its power?"

He squinted into the distance as if he were doing mental calculations. Finally, he focused his attention back on her. "It might just work."

"And if it doesn't?"

"I will need Knox's help, I think. He's as strong as Serqet, and if anyone can spell the piece so she can't find it to start her reign of terror again, it might be him."

"Should we ask Isis, or is that pushing it?"

He worried his lip with his teeth as he stared at her.

"Nash?"

"I'm not sure. Let's go to Thorne Manor and worry about it later."

"If we take it with us, we risk exposing someone else to its evil influence."

"We'll talk to my dad and get this worked out."

They walked hand in hand toward his family's estate. With each foot traversed, Ryanne became more uneasy. She'd lost too much to that damned necklace. Her sister was the greatest loss. Rylee had been too young to die and didn't deserve to go out like that. Anger began at a slow boil within. Pulling to a stop, she reached for his pocket.

"No!" He shouted as he gripped her wrist. "No, Ryanne," he said again, softer this time. "I can feel your rage building along with your desire to strike. It's the necklace again. It seems to affect you more than others. If I had to guess why, I'd say Serqet's blood in your veins."

"Evil attracts evil?" she snarled. "You're saying I'm a horrible person."

He distanced himself from her and shifted his body to put the necklace as far from her as possible. "I'm saying Serqet created this cursed object. It could be the scorpion tempts you more because of it."

The dark, oppressive air that had filled her lungs and clouded her brain moments before eased with each step Nash took away from her. Damned if he wasn't right!

"I can't be anywhere around that thing, can I?"

"It doesn't look like it," he replied grimly.

"What are we going to do?"

He shook his head helplessly. "We'll figure it out. In the meantime, we have to set a safe distance for you from this blasted necklace." Nash eyed the distance between them. "Would you say this is about eleven feet?"

"At least. Maybe more."

"Do you want to lead or follow?"

"I don't know where I'm going."

"Right, but I'm not comfortable turning my back on you right now."

What the hell did he think she'd do? Club him on the head? His distrust tempted her to do just that.

"Come here and we'll teleport. You'll only be next to me for a minute at most."

CHAPTER 27

"Where's my father?" Nash asked without preamble the second he arrived in the front yard with Ryanne.

Spring silently pointed toward the kitchen window.

"Please stay here, babe. You need to be as far away from this necklace as possible for the time being."

As soon as Ryanne nodded her agreement, Nash jogged up the porch stairs and sailed through the large mahogany door to find Alastair. He found his father in the kitchen, a large hunk of cinnamon roll in one hand and a cup of coffee in the other.

"We need to devise a plan to get rid of this cursed necklace. I can't take the risk of surrendering it to the Council. If the wrong person gets their hands on it…" Nash ran a hand through his hair and shot a helpless look at his father. "It's already affecting Ryanne, and if I'm being honest, I've developed a crushing case of anxiety."

"I can feel it." Based on Alastair's grim look, his father was experiencing the same unsettling emotions rolling around inside of Nash.

"We found it doesn't have such a heavy effect if Ryanne stays at least eleven feet away."

"Then let's discuss this outside and put a safe distance between you and the rest of us. Can you handle the strain of the piece for a while longer, or do you need to pass it off to me?"

"I think I'm good for a few minutes more."

"Let's not waste time."

Any family members present gathered on the front lawn and maintained a twelve-foot perimeter around Nash. He explained his fear regarding the pull of the Red Scorpion in addition to the legend surrounding the curse. "I can't, in good conscience, turn this over to the Council. We need to destroy it, or barring that, encase it in cement and bury it a few stories beneath the surface of the earth."

"Put it down on the ground and let Ryanne try to melt it," Spring suggested.

Nash placed it in the center of their impromptu circle and backed away to stand beside Ryanne. He reached for her hand and merged his power with hers as she directed a blast of fire toward the necklace. Everyone shielded their eyes against the silvery-blue light created by her attempt to torch the metal. After fifteen seconds of the constant bombardment, she pulled her magic back.

The necklace remained untouched, with the exception of a seemingly irate scorpion. Light reflected off the ruby stones as the arachnid twirled in a circle, tail raised as if to strike.

"Back farther away." Knox shifted forward and began to pull energy from the air molecules around him. Arcs of light sparked from his fingertips as he built for a lightning strike.

When they were all at a safe distance, he hammered the jeweled piece with bolt after continuous bolt until the ground around them was a charred ruin. It seemed to enrage the Red Scorpion further, and the ruby arachnid scrambled toward Knox with its tail ready to inflict the deadly poison.

Utilizing his ability to freeze, he stopped the oncoming threat.

"Apparently, it can't be destroyed." Alastair sighed in resignation.

"Now I'm curious if it can even be contained? Would it find a way to free itself?" Nash quickly conjured a thick, chain mail-type sack. He scooped up the necklace with a stick and eased it inside the original leather bag he'd been using, then secured it inside the armored sack, melting the opening. *"Colliquefacio!"*

Quickly, so as not to burn his fingers, he dropped it in the dirt at the center of their circle. He hurried away, not convinced the bag would do the trick and keep that fucking scorpion locked away.

"Would it be wise to bury it in the clearing? Maybe we should find a sacred site at the far ends of the earth where no one is likely to discover it," Ryanne said. The strain of the last days dulled her eyes and deepened the grooves around her mouth. "The farther away, the better, to my way of thinking."

Nash gently drew her close and sighed his relief when her arms encircled him. His concern for her mental and emotional state was great. "Not a bad idea. We'll add a magical boost to conceal it while we're at it." Over her head, he met his father's watchful gaze.

"I have an idea. It's risky, and if the rest of you don't want to be involved, I will understand," Alastair said to the group at large.

"I'm in," Knox assured him.

"Me, too," Nash said. He dropped a light kiss on Ryanne's lips before they could form a protest. "I have to see this through," he told her, gently sweeping a hand down her dark hair. "And I need you to stay here."

"That's not happening." She rolled her eyes and lightly pinched his side. "I thought you knew me better than that."

The atmosphere around them grew heavy, and the hair on Nash's arms rose. "We're about to have company."

No sooner had he spoken than his uncle showed up. Ryker grinned and gave Nash a hug. "You're looking a helluva lot better than you did the last time I saw you, kid." He gave the group a cursory look. "Looks like deviltry's afoot. Count me in."

"I thought you were out of the spy game," Nash said dryly. He knew good and well his uncle's wife, GiGi, would have a fit if Ryker were to embroil himself neck-deep into intrigue again.

"I'm not going undercover. Nor do I intend to be gone for any length of time. A singular mission here or there never hurt anyone." Ryker rubbed his hands together, the light of interest flaring brighter. "Now, deal me in."

"This isn't poker, and unless the world is coming to an end, you are to stay out of it." GiGi's strident tone came from behind their group.

As one, they turned to face her. She was curled up on the porch swing with a tall glass of what looked to be iced tea in her hand. Knowing his aunt, Nash had no doubt her drinking glass had something stronger than southern iced tea.

"But, sweetheart..." Ryker's tone softened and his smile cajoled. "... you said yourself, if the family needed me, I could help."

Without looking away from her charming rogue of a husband, GiGi addressed her brother. "Al? On a scale of one to ten, how badly do you need my husband?"

Ryker flared both hands behind his back, fisted them, and flared them wide again. A clear signal to Alastair to say "ten."

"Maybe a five," Alastair delivered with a straight face.

The look of betrayal Ryker sported was priceless. Comical enough to set GiGi off into peals of laughter. Ryker swore and spun to face his best friend. "You jerk."

Whenever amusement lit Alastair's face, he was transformed from austere to approachable, like now. He clapped Ryker on the shoulder and laughed. The family was helpless not to join in. Only Ryanne looked uncertain and somewhat sad.

Nash wove his fingers with hers.

"Ryanne and I are going to take a little walk. I'll let you fill in Uncle Ryker and Aunt GiGi regarding everything up to now. When we come back, we can discuss this plan of yours."

He led Ryanne down the gravel path Spring had so painstakingly created through her gardens.

"This is lovely, but why did you really pull me aside, Nash?"

"I needed to check your state of mind. A lot has happened in the last few days: us, your stasis, your sister's passing." He guided her to a nearby bench. "I can tell you from experience, things are about to intensify. Alastair's schemes are never for the faint of heart. He intends to stop Victor for good."

She studied the roses on the other side of the path as she digested his words. He remained quiet to let her sort through her feelings on the matter.

"I'm okay with that." She spoke softly. Finally, she raised her eyes to his. In those dark depths, he saw determination and the promise of revenge. "He needs to pay for what he's done to my family. For both my sister and my adoptive parents."

"There is no coming back from this, Ryanne. No doubt he doesn't deserve to live, but make sure you can live with his death on your conscience before we go further."

"I'm sure."

He rose and held out a hand. "Then let's go find out what part Alastair wants us to play in all of this."

Her feelings of gratitude were strong, and they wrapped around him through his empathic gift. She needed this. Probably more so than his father, who had waited almost thirty years to exact revenge on Salinger.

Alastair laid out a simple plan to draw Victor Salinger out. He fully intended to taunt Victor into making a move. A basic "come and get me, asshole" tactic to set himself up as bait. It was a given Victor wouldn't be able to resist the opportunity to strike at Alastair.

Ryanne hated the idea.

She preferred to take the necklace back to Victor, pretend she was Rylee, and find a way to strangle that damned asshole with the evil little jeweled beast. Her plan was less likely to ensure survival than Alastair's.

"What about a combination of your plan and mine?" she asked the head of the Thorne clan.

"Please elaborate, child."

Being the focus of all Alastair's clever attention was disturbing, but she forged ahead. "What if Rylee takes you to Victor? A prize for her boss. We pretend I was the casualty of this whole debacle and create the illusion of the necklace around your neck. Attack him in his own home for a change." Under everyone's speculative regard, Ryanne began to sweat.

Alastair shifted his attention to Nash, who stared at her with a deep frown.

"What?" she asked. Her tone was waspish, and she wished she could dial back the attitude. It was harder to do this close to the Red Scorpion.

Nash surprised her when he said, "I think it could work. Your energy is different now. Your light altered."

She jerked back as if he'd slapped her. One of the things that allowed him to distinguish between her and Rylee had been her light, or so he'd told her two days ago.

Two days.

It seemed like a lifetime ago.

"I didn't mean anything bad by it, babe." He touched her shoulder in comfort. "But you are different since your time in the Otherworld. It would be impossible not to be changed by the whole incident."

"I get it." She did, but it didn't make her feel any better. Nerves got the better of her. "If you think it's a stupid idea, just say so."

"I don't, but I can't see how he'll be fooled for long. Nor can I think of a reasonable explanation my father would be standing after that blasted scorpion was attached to his chest. It took me down in less than an hour. Granted, my dad is probably twice as strong as me magically and in physicality, but still."

"Good point, son." Alastair looked at the other family members standing silently by. "Thoughts? Spring, you are unusually quiet. I've never known you to not pipe in with some brilliant scheme."

Her distasteful grimace did nothing to detract from her beauty. "I can't see how anything involving either Victor or that cursed scorpion will turn out positively."

Knox nodded his agreement. "I say we go back to the original idea of burying it in cement at the farthest reaches of the earth. Surely if it *is* discovered again, it will be some time and no longer our problem."

"Victor will not be as easy to dispose of," Alastair told them. "He's every bit as deadly as that necklace."

"Too bad we can't bury his whole compound," Ryanne muttered.

All eyes turned on her, widened in wonder.

"Why did we never think of that?" Alastair asked with a shake of his head. "It takes an outsider to remind us of our power over Victor."

"Could we get close enough with the Blockers present?" Ryker asked.

"We don't need to," Spring replied with a widening grin. "We have two earth elementals and two metal elementals. Uncle Alastair is pretty much Superman, and with Aunt GiGi, they could put the final touches on our sinkhole. We could easily do it from thirty yards out. Perhaps even fifty to be on the safe side."

Ryker nodded his understanding. "We need to make sure he remains on the grounds."

"And we need to make sure there is no more collateral damage," Ryanne added. "I couldn't bear it if I thought more people were going to lose their loved ones."

"Victor only hires people without ties. Even if they did once have family they cared about, they wouldn't for long. Not working for him, child."

Looking into Alastair's serious sapphire gaze, Ryanne recognized the truth of his words. "Do you think it's why he murdered my adoptive parents?"

"Yes. It's why he would've eventually murdered you if he intended to keep Rylee as a pawn. However, I suspect she'd served her purpose. He would've had her eliminated soon enough."

"You speak so casually about death." Ryanne's stomach flip-flopped at the sadness that flashed in his eyes. "Is this what I have to look forward to as Nash's girlfriend?"

Father and son locked eyes. It was Nash who eventually answered. "There will undoubtedly be more enemies in our future, Ryanne. We are Thornes. We were blessed with power most witches only dream about. It builds resentment and hatred. Added to the mix is your ancestor, Serqet." He sighed and shook his head. "As you saw, she will stop at nothing to destroy us." He lifted her hand and held her palm against his cheek. "You need to decide if you can live this way. It might be better for you if you headed for the nearest exit." Dropping her hand, he strode at a fast clip toward the old Victorian house they called Thorne Manor.

Ryanne watched him in dismay, her mouth hanging open. After two years of dancing around their attraction, life-altering sex, and the torturous, fucked-up two days they'd been through, he decided to drop a get-out-while-you-can bomb and walk away?

"Oh, hell no!" she growled right before she charged after him.

She was certain she heard Alastair's chuckle, but she ignored him and ran for the house. She found Nash lingering at the kitchen island, a mug of what she assumed to be coffee halfway to his mouth.

"Are you for real right now?" she shrieked out the question. "No one wants to see that fucker dead and buried more than I do. I have absolutely no qualms about it either." She inhaled deeply, warming to her rant. "You don't get to sex me up and rock my world, tell me I'm your everything, then walk away as if you could take my love or leave it." She punctuated the last sentence with her index finger against his chest. "Your damned arrogance is why you collect enemies. Not your supernatural abilities. I can say this, because I want to throat punch you right now."

The surprise left his face in increments and morphed into roguish delight. Carefully, he set his mug down and clasped the hand that had poked his chest. With a quick, hard tug, she was tightly wrapped in his warm embrace.

"Rock your world?" he teased with a butterfly-soft kiss on the exposed skin just below her ear.

"Shut up. You know you did."

"Oh, I have no doubt I did. You returned the favor. I'm mocking you because no one says 'rock my world' anymore."

"I hate you."

"No, you don't, babe. Not even a little bit."

His mouth lowered to hers and captured her retort. The taste of him—coffee and dark chocolate—drove her wild, and she wanted to feel his naked, hot skin against hers. Wanted to have wild, monkey sex and leave the outside world far, far behind. Wanted him to pound into her and shout her name over and over as he came. She recognized this might be her desire for affirmation of life—a way to warm the cold parts of her soul—but she didn't care. This man was essential to her very existence.

They broke apart to suck in much-needed oxygen into their lungs.

"No," she agreed. "Not even a little bit."

CHAPTER 28

They staked out Victor's compound, using two family members at a time as a precaution. By the end of the third day, Victor made an appearance on Nash's watch.

Touching the tanzanite and platinum ring his father had designed specially for him, Nash sent a telepathic signal to Alastair.

"He's here."

"I'll inform the others."

Twenty minutes later, their sink-hole-production team was in place under the umbrella of Granny Thorne's invisibility spell. It consisted of Nash, Alastair, GiGi, Ryker, Knox, Autumn, and Spring. Ryanne was to torch the entire compound as the others collapsed the buildings and opened the earth to consume them. In theory, they would expand their circle of magic to surround the estate, with the witches spread out evenly around the perimeter. They all now had some form of charmed tanzanite jewelry to boost communication.

"Ryanne, because you are the most inexperienced witch, I'd prefer you stay out of harm's way. If anything goes wrong, teleport back to Thorne Manor without delay." Nash and Ryanne had worked on her skill set when they weren't monitoring Salinger's activities.

She had good control of basic abilities, but she was a novice. Nash wouldn't put her at risk, despite her desire to "fry Victor's ass" as she so eloquently put it.

She lifted her chin, and a steely light entered her dark eyes. "I'm here until the end. I won't be satisfied until I see his eyes closed in permanent sleep."

She was never more beautiful than when she was being stubborn. Yet, Nash's insides were a ball of nerves. He hated to think what could happen to her. There had been enough close calls in his family over the last year and a half. All those involved had grown up with magic. They knew the ins and outs of utilizing their power for their personal protection. Ryanne was nothing more than a babe in the woods. Her first instinct would be to react as a human and not a magical entity.

"You're killing me, you know that?" he complained not so good-naturedly.

She surprised him when she grinned and pressed a firm kiss to his mouth. "Yeah, I get that. But in this, you can't control everything, Nash. I need to be a part of this. I need to be able to verify for myself that he is gone. He, or one of his ilk, was responsible for the deaths of everyone I've ever loved, with the exception of you."

Her response was understandable. Nash didn't like it, but she was also an adult and had to make her own choices. "Stay close to me, okay?"

"I promise."

Once they were all in position, Alastair led the group in a protection spell. He created a boundary around the property's perimeter—a circle within a circle—a four-feet-deep band allowing the witches room to move, but repelling anyone else from crossing through to escape the coming destruction.

Through their tanzanite connection, he instructed the metal elementals, Ryker and Knox, to begin the teardown of the buildings. Knox removed screws and brackets while Ryker removed nails and other fastenings. When they were done, they started on the Rebar supports. Nash and Spring were up next. They manipulated the lime-stone, slowly chipping away at it to create channels underground, as Alastair drew every drop of moisture from the earth beneath the buildings. Autumn conjured a five-feet-high wall of fire to encircle the estate, just on the far side of the security fence. GiGi produced the wind to feed the flames and direct them toward the structures.

Shouts went up in warning, and people crowded in the courtyard and parking area. From his location, Nash could see Victor Salinger stroll out of the main doors as if he had all day and the fire quickly consuming the grassy area of his compound was of no consequence.

The moment Nash saw him, he started a low-rolling earthquake. He derived satisfaction from watching Salinger stagger and scramble to remain upright.

Through the telepathic connection, he said, *"Now, Spring."*

Together, they encouraged the earth to collapse, and Mother Nature complied. The building at the centermost of the clustered structures went down in a pile of rubble and dust. Screams of terror echoed in the early morning air as the rumble of earth became louder and the land beneath their feet opened.

Victor remained calm amongst the chaos, leisurely scanning the tree line around the property.

"Are any of you seeing this? Why is Victor not reacting?" he asked the others.

"It's concerning," Alastair replied.

"It gives me the heebie-jeebies," Ryanne murmured from beside Nash.

He couldn't agree more. Of course Victor would know it was the Thornes. Who else would attack his compound? But to act as if this was an everyday occurrence and no big deal was, as Alastair said, concerning.

Suddenly, Victor smiled and raised his arm to circle in the air above him. The sound of military-style weapons being shouldered exploded throughout the woods surrounding them.

"Teleport now, Ryanne. *Right fucking now! Achoo!"*

"I can't!" she cried.

"Blockers!" Alastair stated grimly through their connection. *"Everyone get as low to the ground as you can and stay where you are."*

"Nash Thorne!" Victor called out. "I can tell by the appearance of raccoons that you're on my property. Step forward with the necklace, and I won't kill whoever else you have hidden with you."

"If other witches were present, why didn't they block the fire and earthquakes?" Ryanne wanted to know.

Nash felt as if he'd been poleaxed. "Why is a darned good question."

"Could it be that you're too powerful as a group?" she asked.

"Dad?"

It didn't take long for Alastair to answer. *"I think Victor's bluffing. I don't know why Ryanne couldn't teleport, but if Blockers were present, we would have met with resistance. I'm going to step out from the shield."*

Ryker's response was immediate. *"Not a chance! If he's not bluffing, he'll gun you down for sport."*

"How about we take a page from GiGi's book and levitate like she did in the clearing when she confronted Harold Beecham?" Knox asked. *"For the record, I had no idea that was even a thing."*

"That gives me an idea." Alastair slowly spun in a circle, surveying the lay of the land. *"Everyone, come toward me."*

"Mr. Thorne, I won't ask again," Victor shouted.

"No, son," Alastair responded. *"Don't listen to him. Bring Ryanne here. We'll get her to safety."*

Staying low in case the gunmen opened fire, Nash ushered Ryanne to Alastair. They all squatted in a small cluster. "What now?"

"Join hands," Alastair instructed. When they had all complied, he said, "Now, lie belly down on the ground. You three, send a shockwave in Victor's direction, and the rest of you send a shockwave toward the trees." He locked eyes with Ryanne. "In the clearing, Serqet stated you had the power to destroy all of us. If

214

unleashed, do you have the confidence in yourself to control that power?"

"What do you mean?" She cast an anxious glance Nash's way.

"Stand here, child. Put your arms up, palms facing Victor. Good." He placed his hands on her shoulders. "I am going to add to your ability with my own, but I need you to concentrate. Your magic could hurt me when it ignites. Don't look anywhere but at your intended target. Feel your cells heat and shove that energy toward your palms. Visualize it turning Salinger into fried bacon."

"Got it!"

As Victor opened his mouth to give the order to fire, Ryanne blasted him with all she had. It tore through their cloaking shield, exposing them all. Into the action, she poured all her grief for her birth parents, for the Joneses, and for Rylee. The apprehension she felt regarding the control of her magic was small in comparison to the revenge driving her. She intended to blast that bastard back to hell.

As the soldiers shifted to take aim, Nash, GiGi, and Ryker combined their efforts and buckled the earth separating them from Victor's mercenaries. The trees toppled outward, taking down the men who hadn't initially lost their footing to the small quake.

Spring, Knox, and Autumn copied the maneuver.

"Bury the bloody compound," Alastair barked. "Now!"

The Thornes joined hands and executed their initial plan. The employees of Victor who had survived their first attack ran toward the ring of fire Autumn had initially created, choosing what they must've felt was the lesser of two evils. GiGi sent hurricane-force winds in their direction and made it impossible for Victor's panicked minions to go anywhere but back the way they'd come.

"Ryanne, you can stop now, child."

But she couldn't. A sob tore from her throat for all she'd lost. Rylee's death was the freshest and grated the worst. Pointless even. The whim of a man seeking revenge.

Strong, warm arms wrapped around her.

Nash.

In slow increments, she felt her anger dissolve. Somewhere in the back of her mind, she understood Nash was taking her pain, helping her to get a grip and control herself once more. Embarrassed by her lack of control, she averted her eyes from his family. It was only then that she noticed his burns.

"Ohmygod! Nash!" Instinctively, she reached for him.

His harsh, indrawn breath made her snatch her hands back. Blisters formed along the smoother skin on the underside of his forearms where he'd touched her body. She'd done that! She wanted to weep due to the excruciating pain she'd caused him.

"*Oh, Nash!* I'm so very sorry. Tell me how to heal this?"

GiGi stepped close, careful not to touch her, but offering her comfort. "You can't, dear. Please step aside. My brother and I will take care of Nash."

"I didn't mean to. I swear," Ryanne babbled.

"I know, babe," Nash assured her through gritted teeth. "I know."

She had the feeling he did, but her remorse for what she'd done to him weighed heavily upon her.

GiGi stood next to Nash's right arm as Alastair positioned himself at his left. By silent agreement, they transferred healing energy from their bared palms to the skin on Nash's forearms, running it up one side and down the other in an attempt to cool and restore his burnt, abused flesh to normal.

Because Ryanne couldn't face what she'd done to him, she pivoted away to stare at the destruction she'd wrought to the compound. One figure lay balled up on the only parcel of land untouched by the Thornes.

Victor Salinger.

Since the fence was long gone, Ryanne walked slowly toward the man who had brought so much misery to her world. Staring down at his blackened remains, she was hit by exhaustion. Fatigue so deep, it nestled into her bones. Then came the numbness. In the span of two days, she'd morphed into a completely different person. Gone was any innocence or remaining illusions she'd had of her childhood. Of unhealthy past relationships. Like an onion, the layers had been peeled back, revealing a severely dysfunctional family at its core. No wonder she'd shied away from romantic involvement. The pain was too great a risk to take.

As Ryanne continued to gaze dispassionately down at Victor, Autumn approached.

"You okay?"

"Far from it," she managed past the lump in her throat. "I murdered a man."

"No. You rid the world of one evil twatwaffle, Ryanne. Don't lose a single night's sleep over it."

"I burned Nash," she whispered.

"Not on purpose."

"But I still hurt him."

Autumn sighed and shifted to stand in front of her. "Listen, he knew the risk he was taking when he touched you. Your skin took on a scarlet glow, Ryanne. Like a molten-lava chick. I've never seen anything like it."

Ryanne lifted her gaze to meet Autumn's steady, non-condemning eyes.

"It wasn't your fault, and he's going to be fine."

"You don't know that!" Ryanne cried in her fear. "What happens if we argue and I accidentally lose control again?"

"Why would you argue?"

"Have you met the man?"

Ryanne was thrown by Autumn's laughter. She couldn't find a single thing funny about the situation.

Finally, the other woman calmed enough to say, "If you're wise enough to worry, you're wise enough to control your temper moving forward. If all else fails and you're truly that concerned, have my uncle bind your powers again." Autumn shrugged and patted her shoulder. "Nash loves you. You love him. Everything else can be worked through."

Ryanne looked back at Nash. As she watched, he kissed his aunt's cheek and said something to make her laugh. Relief and a whole lot of angst filled her for causing him such horrific pain. Maybe she should have Alastair bind her powers. Did she dare take the risk of hurting anyone ever again?

Suddenly it was all too much. Her throat felt as if it were tightening, and her breathing became labored. She had to escape. Had to get away from Nash, his family, and the death around her. Without any thought other than a mental image of her apartment's interior, Ryanne fired up her cells to teleport home.

She realized her mistake the moment she arrived in her living room. Death was still with her in the form of her sister's ghost. Although Alastair's men had retrieved the body for burial sometime within the last two days, Ryanne could still imagine Rylee lying on the bed, eyes closed in permanent slumber.

Sinking to her knees, she gave in to the grief and sobbed. She was so tired. So raw and disillusioned with life. Five days ago, everything had seemed exciting and new. She'd been about to explore a relationship with Nash after being more than half in love with him for nearly two years. She'd just discovered she had magical abilities. At the time, it was cool. The idea of conjuring food and moving between places with just a simple thought was sublime. Now, she'd give it all back for the blissful ignorance.

The skin on the back of her neck prickled, and the air grew heavy. This was the sign she was beginning to associate with an incoming witch. Ryanne lifted her head just as Nash arrived.

As he stared at her, his expression thoughtful, Ryanne wanted nothing more than to jump up and run to him. She couldn't. She was completely depleted. The new problem remained. Dare she stick around and take the chance she might cause irreparable damage to him?

"Go home, Nash," she ordered tiredly.

"Can we at least discuss this?"

"What's to discuss? I'm a ticking time bomb. I fried your ass without even trying," she cried raggedly.

"Nah, just my arms." He gave a half-grin that never failed to wake the butterflies in her belly. Lifting his arms, he rotated them back and forth to show the undamaged skin. "I'm all better. Not even a red mark. Swear."

"You don't get it." Frustrated, she rose and crossed to the kitchen for a glass of water to ease the dryness in her throat.

"Then explain it to me."

Ryanne gulped down three-quarters of the glass before she answered. "You were in agony, Nash. I saw your face. What if your aunt and father hadn't been there after it happened? I wouldn't have known how to heal you."

He crossed to where she stood and rested those sinewy forearms on the counter, then he bent forward to meet her eyes on the same level. "You wouldn't have needed to heal me, babe. A simple call to my father or aunt would bring them running."

"Yeah, because I have their numbers memorized and you would be able to simply dial them with charred fingertips," she retorted.

"Ryanne, how upset are you right now on a scale of one to ten?"

The question threw her. She wasn't sure how to answer, so she remained silent.

He raised a dark blond brow and waited.

"I don't know. Pretty damned upset," she finally said.

"Are you going nuclear now? Or are you having a discussion like a reasonable adult?"

She glanced down. No glowing, no fire, not even a warming of the glass in her hand.

Nash moved to her side of the counter and wrapped his arms around her middle, just as he had done to pull her back from going nuclear. She flinched at the contact.

"See?" He said softly, his cheek pressed to hers. "Even upset and angry, you're controlling yourself. You wouldn't knowingly hurt me."

"No, I wouldn't," she croaked. "But what about the times when I can't control myself, Nash? I can't risk hurting you or anyone."

"We will work each day, and you'll get stronger. You'll learn how to manipulate your magic so this never happens again."

"I can't."

"You can." He turned her to face him, and lifted her chin. "You *can*."

She closed her eyes against the sting of tears. Her nasal passages burned, and she knew she was about to cry the big ugly for a second time.

"It's okay, babe. I promise you. It's okay."

"I don't want to hurt you again. I couldn't bear it."

"I doubt you'll ever be as enraged as you were when you served Victor up his Karmic spoon of medicine." He settled a soft kiss on her lips. "But if you ever do get to that point again, you'll have tricks to cool down. I guarantee it."

"What if we get married and have children? What type of power would they have? What if they walked around setting things alight or burning people?"

"I don't have all the answers right now, Ryanne. At some point, you're going to have to take a leap of faith."

"Will you just go? Please?"

He stepped back, and Ryanne felt the loss of his touch keenly. Her soul felt colder without him close. She almost changed her mind then and there. With a simple nod, he was gone.

Ryanne closed her eyes and let the tears come.

CHAPTER 29

It only took Ryanne twenty-seven hours and eleven minutes to realize how much of an idiot she was being. Nash was right. She *could* learn to control her powers. Other witches did it all the time. Now, she owed him an apology. Being wrong was a lot harder to own up to. Basically, she said she didn't trust in them enough to try. Her only excuse was fatigue. She'd been so emotionally wrung out, she didn't know if she was coming or going. She hoped like hell Nash would understand.

In all the time she'd been his assistant, she'd never been to his home. It wasn't as odd now that she realized what he was and under-stood he needed privacy to protect his secret. A quick call to Liz obtained Nash's home address, and Ryanne wasted no time high-tailing it to his place. As she pulled into the driveway and stared at the palatial house, her nerves got the better of her. What if now that he'd had time to think about it, he didn't want her? Her insecurities assailed her. She'd had to be many things to many people in the past. Never her true self. She'd be asking him to accept her as she was. That woman might not be who he truly wanted.

The front door swung open, and Nash filled the doorway. Even in his jeans, tee-shirt, and bare feet, he looked like the lord of the manor. His inherent, commanding presence couldn't be denied. He crossed his arms and leaned against the doorjamb, waiting for her to come to him. It was a very Alastair move. She'd seen his father do the same many times when he visited Thorne Industries. It made others uneasy, this watchful casualness. Would Nash grow more like his father in the coming years? A force to be reviled because he was feared?

During their time surveilling the Salinger compound, Nash had told her the story of Alastair's imprisonment by Zhu Lin and Victor. Alastair was forged into the formidable warlock he was today due to torture at his enemies' hands. Yet, she saw so much of his father in Nash. At their core, they were the same. She had no doubt.

On shaking legs, she approached. He didn't appear to be all that welcoming.

"I'm sorry," she said.

His features softened, and it occurred to Ryanne that he'd been just as nervous as she was when she arrived.

"You have nothing to be sorry for, Ryanne. You had an insane week."

She nodded, her eyes dropping to his crossed arms. She reached out and stroked the top of his forearm, running her fingertips along the blond hair. He didn't flinch or withdrawal. A good sign.

"Can we talk?" she asked softly.

"No."

She yanked her hand back.

He laughed and scooped her up. "No, but not for the reason you might think. I'm talked out, and I just want to hold my girlfriend. Maybe make out and see if she'll let me get to second base. How does that sound?"

"Wonderful," she gushed. She gave him a tentative smile. "And, Nash? If we're going with the whole baseball analogy thing, you're assured a home run."

His grin widened. "Excellent."

Ryanne laughed when he kicked the door closed with his heel.

Two hours later, when she could finally drum up the energy to move, she padded to the kitchen to forage for food. She stopped in the doorway and gaped at her dream kitchen. The nerve endings along her spine went haywire right before he rested his chin on her shoulder to survey the room with her.

"Do you like it?"

"I love it!" Everywhere she looked, there was beauty. From the white cabinets to the pewter-and-glass-tiled backsplash to the top-of-the-line stainless appliances. Splashes of contrast peppered the room and massive island from brightly colored pottery, most in shades of purple—*her favorite color.* "Nash, this is gorgeous. A good thirty or more people could mingle about in here."

"I heard you and Liz discussing HGTV one day. When I pressed her for information about your favorite designs, she gave me a few magazines. This is what I conjured with you in mind. The purple dishes are the various hues your highlights made when they caught the sunlight."

She dragged her attention from the magnificent room and twisted to face him. He had observed her that frequently? How had she missed it? "That was the most romantic thing you could say to me."

He chuckled as he captured her lips in a searing kiss. When they parted, they were both a little breathless. "I worried it was obsessive because I couldn't stop thinking about you and what you might like. I began surrounding myself with anything that reminded me of you."

"Oh, Nash."

He went still, his expression serious. "I'm crazy about you, Ryanne. Tell me this is meant to be. Tell me we will have a forever kind of love. You're essential to my happiness."

When she remained silent, too wonderstruck to speak, he continued. "I don't want to put undue pressure on you. I get it if you don't feel the same. I just—"

Ryanne heard the nerves in his voice. She understood his fear of rejection because she'd dealt with it herself many times in the past.

Placing her fingertips against his lips, she halted his flow of words. "I do feel the same. I think I always have."

"Thank the Goddess!" he said on a breathy exhale.

"Oh, and while all this…" She gestured to their surroundings. "…is definitely a little stalker-like, I won't hold it against you, because I love you."

Wicked intent filled his jade eyes. "In that case, we should definitely break in this counter."

She raised her arms for him to lift her up. "I thought you'd never ask."

Knox Carlyle pulled the chain mail bag from inside his leather satchel and laid it upon the stone altar in the clearing. Normally, to request an audience with the Goddess, one would place a gift where the sack now rested. However today, this was all he had. He hoped she'd take this offering for the sake of all mankind.

It didn't take long before pure white light illuminated the glen. It flared brightly for a moment, then calmed to a muted golden glow.

Isis.

Today, she was gowned in gold silk. Her black hair was gathered up, and a cascade of curls tumbled down the back of her neck and across one shoulder. Her expression bordered on irritated as she sashayed forward.

"Why did you call me, child? You are not one of mine."

"Exalted One," he intoned as he bowed low. "I've come to present you with the Red Scorpion. I'd hoped you might find a way to contain or destroy it for the sake of humanity. This cursed object is too dangerous to entrust to a mere human."

Her eyes dropped to the metal bag on the stone surface. For a split second, her lips tightened before she once again smoothed her features to serene. "You are more than human, Knox Carlyle. Why do you not become the keeper of this object?"

"I can't risk my wife's safety."

"Your attachment to the woman is unnatural," she snapped. With a deep inhale and a casual wave of her hand, she dismissed their conversation. "Go. I shall see to the Red Scorpion." She spoke the last words almost lovingly.

Alarm bells began clanking inside his mind. Surely Isis wouldn't revere such a deadly object.

"I shouldn't have bothered you with this," he said as he shifted to reclaim the bag.

She beat him to the altar and scooped up the armored sack. "I appreciate that you returned my necklace, lover."

Her tone of voice changed seconds before she morphed into the goddess Knox never wished to encounter again—*Serqet!*

Fuck!

He backed away, gathering elements to strike. "Where's Isis?"

"Oh, I'm sure she's around. As the creator of your little gift, it called to me first. Now, it has been returned to its rightful owner."

"The gift was not meant for you, Serqet. Return it to me immediately."

"No, I don't think I will." Her smile was as malevolent as the cursed object she cradled to her chest like a precious babe.

Knox didn't offer a warning, he simply struck, sending a lightning bolt straight for her heart. But he was too late. She'd already disappeared in a flash. He roared his frustration and mounting fury. He'd lost the fucking necklace, and now he had to tell the Thornes that Serqet had the ability to stir up her special brand of mischief for their family again.

Keep an eye out in the coming months for MOONLIT MAGIC. Liz's story is sure to delight.

FROM THE AUTHOR...

Thank you for taking the time to read ***ESSENTIAL MAGIC!*** If you love what you've read, please leave a review. To find out about what's happening next in the world of The Thorne Witches, be sure to subscribe my newsletter.

Books in The Thorne Witches Series:

SUMMER MAGIC
AUTUMN MAGIC
WINTER MAGIC
SPRING MAGIC
REKINDLED MAGIC
LONG LOST MAGIC
FOREVER MAGIC
ESSENTIAL MAGIC
MOONLIT MAGIC

You can find my online media sites here:

Website: tmcromer.com
Facebook: facebook.com/tmcromer
TM Cromer's Reader Group: bit.ly/tmc-readers
Twitter: @tmcromer
Instagram: @tmcromer

How to stay up-to-date on releases, news and other events…

✓ *Join my mailing list. My newsletter is filled with news on current releases, potential sales, new-to-you author introductions, and contests each month. But if it gets to be too much, you can unsubscribe at any time. Your information will always be kept private. No spam here!*
Sign Up: www.tmcromer.com/newsletter

✓ *Sign up for text alerts. This is a great way to get a quick, nononsense message for when my books are released or go on sale. These texts are no more frequently than every few months. Text TMCBOOKS to 24587.*

✓ *Follow me on BookBub. If you are into the quick notification method, this one is perfect. They notify you when a new book is released. No long email to read, just a simple "Hey, T.M.'s book is out today!"*
Bookbub Link: bit.ly/tmc-bookbub

✓ *Follow me on retailer sites. If you buy most of your books in digital format, this is a perfect way to stay current on my new releases. Again, like BookBub, it is a simple release-day notification.*

✓ *Join my Facebook Fan Page. While the standard pages and profiles on Facebook are not always the most reliable, I have created a group for fans who like to interact. This group entitles readers to "fan page only" contests, as well as an exclusive first look at covers, excerpts and more. The Fan Page is the most fun way to follow yet! I hope to see you there! Facebook Group: bit.ly/tmc-readers*

ALSO BY T.M. CROMER

Books in The Thorne Witches Series:

SUMMER MAGIC

AUTUMN MAGIC

WINTER MAGIC

SPRING MAGIC

REKINDLED MAGIC

LONG LOST MAGIC

FOREVER MAGIC

ESSENTIAL MAGIC

MOONLIT MAGIC (coming soon)

Books in The Stonebrooke Series:

BURNING RESOLUTION

THE TROUBLE WITH LUST

A LOVE TO CALL MINE (coming soon)

THE BAKERY

EASTER DELIGHTS

HOLIDAY HEART

Books in The Fiore Vineyard Series:

PICTURE THIS

RETURN HOME

ONE WISH